REGRETTING IT

REGRETTING IT

Jennifer Chapman

C

CENTURY

LONDON MELBOURNE AUCKLAND JOHANNESBURG

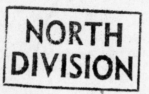
Copyright © Jennifer Chapman 1987

First published in Great Britain in 1987 by
Century Hutchinson Ltd
Brookmount House, 62–65 Chandos Place
London WC2N 4NW

Century Hutchinson South Africa (Pty) Ltd
PO Box 337, Bergvlei, 2012 South Africa

Century Hutchinson Australia Pty Ltd
PO Box 469, 16–22 Church Street, Hawthorn
Victoria 3122, Australia

Century Hutchinson New Zealand Ltd
PO Box 40–086, Glenfield, Auckland 10
New Zealand

ISBN 0 7126 1457 5

Typeset by Inforum Ltd, Portsmouth
Printed and bound in Great Britain by Anchor Brendon Ltd,
Tiptree, Essex

Chapter One

They were back. The years in America seemed as long or as short as a fortnight's holiday, removed and condensed, like an old car crushed to a metal cube.

Charlotte had seen it happen once, the strange, encapsulating destruction of a car. She'd stopped for a few minutes on the perimeter of the dumping ground and watched, fascinated, as a mangled Trans-Am became something else, unrecognisable yet made up of all the same bits and pieces that had been the car. Somebody had seen it as an art form, years back, and had hoodwinked a section of the public into believing it too; perhaps there was something like it still at the Tate. These loosely connected thoughts ran on, taking her back to the time when she was still married to Dan but hoping not to be much longer: the time when Nick had come back from America alone and she'd met him at the airport and in order to prolong the time together before returning to their separate houses they'd gone to the Tate.

She tried to remember the pictures they had seen that day but not one of the enduring works of art sprang to mind, only a sense of sad curiosity at the memory of how she had felt about Nick. It had been a quite overwhelming physical desire which she had chosen to identify as being in love because she'd wanted so badly that kind of intoxication – the lofty, intense emotion, sufficient to justify the wickedness of destroying two marriages, splitting two families.

This sort of thought pattern was not new to Charlotte. More and more over the past year otherwise inconsequential memories had led on to the same wretched feeling of dissatisfaction; and now, as before, she tried to find excuses. For goodness sake! She'd just spent nine hours on an aeroplane. She'd missed the better part of a day (or was it a night – she'd lost track) surely this was classic jet-lag.

She'd been lying on the bed but sat up as the door opened and Nick came in. His face was pale and greasy from the long flight, his eyes dull for want of sleep. He'd worked through a wad of files most of the time they'd been on the plane but Charlotte could hardly remember a time when he wasn't, when she wasn't, subject to the tyranny of paperwork. A long time ago he'd told her that he always worked during flights because deep down he was a nervous passenger, but she couldn't remember now whether he might have said this in a rare exposure of vulnerability or merely as a palliative to her complaining of neglect.

'My ankles are swollen,' she said, peering down because it was better not to observe too long the details of Nick she now found unattractive.

'No telexes,' he said. 'I just hope the goddam office in 'Frisco has got the number right.'

A twinge of irritation knotted in Charlotte at his use of Americanisms.

'They're probably all still in bed,' she said. 'Darling, why don't we get a few hours sleep?'

She waited for him to say something unpleasant to her. He was tired and restless, worried and bored, and Nick's way of counteracting all these things was to pick an argument. He'd gone over to the window, his back to her. Outside, the noise of London traffic created a sense of vacuum in the hotel room: everyone else was moving about the city in purposeful pursuit while the two of them were caught together in mutual lone-liness, the empty space between one phase in life having come to an end and an invisible question mark hanging over what might happen in the next.

He moved away from the bright daylight and sat down heavily beside her, then unexpectedly he tilted sideways and rested his head in her lap, his arm stretching round the back of her waist and suddenly holding her tightly. Charlotte, con-fused and disarmed, and in need of comfort herself, put her hand against his hair and stroked down the nape of his neck

2

where the skin was brown from Californian sun.

They had spent almost three years in America, just six months less than they'd been married. They'd given up the rented house near Cambridge where they had lived their first year together after leaving their previous marriages. They had gone to America with no thought of coming back, and now that they had there was a sense of having been dispossessed. But for Charlotte, and maybe Nick too, this self-inflicted insecurity amounted to more than the lack of a home base. Their relationship had begun with mutual dislike, both rightly thinking the other arrogant and self-centred. Then it had changed with the sudden and inexplicable attraction that can happen when dislike has become obsessive and engrossing. They had surprised themselves with the degree to which they had fallen in love and such intensity had seemed to justify the hurt and damage they had inflicted upon their respective families. But neither Charlotte nor Nick was sufficiently ex-ceptional to maintain the level of passion that is there at the beginning of such a relationship. They argued a lot, that had never changed, but while in the first year these disagreements served largely to heighten desire and invariably led to near violent bouts of lovemaking, the sex act had subsequently become a different sort of weapon, one to be withheld.

Nick had fallen asleep, his head now uncomfortably heavy against Charlotte's thighs. She eased herself from under him and went over to the place by the window where he had stood a few minutes earlier. She felt like a foreigner in her own country, everything in her life mixed up and out of place, most of all in this precise moment, Vicky, her daughter but not Nick's. She was seized by the thought of her stroppy little girl, still in California. Only nine years old and thousands of miles away. The decision to leave Vicky at the school in Piedmont until things were more settled and a house found in England, had been one of the few issues over which she and Nick had not argued. Of course it had been made a lot easier with Frances there, Charlotte's friend from childhood who had married an American and had managed to get Vicky into the exclusive school soon after Charlotte and Nick had arrived in San Francisco. Vicky spoke with an American accent now, said Mummy with a long 'o'.

3

The ache of separation caused Charlotte to wrap her arms round her stomach and subconsciously she had begun a slight rocking movement as she gazed down on to the London street.

It was an entirely selfish longing that she felt for Vicky who had smashed a full tumbler of strawberry milkshake on the restaurant floor and yelled hatred of everything English, most particularly her mother when Charlotte told her they were coming home.

'You're not having another one,' Charlotte said.

'It wasn't my fault!' Vicky said with a pout.

'Well, it certainly wasn't mine,' Charlotte rejoined, though she felt wretchedly guilty.

'Oh my, oh my,' murmured the waitress.

'It wasn't my fault,' Vicky repeated, loudly.

'Course not, sweetie,' the waitress said, looking to Charlotte.

'I'm most terribly sorry,' Charlotte offered, abjectly, and when the bill came she massively over-tipped and felt even more uncomfortable that she had allowed herself to be intimidated.

Outside, on the broad Oakland sidewalk she made the mistake of attempting bribery.

'Just think of all the lovely things you can have when we're back in England, your own dog, even a pony.'

'But I won't have my friends,' Vicky wailed. 'Oh, Mommy, please, please can't we stay here. If we can I'll never be rude to Nick again, really, I mean it.'

'Vicky, darling,' Charlotte paused, they'd reached the car and Vicky had to be back at the school in twenty minutes. 'Vicky, going home to England is not a bargaining point,' she said, gently. 'Darling, you're old enough to understand that.'

The uphill journey back to Piedmont went badly.

'Why can't I stay here. I'm a boarder anyway and weekends I could go to Frances and Leonard,' Vicky suggested in an inspired tone.

Charlotte lost her temper then.

'You'll do as you're told,' she snapped.

When they got to the school, a dazzlingly white building of colonial proportions, Vicky didn't get out of the car when it stopped. Her head bowed she asked quietly and pathetically:

4

'How long before we have to leave?'

'Perhaps you could stay on until the end of term,' Charlotte answered, softly now. 'I'll have a word with Frances. It might be better if Nick and I find a house and get things more settled before you come.'

Vicky stepped out of the car, her head still down. Charlotte stretched across and spoke through the open window of the passenger door:

'Vicky, it'll mean you'll see more of Daddy.'

In the London street it had begun to rain. Charlotte, her thoughts flitting back and forth across the Atlantic, now indulged in that one most particular notion, the one that had made her agree so readily when Nick asked how she felt about coming back. She had not seen Dan for nearly three years.

Chapter Two

While Charlotte stood by the window of her London hotel room Dan was in a plane somewhere between New York and San Francisco.

The man sitting next to him was going to start a conversation, any minute, Dan could tell. He'd glanced over several times, seemed fidgety; perhaps he was a nervous traveller and needed to talk. Instinctively, being English and from the south, Dan was vaguely repelled by the possibility of having to respond to this total stranger, and yet he knew he would say something in return, decency and good manners demanded it.

When the opener came it was more direct than he had expected.

'I'm going to visit my son on the West Coast,' the man said. 'I sure am looking forward to spending some time with him. I've not seen him in nearly three years, not since my wife and me split.'

'How long will you be spending with him?' Dan enquired, glancing at the clean-cut open face of his neighbour. He had the very blue eyes that go with fine pale hair like the remaining strands on his balding head. He was wearing one of those bold check jackets that put him out of the professional class and placed him somewhere between car salesman and something connected with plumbing.

'Just a week. I gotta big exhibition coming up at the end of the month. Gotta be back for that. I'm in the leisure industry. Campers. I fit them out de luxe. Yes sir, some of the folks that buys them lives in more comfort on four wheels than they does the rest of the time.' He was warming to his subject and Dan, who had always found the thought of camping and caravanning rather depressing, resigned himself to the inescapable monologue that would take up the rest of the flight.

Fortunately, it seemed unlikely his companion would want to know why he was flying to the West Coast or what he did with his life. Dan no longer knew which he found more irksome, the people who talked only about themselves or those who, when they discovered him to be a Member of Parliament, plunged headlong into the rhetoric of uninformed opinion as to what was wrong with the running of the world.

'Do you have a family?'

'I'm sorry?'

'Are you a married man, sir?' Mr Camper rephrased his question.

'Yes and no. The same as yourself,' Dan replied.

'Half the world is divorced these days,' the man observed. 'You know, most of the used campers I sell are from folks splitting. Sometimes half the fitments have been ripped out. You know, she wants the split-level so he takes the refrigerator.'

Dan laughed and the man seemed pleased to have amused.

'Folks are crazy,' he went on. 'Though I shouldn't be complaining. I pick up those divorce campers for half what they're worth.' He chuckled to himself then quickly glanced at Dan. 'Mind you, I wouldn't like to give the impression I don't make a fair deal. You won't get a better in New York state, no sir.'

The man seemed a little uneasy now, as if maybe he'd failed to convey adequately the sincerity of his business dealings. He launched on a new tack to emphasise the point further.

'It's the wives that want it that way, everything split down the middle to the last cent. My wife, she took me for half the business even though she never did nothin' for it 'cept complain I was never home. Still, I suppose we have to do right by them and I'm a happy man if I feel I've struck a fair deal.'

Dan had a mental picture of Mr Camper's wife for whom he felt pity though the image centred on a wide American mouth from whence came harsh words and whining complaint, scathing condemnation of the camper trade which paid her alimony. This check-jacketed man sitting next to him had

7

probably made her truly miserable, though who was he, Dan, to judge another man's capacity to cause misery.

Every now and then a thought such as this nudged at his happiness, because he was happy, and for the first time in years, including many of those he was married to Charlotte. He'd loved Charlotte too much and with too great a sense of the inequality in their loving; there was no comfort or respite in wanting someone so much more than they did you. He had made her miserable because their marriage had not been enough for her. After she'd left him he'd closed in on his vulnerability, eschewing the possibilities for anything lasting with someone else. That was until a few days ago.

Suddenly, and quite uncharacteristically, he'd done something ill-considered, even stupid. He had tossed a single change of clothing into an overnight bag, driven to Heathrow and jumped on a plane to New York. He had arrived in the middle of the night and only then called Mickey and told her he was coming to see her.

Months earlier he'd said goodbye to her in London the day she went to New York. They'd parted as friends but as soon as she was gone Dan wished he'd said more, taken the risk; and yet the whole of the summer had passed before he'd stopped vacillating and caught that flight to New York.

Arriving at Mickey's apartment he felt quite ridiculously nervous, or perhaps nervously ridiculous. He was old. Four days ago he was uncertain and old because Mickey was still in her twenties and he was in his forties and although this age gap had never been noticeable in their friendship it suddenly seemed huge and a little obscene now that he wanted to declare himself.

And Mickey, still too thin after the trauma of her own broken marriage, but appearing hopelessly youthful in a blue running suit with her dark hair hanging loose round a face without make-up, greeting him with low-key affection, assuming that nothing had changed.

In the elevator going up to the apartment he mouthed a feeble rehearsal of what he might say to her, but when it came to the point he couldn't get his tongue round the eloquent phrases of love and as far as he could remember he'd said something pathetically inadequate along the lines of 'giving it a try'.

8

'I think we'd be mad not to,' she answered, making the hope-against-hoped response sound peculiarly slight in content and meaning. But Mickey had the same background of injury to guard herself with equal caution, and the tone of her words was chosen carefully not to exceed the level of his own.

And Dan was happy. At least, he believed himself to be so, though perhaps more importantly, he anticipated a future with the sort of calm happiness he thought he'd always sought and hitherto utterly failed to achieve.

'Your kids are back in England, I guess?' his fellow passenger was enquiring after some minutes silence.

'No, I've only one. A daughter. That's why I'm going to San Francisco. She lives there with her mother.'

'A little girl, huh,' the American remarked appreciatively. 'Tell me, sir, if you don't mind, how do you and she get along?'

Dan was rather taken aback by the directness of the question, but sensed a genuine interest which probably arose from some problem the man had with his estranged son.

'I haven't seen her for three years which is a long time when they're growing up,' he answered, somewhat obliquely, he felt, but he really didn't know how it was going to be with Vicky.

'My boy is kinda his mother's son,' the American said on a down note. 'Oh, don't get me wrong, he's a real fine son and I guess one day he'll see the both sides of why his mother and I didn't get along. Trouble is I get the feeling every time I go visit that he sort of expects me to pay – literally. It's probably his mother who tells him to do it, but if I don't deliver, don't buy him all the things he asks, well, he makes me feel about as welcome as a lump o' pig meat in a synagogue.' He seemed to ruminate on this unsatisfactory state of affairs for a moment or two, and Dan reflected on the insularity of plane journeys, bringing forth candour and confession between total strangers.

When they left the plane and by the time they were waiting beside the baggage carousel, the contact was already lost and they no longer knew one another.

Dan rang Mickey in New York before going to find a taxi outside the airport.

'I hope it goes well,' she said.

'I'm sorry you couldn't come too.'

9

'Next time.'

They'd agreed it was too soon for her to meet Vicky, especially as it had been such a long time since Dan had seen his daughter, and in the taxi to the hotel he thought more about Mickey, whose shape and feel and smell lingered in his senses.

The following morning he woke with the semi-conscious sense of doom that so often began his day; but rousing himself into full consciousness he was relieved, even mildly joyous, to know it was no more than habit and without cause. He got out of the broad hotel bed and ran a bath. He drew back the curtains and let in a shaft of Californian sunlight, and gradually the new experience of pleasurable anticipation of what the day might bring spread through him, producing a feeling of vigour in his less than taut body.

In the bath he paid some attention to the state of his physique, something that had not greatly interested him over the past few years. He was not much overweight but his muscles were hardly evident and his skin the pale pink of hidden flesh. Perhaps he should take up some sort of physical punishment, press-ups, or maybe buy one of the instruments of torture sold by Charlotte's husband, one of those expensive weightlifting contraptions.

He got out of the water, wrapped a huge, soft towel round himself and energetically brushed his teeth over the basin.

He dressed, having little choice but the dark suit he'd arrived in at New York, and went down to the restaurant where an appallingly decadent and delicious array of foods was set out in tier upon tier spread over a massive serving table; black and white grapes dripping from crystal pedestals, water melon, oranges; rolls of pink meats, smoked fish, and an abundance of every type of bread. The menu suggested the most original combinations of fruits and protein and Dan breakfasted on strawberries piled over waffles with rolls of thinly-sliced ham.

It was, of course, quite unlike the sort of thing he would normally choose, but experimentation suited his mood. He was a little nervous now at the imminence of seeing his daughter, and Charlotte. He found he was making slow progress with the strawberries as his mind focused upon the prospect of presenting himself to his former wife. Almost certainly they would be civil, even friendly to one another. He knew no other way himself and could foresee no cause for Charlotte to be other than pleasant to him. But the more he thought about the meeting the more difficult he found it to eat.

He was wise enough to accept that in any dealings he would have with Charlotte hers would be the upper hand, simply because he had loved her so much more than she'd ever loved him. It was an imbalance that couldn't be made even. She was the leaver and he the left, and much as he hoped for new happiness with Mickey, this had nothing to do with him and Charlotte. They'd both moved on, but the past would be the present when they met again and each would be too keenly aware of this for the roles to change. It would be victim and aggressor beneath the paper-thin veneer of civility: winner and loser, just as it had always been. The inevitability of it oppressed him, and yet a vestige of the old excitement was still there.

Back in his room he found the number in his diary and lifted the telephone. It rang for some time and he was about to replace the receiver when an American voice answered.

'Could I speak to Charlotte Matthews,' Dan said.

'Who d'you want?' the voice asked, without interest.

'Mrs Matthews. Is she there? I hope I've got the right number.'

'Oh, yeah,' the voice drawled. 'You mean the English couple who were here. They've gone.'

'Do you have a forwarding address?' Dan asked, registering with irritation that it was typical of Charlotte to move without letting him know where he could contact her — and Vicky.

'They went back to England,' the voice announced, flatly.

'Are you sure?' Dan said, while he took in the enormity of his mistiming.

'Look fella . . . ' the voice began.

'Of course. I'm sorry to have troubled you.'

The line went dead.

Chapter Three

The next day Charlotte woke feeling much better. The tiredness had gone and she was ready to get on with the huge list of tasks that included finding somewhere to live, a new school for Vicky, contacting her old friends and having lunch with her mother.

Nick was utterly preoccupied with the sending and receiving of telexes, seeing business associates and bankers. He'd already left for the day long before Charlotte emerged from the bathroom.

She was glad to have so much to occupy her. It cut down on thinking time, pulled her along on the conveyor belt of practicality.

Her mother, the only living member of the quartet that had produced Charlotte and Nick, had a small, first-floor flat in the less interesting part of St John's Wood. Charlotte referred to her as and called her Mother because the word sounded formal rather than close. Any of the derivatives, Mummy, Mum, Ma, would have been too intimate for the person who had allowed what was supposed to have been forgotten.

Oddly, the memory was always more vivid after a long interval of not seeing her mother. It related to only a few months, when Charlotte was in her early teens, that hideous period when life became unbearably intense, society in general seemed hostile and devoid of understanding, and at home there was only terror.

Her father's illness had come on gradually at first but in the later stages he galloped into insanity like a raging bull. And at the time, right up until his death, Mother had pretended that none of it was happening, that everything was normal and to be expected and the only person behaving unreasonably was Charlotte.

It was particular incidents rather than the whole that she remembered; isolated pockets of the most dreadful fear and bewilderment. Father had always been on the stern side, but before the illness this had been tempered with kindness and the particular attention a parent gives an only child. He would come and read to her at night when she was in bed, without fail, even if he was late home and had not yet eaten his supper. He liked to take her to places such as the zoo and Madame Tussaud's; he'd opened her eyes to the great paintings in the National and the Tate, and her ears to the glorious music other children found boring and oppressive. They did all these things, just the two of them, while Mother stayed at home making cakes to be eaten on their return and nurturing her own insidious illness which would eventually prevent her from going out at all.

'Mummy doesn't like crowds,' Daddy said one Saturday when Charlotte asked why she never came with them, and Charlotte had not asked again because really she didn't want Mummy with them, and naturally assumed this arrangement suited her father as well.

These outings remained in memory but became relegated to a part sealed off beyond reality. They were part of a perfect world that came to seem no more real than the tales of Dr Dolittle and the other stories Father had read to her.

The first time he lost his temper was on a Friday evening when Charlotte came home from Girl Guides. On the way back she and Frances, who lived nearby, had got themselves into a state of helpless giggles over the prescribed reading for Guides, at that time, *Scouting for Boys*. The two girls had just become aware of the opposite sex, and the delicious, self-conscious mystery of this new interest could only be contained within silliness.

The larking about on the way home, the renewed fits of laughter each time Frances looked at Charlotte or Charlotte looked at Frances, meant they were later than usual getting back. Charlotte was unaware of this until she reached the corner of the road where she and Frances went different ways.

Perhaps she was, even at that stage, vaguely conscious of a change in the atmosphere at home because she ran the last bit, as fast as she could, and got in, panting for breath.

'Where have you been?' Father bellowed, meeting her in the hallway.

'I didn't realise,' she gasped between gulps of air. 'I didn't know I was late.'

'Liar!' Father shouted. 'You're out of breath. You knew!'

Instinctively, Charlotte tried to get past him and to the lounge where she knew Mother would be watching television. She could hear the muffled sound of audience laughter.

Father moved to prevent her passing. She glanced up at his face which was grey and frowning, a strand of hair had fallen at an angle across his forehead which was glistening as if he'd been exerting himself.

'I asked you a question,' he demanded.

'I've been to Guides,' Charlotte said, standing very still. Something in her father's voice was strange and unknown to her. She didn't like it. She saw his arm swing back but she was completely unprepared for the blow that landed against the side of her head. Her ear blocked and she didn't fully catch the next ranting accusation. Then she managed to dodge round and flew towards the closed door to the lounge. She could feel him behind her as she pushed down on the handle and the door burst open, letting out a great wave of hilarity from the programme Mother was watching.

Charlotte stumbled into the room but Father had caught hold of her arm and the second stinging blow went into her cheek. She started to cry, which she hadn't done in years. It was an ugly, gulping sort of whimper.

'Stop it!' Father shouted into her face, his hand still gripping her arm. He started to shake her, as if she needed bringing to her senses.

'Mum,' Charlotte called, but her mother had remained seated throughout, though stiffly and on the edge of her armchair. Charlotte saw the anxious, bird-like movements of her head. She glanced from the television to the scene by the door, then into the knot of her fingers in her lap, repeating this triangle several times. Why didn't she do something? Why didn't she leap up and dart across the room to intervene and prise Father's hand away? Why didn't she stop him! But in that moment he let go.

The sense of horror welled and then receded as if it wasn't possible to believe what had happened. Charlotte looked at her mother whose gaze seemed fixed, unseeingly, on the television screen. Father she couldn't look at. She ran from them and in a matter of minutes was in bed, in the dark, every part of her body trembling as she prayed that neither of them would come to her but fell asleep utterly bereft that they had not.

That was the first of several similar episodes that took place over the next months. Charlotte was silent with shame after each occasion and became part of the conspiracy that pretended everything was normal. She couldn't remember how she discovered what was wrong with her father, that he had a tumour growing into his brain, because Mother never said anything and continued, right up until the end, with that unseeing attitude that had kept her in the chair the first time and subsequently.

Charlotte thought of the tumour like a carrot growing and swelling in her father's head. She even imagined it as being orange. And the memory was there, the confusion between tumour and tuber, as she sat in the taxi to St John's Wood.

'Lottie, Lottie!' Mother twittered as she opened the front door. 'Oh, Lottie.'

'Hello Mother,' Charlotte bent and kissed the person who seemed to have lost several inches in height over the last three years.

It was rather a shock to see her mother so shrunken, so old.

'So thin!' Mother exclaimed.

Charlotte smiled. She was, actually, feeling vaguely hefty, the obsession with body tone, by necessity, having caught hold of her in California. It was, after all, the reason she and Nick had gone to America, his involvement with the health and fitness business. The Fortress Against Fat chain of gymnasia and work-out studios had provided them with a comfortable life style, but one in which it was imperative to keep the weight off. You really couldn't expect to make a success of such an enterprise if you didn't set a good example. Jane Fonda had made that clear.

Mother had gone a funny shape, probably because she never went out. Her hair, which had turned grey, was evidently long, doubtless for the same reason. She wore it in a large bun pinned on the top of her head and further emphasising the old lady look. Her clothes were as neat as they had always been, but many seasons out of fashion. She appeared a sad and neglected little figure, despite the smile, and Charlotte felt pricked with guilt and a longing to be anywhere else.

'It's so nice to have you home again. And Vicky, I'm so looking forward to seeing her,' Mother said, still drinking in the real live presence of her daughter.

'Shall we go and sit down?' Charlotte said.

'Of course, of course. Lunch is all ready.'

They went into the living room which served the dual functions of dining and sitting. It was a square room with a bay window and originally must have been the main bedroom of the house. Heavy net curtains dulled the daylight and cast a gloom over the familiar furnishings, the brown armchairs that were at least thirty years old, the drop-leaf dining table and wheelback chairs. Even the carpet, olive green with an abstract pattern of ochre and beige, was the same piece that had lain in the dining room of the larger flat where they'd lived as a family. And the reason it all remained the same was not just the agoraphobia that kept Mother from going out to furniture stores; that could have been overcome in the same way she arranged delivery of everything else; it was more that she was able to cling on to the past by retaining the setting.

The smell of unseasoned food, steaming vegetables, hung in the room. Charlotte longed to light a cigarette but she knew she would not be comfortable smoking it and therefore resisted the urge.

'How's Nicholas?' Mother asked, an edge of stiffness in the question.

'He's fine. Terribly busy. He wants to get Fortress Against Fat going over here.'

'Such a funny name!' Mother said, that slight note of deprecation in her voice, the one that was always there when she spoke of anything connected with Nick.

'It's rather clever really,' Charlotte said. 'It's easily remembered and it says what it is.'

16

'Oh yes, I'm sure it's very successful,' she smiled and wrung her hands.

I mustn't start being defensive, thought Charlotte. Mother loved Dan. She always had, even when he was a child, the son of their friends, hers and Father's closest life-long friends. But the Lovells had never loved Charlotte. They'd recognised her as being not quite right long before she and Dan were married; and when the wedding had come Charlotte remembered there being an awful atmosphere of sadness and disappointment in the Lovell household. It had been a time of brave faces, everyone, including herself, going along with what was happening in order to please other people rather than themselves. The only person who'd got what he wanted was Dan. Poor, dear, thoroughly good Dan. And Mother perhaps too. She had wanted the marriage, but the occasion had been too much for her, going out, being the impoverished widow at her daughter's wedding paid for by the groom's family.

As if cueing into these thoughts, Mother asked: 'Have you heard from Dan?'

'Not for a long time,' Charlotte answered.

'He knew you were coming back, though?'

'No, actually he didn't, I mean, he still doesn't now.'

Mother's lips pressed together and her gaze dropped to the olive green floor.

'I'll fetch the lunch,' she said in a moment. 'You sit down at the table.'

'Can't I help?' Charlotte called after her as she went out to the kitchen. Mother never had to put her reproaches into words – there was never any need. Charlotte, seemingly forever destined to do the wrong thing, didn't have to be told; and perhaps there would always be the margin of reserve, Mother's own unspoken guilt over the time when Father was ill, that prevented her from blaming Charlotte in any manner beyond a moment of silence, a glance at the floor.

Charlotte sat down as she'd been bidden, and gazed across the room at nothing in particular, her attention within herself. Several times she'd thought of writing to Dan, and of course she should have done so. Why she had not made little sense and it would seem, as evidently it had to her mother, that the omission was yet another piece of ill-treatment, lack of

17

consideration. After all, Dan had a right to know Vicky's where-abouts, any plans concerning her future. And it wasn't as if she had not wanted to tell him. She wanted badly to be able to tell him everything: to sit and talk and be soothed and understood. She turned her head in a restless, despairing movement. It was no good thinking these thoughts, apart from anything else she wouldn't be able to eat any lunch and Mother would be disappointed. . .

Chapter Four

It was Friday, at midday Frances was due to collect Vicky from school and bring her back for the weekend. Concentrating on the positive, she'd planned the two days with care, thinking up a menu that would please both Vicky and Leonard (which was difficult now that he'd gone vegetarian as well as kosher); working out a programme of activities to keep Vicky amused and away from thoughts of her mother in England. But there was more to it than this. Frances had agreed straight away when Charlotte asked her to have Vicky weekends until the end of term. How could she have refused? She couldn't. It was just unfortunate that Vicky seemed to have inherited all Charlotte's bad points and none of the good, or rather, the attractive, because long ago, maybe as far back as childhood, Frances had formed a clear and accurate summation of her friend. Charlotte was over-ridingly selfish in every aspect of her life with the single exception of Vicky, who perhaps might have been a nicer child had she been less adored by her mother.

Having no children herself, Frances was doubly concerned about the weekends that stretched ahead. She and Leonard had no experience for this surrogacy. Their life style at home was quiet but intense; after three years of marriage they were still fingering each other's emotions with wonder and confusion. It suited them to be alone.

She was upstairs, standing in the spare room where Vicky would sleep, trying to think what else could be put in it that would not be too young or too old, when the telephone rang and it was Dan.

Half an hour later he was sitting in her living room and

looking older than he should in the four years since she'd last seen him.

'Charlotte didn't tell you?' she said after briefly explaining the situation.

He shook his head and smiled sadly. They were the two people who had always known her best and with love. If it had not been like this they might now have launched into the criticism she deserved, the expressions of indignation they'd have been justified in sharing. Instead Frances went out to the kitchen and made a jug of coffee. When she returned to the living room Dan was standing by the window, looking down to the steep decline of the wooded garden.

'What a lovely place to live,' he said.

'I've always felt it's a bit like your place. I think it's the trees,' she answered.

He turned to face her.

'Has Vicky changed a very great deal?'

Frances set down the coffee tray.

'Not really. She's just like Charlotte. More and more so.'

He came back into the centre of the room and sat down again.

'How is she? Charlotte, I mean?' He asked the question in an even tone but it was more than a casual enquiry.

'Not happy,' Frances said.

They both glanced up from their cups.

'She's not very good at it – being happy. Only in short, sharp bursts,' Frances added.

'Poor Lottie,' Dan murmured, winding a spoon in his black, sugarless coffee.

'What about you?' Frances asked.

'I'm all right. The past year has been difficult. I've had a few problems, but things have been looking up.'

Frances thought back to the last time she'd seen Dan. It had been the night she'd gone to his house near Cambridge and found him alone with Vicky. There'd been a power cut, and the darkness, lit only by a solitary candle, had added to the feeling of abandonment within the house. Charlotte, out somewhere with Nick, must already have told Dan she was leaving and taking Vicky with her. The candle had been in the child's bedroom. Frances had gone into the house after hearing

20

Vicky's nightmare scream. The memory was a vivid one: she'd thought something must have happened, something awful for the house to be so dark and Vicky screaming within it. She'd been quite terrified herself but had gone in and crept up the stairs. The screaming had stopped but from the landing she had stepped towards the open doorway and unnoticed at first she'd seen Dan cradling Vicky in his arms, sitting on the edge of the bed, by the flickering candle, his face damp with tears. They were probably Vicky's, the child had been hysterical, but the despair in Dan's expression had been unmistakable.

It was only then, that night when she had sat and talked with Dan, the first time in all the years she'd known him they had been alone, Frances realised what a thoroughly nice man he was. She'd never thought him exciting enough for Charlotte, and perhaps she was right in that, but he was so much more in other ways, magnificently fair towards a wife whom he loved and who had behaved towards him with all the unfair malice of guilt. Dan was dignified and decent and Charlotte should never have left him, more particularly, not to go off and marry Nick.

'She's all right with Matthews? He's treating her well?' Dan asked.

It was impossible for them not to talk about Charlotte. She'd dominated both their lives in the past.

'Yes,' Frances answered, and this was true. Nick was almost as selfish as Charlotte but he loved her and the fact that he was all wrong for her was not his fault. He treated her, as they say, as well as could be expected. It would have been too easy now to share with Dan her own misgivings over her friend's marriage, but to do so would not achieve anything other than worry for Dan over Vicky, stuck in the middle of an unsuitable alliance. And there was the old loyalty to Charlotte who surely wouldn't want her first husband to know the shortcomings of her second.

Charlotte and Nick had stayed with Frances and Leonard when they first arrived in the States. It had proved an awkward time with Vicky having tantrums over the slightest thing and Charlotte, ridden with guilt, being an over-tolerant mother. At that stage she'd probably already fallen out of love with Nick but was overt in the way she attempted to make it seem

21

otherwise. And Frances had seen that she was trying to convince herself as much as the rest of them, and felt the same sort of pity and revulsion she had years before when Charlotte had been brave and secretive and proud about her father's illness so as to hide its mundane awfulness.

Ultimately, Frances had come to feel more sorry for Nick than Charlotte. He was a man struggling to be what he was not, and his marrying Charlotte was part of this struggle. With the sort of perception she disliked in herself, Frances heard Charlotte's BBC accent and Nick's attempt at it. She observed the expensive quality of his clothes but also the heavy gold jewellery he wore and the Italian shoes. She told herself she was a snob and that none of these things mattered, and of course they wouldn't have in the least if Nick had not been so concerned with them himself, if he'd simply been himself. Frances could see that Charlotte would probably destroy him, just as she had Dan.

All this Frances had seen at the beginning during the two or three weeks Charlotte and Nick and Vicky stayed with her and Leonard. Since then they had met seldom as couples, largely because Leonard and Nick had so little in common. Nick had shown some interest in Leonard's academic work at Berkeley, but this was superficial and part of the struggle, which made it uncomfortable for both men. And Leonard, his initial curiosity about Nick's health and fitness enterprise was far too anthropological.

So Charlotte and Frances had continued their friendship at lunchtimes without their partners, and although Charlotte couldn't resist complaining about Nick, she never admitted that she didn't love him – that would have been going too far, conceding too great a failure. And because Frances was a true friend she listened and didn't comment and tried to make the major part of their conversations about other things. Despite her own intense love of Leonard, she thought it narrow and unwise to concentrate too much on this part of life.

The lunches with Charlotte had continued and for more than two years Frances had barely exchanged a sentence with Nick. And then one afternoon he turned up at the house.

He didn't explain or excuse so unexpected a visit. He just came in and sat down and started talking.

'It's so quiet here,' he observed, as if tranquillity was a new discovery. Frances noted how American his voice had become, while Charlotte's had remained as English as the day she'd arrived.

'You're looking well, Frances. Well and happy and not too thin,' he said, looking at her in an appreciative way that made her feel slightly uneasy. Why had he come?

'I don't know quite how to take that,' she replied, laughing a little.

'Oh, I shouldn't knock thinness, should I. After all, I've done so well out of it, haven't I.'

Frances wondered whether he'd been drinking. He seemed rather strange, almost belligerent.

'I had a letter from my son the other day. He thinks it's obscene that half the world is spending a fortune on trying to lose weight while the other half hasn't enough money to keep it on. What do you think, Frances. Do you think it's obscene?'

'How old is your son?' she asked.

'Sixteen.'

'Didn't you see the world in those terms at that age?'

'I doubt it. Paul takes after his mother.'

Frances had sat down opposite him. A patch of dappled sunlight jostled about on the carpeted space between them. Outside the wind had got into the trees.

'He's got it wrong, though,' Nick shifted his weight, crossed his legs and looked into his hands.

'He was trying to get at me and I suppose I can't blame him for that. The trouble is the half of the world with the money is no longer spending it as they once did.'

'Is something wrong?' Frances asked, seeing that there was.

'Fortress Against Fat is going to have to file a chapter eleven,' he said flatly.

'I'm sorry, I don't understand,' Frances said.

'I'm one step away from going bust.'

'But the Fortresses have been so successful,' she protested.

'They were, past tense. Fashions change. I think the rot began when Jimmy Carter made a fool of himself jogging. Everyone saw it on television, that moment when he looked as if he was about to have a heart attack.'

'But that was years ago.'

23

Nick stood up and began pacing about the room.

'It's diet and dancing now. Everyone's dieting and dancing.'

'Can't you change your business to that?' she asked.

'It's not that simple. I've invested an enormous amount in gymnasium equipment, weight-lifting apparatus, that sort of thing.'

'What are you going to do?'

'Go back to the UK.'

'Does Charlotte know?'

'Not yet.' He came and sat down beside her on the sofa.

'The UK follows the States. What they were doing ten years ago in California they're doing in England now.'

'Are you sure?'

His arm was resting along the back of the sofa behind her.

'Not entirely,' he answered.

He was studying her closely, and suddenly she understood that it needed only the slightest sign, the smallest indication from her for him to make a pass.

For another moment she remained very still and then she stood up and walked away from him, her heart beating hard with alarm.

'I'll make some tea,' she announced.

After he'd gone she thought of him with loathing. It was not because the possibility of the pass had been there but because she felt so powerful in refusing it. She'd enjoyed that moment too much. It had to do with all the years she'd known Charlotte and seen her eating up life with so enviable an appetite. It was to do with all the times she had stood in the shadows of Charlotte's dramas. But it was a demeaning glory and she hated it and felt as guilty as if she'd let Nick kiss her and take her to bed.

She looked across to Dan. There was a culpability there too, cause for guilt. She had encouraged Charlotte to leave him. She'd thought him too dull a husband for her friend.

'Vicky has to be collected from school at midday,' she said. 'Why don't you go and meet her.'

'Yes,' Dan answered, a little hesitantly.

Frances looked at him.

'Would you mind coming too?' he said. 'It's been three years. She might not recognise me.'

24

Chapter Five

Paul was not looking forward to seeing his father again. He didn't like him, in fact he hated him, and yet he couldn't approach the meeting with the indifference he'd decided to display. He was furious that he had so many spots at the moment and he'd gone into his mother's room to see if he could find some make-up to cover them up for a few hours.

'Paul?' His mother stood in the doorway, brought up short to find him rummaging through her dressing table.

He turned and felt the awful beetroot flush burn hot from his face.

'I wanted to see if you'd got anything for spots,' he croaked.

'Why didn't you ask me. There's some TCP in the bathroom.'

She disappeared, returning a moment later with the bottle and a wad of cotton wool. She unscrewed the top and tipped some of the evil-smelling stuff on to the wad, handing it to him so that he had to stand there in front of her and dab it on his face. He smelt like a medicine cabinet. The spots stung. The doorbell rang.

'That must be him,' his mother said. He couldn't make her out, not over this. She looked absolutely dreadful. Her pale hair hung long and ratty round her face, she wore no make-up, but then he couldn't remember if she ever did. And she had on his old jeans, a pair he'd outgrown two years ago, and a horrible acrylic jumper with a few old sequins that hadn't been ripped off like the rest by the washing machine. He hated that washing machine. It had reduced all his stuff in size and colour.

'You go, Paul. It's you he's come to see,' she said.

He went out on to the landing and caught sight of himself in the oval mirror that threw back distorted shapes as if it was the eye of the house, forever mocking the people in it.

His nose leered out at him, big and red. The doorbell sounded again. He pinched his nostrils together and started down the stairs. The shape of his father blocked out the light from the opaque glass of the front door.

He pulled on the latch and there he was, grey-haired and looking rich, a smirky smile spread across his face.

'Hello Paul,' he said.

God, he sounded like an American!

'Hello,' Paul responded, stiffly. He heard footsteps on the stairs and saw his father's eyes focus behind him.

'Paul, aren't you going to ask your father to come in?' his mother said beyond him.

'How are you Marion?' his father said.

'Hello, Nick.'

They all stood where they were for a few seconds, the three composite bits, but it was the smell of TCP Paul would remember.

He moved away from them, surreptitiously, and told himself he was glad they were no longer the two most important people in his life. Paul was in love.

They went through to the living room which was in its usual state of mess, the comfortable, homely disarray that was Marion and at which Paul now felt a mixture of shame and irritation. Why didn't she make an effort? It didn't have to be like this. He had a very clear picture of the sort of setting in which he imagined his father lived in California. It was the type of place in which Joan Collins would look at home.

'Have you still got your nursery?' Nick asked, for something to say, that was how it sounded.

'My playschool. Yes. We use the scout hut now though. It got too big for here.'

'Sounds as if you're doing pretty good.'

'Oh, mustn't grumble, you know,' Marion answered, adding an unnecessary burst of laughter. She always did that when she was nervous, and Paul could see she was right in it now, her hands quite visibly trembling.

26

Don't ask him to sit down, he begged inside his head. Don't.

'Sit down, Nick. There're plenty of chairs.'

He won't. He'll spoil his clothes sitting on our chairs. Why can't we just go out and get it over with.

His father sank into the nearest chair.

He doesn't want to be alone with me.

'So you're coming back to live here?' Marion said.

'Yes. We're looking for a flat.'

The plural still grated.

'I'd thought you'd stay in America,' Marion continued. 'I thought you liked living there.' She laughed again.

Nick, who had been the only one sitting down, now stood up again.

'We'll have a chat later,' he said. 'I think maybe Paul is waiting for us to go.'

'Of course. I'm sorry,' Marion said. 'I may see you later, then,' she added as they headed towards the front door, and then, by way of further apology 'It's been such a long time . . . ' her voice trailed off.

Outside, at the end of the cul-de-sac, Nick's hired Ford Granada was blocking the neighbour's drive.

'Going now, are you?' the neighbour, Uncle Lionel, as Marion still referred to him when speaking to Paul, commented brusquely. He was holding a pair of hedge clippers and bore no signs of having been about to go out in his own car, an orange Lada, parked in the drive.

Nick smiled at him offensively and got in the car without saying a word. Paul looked away, as if Uncle Lionel was a total stranger, and slouched round to the passenger side.

'I'd forgotten the narrowness of the roads and minds in the UK,' Nick said as he turned the ignition. 'It's twelve o'clock. How do you fancy a beer?'

'I don't mind,' Paul said in a tone he hoped lacked any enthusiasm. He'd no intention of making this father and son getting to know one another session an easy thing. He had wondered how his father would play it, whether he would treat him like a child, or try and make friends with him. It seemed the latter.

'I don't drink,' he said, sullenly.

'Well I do,' Nick countered. 'Can you at least suggest a

decent pub round here, or shall we go to Cambridge?'

'Cambridge, I suppose.' The further away, the better. He wanted to keep this meeting separate from the everyday places of his life.

They turned out on to the main road and did the ten miles to Cambridge at an aggressive speed sufficient to negate the need for conversation, but it was a Saturday and the Cambridge traffic at its worst. It took them twenty minutes to get in a car park.

'How are you doing at school?' Nick began as they waited in the traffic queue.

'Okay,' Paul murmured, noncommittally. He didn't feel like delivering the gratifying news that he'd just got twelve 'O' levels. He waited for the next question: have you decided about what you want to do when you leave? He planned to be facetious.

'Have you got a girlfriend?' Nick asked.

Paul felt the beastly beetroot rise into his face. He didn't want to tell his father about Stacey Middleton, who walked down the street saying 'Fuck' in a loud voice and laughed in that hard, mocking way of girls in a gang. Stacey, whom he hated and adored and who'd cried when she let him do it and said his prick was too big and had hurt.

He'd read Somerset Maugham's *Of Human Bondage* that summer and identified strongly with the sorrowful hero. The book had enabled him to recognise himself as a romantic cynic, and Stacey had so perfectly fitted the part of Maugham's shallow cruel and vulnerable girl, the reality of their relationship had allowed him to live out the part. The thought of it, the whole, the addictive degradation of being in love with someone like Stacey, induced a sensation in the pit of his stomach that was both revulsion and desire.

'No girlfriend?' his father said.

'No.'

Stacey was a year younger than him. She had red hair and a freckly face and legs the shape of bananas. She was at the same school as Paul, and continually in trouble for deviating from the uniform, wearing overt make-up and generally being what was described as a disruptive influence. She was often to be seen in huddles in the school corridors, she and two or three other girls, slouching against one another, always vaguely chewing, always full of disdain.

Paul, who was a willowy person, taller than his contemporaries, had been nicknamed Shoot, a slightly unfortunate handle that had reached the ears of Stacey. At the beginning of term she'd taken excessive delight in calling out 'Hi there, Shoot' accompanied by a most vulgar gesture and great choruses of laughter from the corridor gatherings.

How he hated her. He'd been rather touched by the nickname, pleased that someone had bothered to think about him to this degree. Paul had friends, but they were casual rather than matey. He spent a lot of time alone, mooching round the town after school, frequenting record shops, avoiding the acne-inducing sweet shops where the year before he'd bought Mars bars and cigarettes. (He'd given up both.) He rarely went out at night and had never been a joiner of clubs or organisations like the Scouts; besides, he'd had a lot of homework for the twelve 'O' levels.

At the beginning of the 'A' level course the pressure had eased a little and he felt at a bit of a loose end some evenings. His mother watched television from six o'clocks onwards, every night, after she'd given him his tea, but Paul was uncomfortably aware of the habit being a way of avoiding real life and he was beginning to get fed up with waiting for that to start. He'd spent the long summer holiday working on a farm on the outskirts of the town and had saved up nearly two hundred pounds. But for what? It came over him one evening, a few days into the new term, that if he was not careful (or perhaps not less careful), he'd become a miser.

Restlessly, he moved about his bedroom, flipping through his record collection, ripping down the Driller Killer poster on the wall over his bed, suddenly finding it puerile as well as sick. He went downstairs. The smell of singed beefburgers still hung in the hallway and from the living room came the first few notes of the Nine o'clock News signature tune, swiftly cut off as his mother switched to another channel.

He sort of drifted out of the house and along the cul-de-sac. It was not yet completely dark and the evening was warm. He'd no idea where he was going, just out, somewhere that might be where it was at.

Down in the town it was quieter than he'd imagined it would be. It was a family town. People had big mortgages and didn't go out at night. There was little to entertain in the place because there was so little to be spent. He ambled along the deserted pavements, past the brightly lit shoe shop and the darkened greengrocer's and turned into Gabriel Precinct, the town's seedy attempt at modern shopping.

There was a burnt-out litter bin outside the electricity showroom and a vandalised plant trough by the building society, and as Paul approached the farther end which opened out to the car park, five girls turned into the precinct and started towards him. Instinct inclined him to turn back the way he had come but the potential ramifications of such a move kept him walking towards the group of girls, among them, Stacey Middleton.

'Hey, it's Shoot!' she cried out.

A ripple of giggles ensued. Paul kept on walking, his hands in his trouser pockets, his gaze set squarely ahead and beyond the girls.

'Hey, Shoot. What yer doing with your hands in your pockets!' Ooh, whoo, how they laughed.

Before he had time to think, Paul withdrew his hands. Mortification flooded through him, then anger. The girls stood in a taunting row across his path, one of them, though not Stacey this time, enacting the crude charade of masturbation.

Suddenly Paul leapt forward. His hands grasped hold of Stacey's shoulders. He saw the surprise in her face. The giggling faded. The others seemed to melt away as if absorbed through the plate glass of the shop windows. He held on to Stacey's bony shoulders and pushed her round against the end wall so that her back was pressed into the bricks. Her eyes remained wide and frightened but she was letting him hold her there, as ripe as he for something, anything, to happen.

'You're a crude little bitch,' he said to her, the words catching in his throat.

She said nothing, just carried on staring at him, her eyes bright and moist.

His chest felt so tight he thought he'd never get another breath but in the next moment he jammed his mouth against hers.

30

He saw stars.

This first and somewhat overdue encounter with a female body was not the terrifying thing he'd imagined. It was bliss, and though he didn't know it, made the more so because he had been so angry the moment before.

The kiss came to an end, and Stacey, her arms now looped round his neck, rested limp against him. The others had not reappeared or maybe they'd crept back and seen, and fearful of Stacey, left well alone.

Paul was eager for more, but not where they were, not by a car park which at any moment might be lit up with the glare of headlights.

'Let's go to the park,' Stacey whispered.

They moved away from the wall and went along the unlit path behind the precinct, not touching now but purposefully heading for the park. They went through the broken-down gateway that had been erected as a memorial to the town's war dead, and on into the rustling dark of the park. The light had faded quickly since Paul had left the house and the blanket of night settled round them.

They went along a pathway lined either side with heavy bushes, and on to a small clearing where there was a metal bench. Their pace slowed to a dawdle. They gazed at their feet and idly kicked at the first crop of autumn leaves. Then, abruptly, Stacey sat down on the bench. Paul skirted round her, as if they were about to engage in a fight, then he dropped down beside her. It had been so easy a few minutes earlier. It had just happened, without any thought. But now. He'd begun to shudder, as if the warm evening had suddenly turned cold.

They sat side by side, on the bench, for what seemed like a very long time but was probably only minutes because when he got home it was only twenty-five to ten. Stacey had stood up as abruptly as she'd sat down and walked off the way they had come. Neither had said a word.

From ecstasy to misery in less than half and hour; and the next day Paul had become Shoot the Mute.

A few days later on the Friday night, the school was holding a disco for the fifth and sixth years. Paul never much enjoyed these occasions and thought them more for the benefit of the teachers than the pupils. Last time, Huffer who taught PE had got off with the new biology teacher and everyone had found it revolting to have to witness such middle-age people groping one another on the dance floor. The boys and the girls never danced with one another, in fact the girls hardly danced at all; it was left to the boys to exhibit their break-dancing skills, the narcissistic contortions that used up all their energy and left nothing for the girls.

Paul, of course, had never attempted such a display, though he was uncomfortably envious of those who did. It was strange really that he bothered to attend these discos, but something drew him there, even more so this time, although he quite dreaded it as well, dreaded the gang of girls, the seething female blob.

He arrived late, aware of this being the cool thing to do, though he didn't intend his presence to be noticed. He sidled along the back of the gymnasium, beyond the penetration of kaleidoscopic disco lights, and found an acceptably inconspicuous piece of wall against which to lean. He remained there for some while, his heart beating harder and harder as he watched the others jerking and twirling, as he waited for something to happen. It wasn't a conscious, thought-out anticipation; it was just there, a certainty. But by a quarter to ten, with only fifteen minutes of the evening left, absolutely nothing had come his way. Everyone else seemed to be having such a good time, the dancing boys, the watching girls, at their forefront, her hair like a porcupine, Stacey, pointing and screeching. Was he relieved or disappointed that neither had been directed at him? A sense of frustration he didn't understand gripped his whole being. He felt let down, cheated, and he hadn't any idea why.

He retraced his shadowy route round the back of the gym and went outside, nearly bumping into Huffer and the biology mistress who were engaged in a clinch. He moved away from them as if they were hot coals, but the sound of Huffer's big fat lips, even if he hadn't heard them, squeaking and sucking on Biology's seemed amplified inside his head. He carried on, across the volleyball court, anywhere to try and escape the wretchedness within him, made so much worse by the noise and excitement of which he felt not the least part.

He reached the bicycle sheds and halted. He was not alone.

He didn't see her at first but picked up the small sounds of flesh and blood close by. Then she came partially out of the deep shadows and was no more than a foot in front of him.

'Paul,' she said. 'It's me, Stacey. I saw you go out. I came round the other way.'

She sounded incredibly meek. She'd never called him Paul before.

She stepped fractionally closer and he didn't hesitate a moment longer. The awful cliché of the bicycle sheds flashed through his brain but Stacey smelt of chewing gum and hair gel, a wonderfully erotic combination he breathed in with a gasp of lust just before the first repeat of that star-studded kiss behind Gabriel Precinct. There were lots more, long ones and short ones. Most were clumsy but it didn't matter. It was sex and it was new and overpowering.

'You can do it,' she urged in a trembling whisper. 'I want you to do it.'

And he did, though how he, they, managed it, standing up, leaning against something rusty in the shed, seemed quite incomprehensible in retrospect.

In the sudden calm that followed, the atmosphere thick with vulnerability, Stacey began to whimper: everything hurt, it really did, and he had to promise faithfully not to tell anybody what had happened, oh, he had to promise!

Paul, awkward now because emotion had taken over from the physical part, promised, wanted to put his arms round her in a gesture of protection and comfort. His heart felt bloated with love, the more so because its object was so very unsuitable. The degradation of having done it with Stacey Middleton in the bicycle sheds thrilled him, but to discover that he loved her as well promised an abject humiliation that appealed to him more. It never occurred to him that they could have a fairly normal boy/girl relationship, that, in fact, this was exactly what Stacey wanted.

So the cruel catcalls continued and Paul took them like the martyrs took stones, head bowed but faithful to a promise. It was in the evenings that things were different. They met in the park, in secret, as if each was in some way being unfaithful, which, in a way, they were.

These meetings had been going on nearly a month when

33

Nick telephoned to say he was back and coming to see Paul. The night before the visit, Paul sat in the park with Stacey for longer than usual. So far there had been no repetition of what had happened in the bicycle sheds, though Stacey often maddened him to extreme arousal and insisted he mark her neck with love bites.

On this night they sat and talked, their arms round one another, like real lovers.

'My father's coming tomorrow. I haven't seen him for years,' Paul said.

'You're lucky!' Stacey said. 'Wish I hadn't seen mine for years. He's always going on at me – about the way I dress and my hair and the way I speak. All the fucking time!' She shifted a little in Paul's embrace so that her head rested against his chest.

'I wish you wouldn't say that word,' he said, tentatively.

'Don't you start!'

'No, I mean it, Stace. I don't like it.'

'You like doing it though, don't you,' she said in her stroppy voice.

He didn't answer.

'Oh well, if you don't like it – if you don't like me – I don't know why you bother to keep following me into the park,' she continued, pushing away from him.

'Why do you have to be so angry all the time?' he asked as she stood up.

''Cause you make me angry, fucking angry!' she shouted at him.

'Why?' he said in a tone of genuine bewilderment.

'Oh, I don't know,' she said, sitting on the bench again. 'Everything makes me angry. I don't know why. Perhaps it's because I've got red hair.'

Paul dived towards her, grabbing her round the waist.

'I love you Stace,' he said, knowing it was completely foolish to let her hear this, but unable to hold it back.

'I know,' she said, 'but you shouldn't have told me. I'll be horrid to you now.'

'You're horrid to me anyway,' he said, pulling her towards him.

She became coy.

'I don't mean to be. I can't help it,' she said. Her moods changed so quickly. He couldn't keep up with her. He felt pathetic when he was with her, sort of weakened and defenceless. He nauseated himself. Even the way he called her Stace, seemed a pitiable attempt at ingratiation.

'What's your father like?' she asked now.

'I don't know. I never really got to know him.'

'Why did he and your mum split up?'

'He went off with someone else.'

'What's she like?'

'Ghastly.'

'I mean what does she look like?'

'Oh, she's got blonde hair. She's a bit fat, I think, at least, that's how I remember her.'

'Why didn't your mum marry again?'

'I should think she'd had enough after Dad. They were always rowing. I remember that. I used to sit on the stairs and listen to them. He always made her cry.'

'You shouldn't have.'

'What?'

'Spied on them.'

'Why not? The noise they made used to wake me up.'

'I can hear my parents at it some nights. Not rowing. Doing it. You know. It makes me feel sick.'

'They are married.'

'Of course they are dummy! But it's disgusting – your mum and dad. You know what I mean,' she whined impatiently.

They were silent for a while but couldn't start kissing again because the conversation about parents had put them off.

'It'll be funny seeing your dad, funny strange,' Stacey said, as if she'd been giving the matter some thought. 'You won't know what to say, will you.'

'I don't intend saying anything. I don't even want to see him. He left us and now he thinks he can just pick up the phone and say he's coming over. I don't want him to know anything about me. He thinks he's something special. The big, international businessman.' Paul's voice had taken on a sneering bitter edge.

'I'd like to meet him,' Stacey said.

'Well you can't. You're too capricious,' Paul said.

'Big words is it now! What's the matter? Ashamed of me, are you?'

'I thought it was the other way round. I thought you didn't want anyone to know about me.'

'Maybe I don't,' she replied, offhandedly. 'But I'd really like to meet this father of yours. I'd dress up in my best behaviour,' she added, wheedlingly.

'I used to write to him when he was in America and he'd get someone else to reply.' Paul went on in his train of thought. 'All the letters were typed. I think he just told one of his secretaries to dream up something to send back.'

'I've never had a typed letter,' Stacey murmured.

This strange little admission flew to Paul's heart; somehow it seemed hugely endearing. He tightened his arms round her. He felt as if he might explode with love and hate, confusion and impatience, with her, with his father.

'You're crushing my fucking ribs,' she announced.

'I'm sorry,' he said, letting her go.

'So you should be!' she said, pertly. 'I'm going home.'

'Can't I take you?'

'Leave it out,' she said in her harsh voice. 'I'm off. And if it was my father,' she called over her shoulder, 'I'd get back at him in some way. I would!'

As usual she left him on an edge of uncertainty. He followed her to the park gates and watched her hurry away down the street, her strange shaped legs giving her a vaguely ape-like appearance. In school on Monday she'd be rotten to him again. He felt slightly uneasy about having told her so much of his feelings towards his father. Really he didn't know what he felt, only that he couldn't stop thinking about it and had alternated between wanting to do somersaults, cut his throat, disappear.

'You won't know what to say,' Stacey had said, with uncharacteristic perception, and she was so right. Nothing he said could be enough and therefore it was better to be a deliberate disappointment. Besides, why should he take the trouble to be otherwise: hadn't his father let him down, let Mum down, and all the time he'd been in America, making all that money doing something totally unworthwhile, he'd never even suggested a visit . . . he hadn't wanted to see him then. He

36

couldn't be bothered until it was easy and didn't cost him anything.

Paul felt like a child when he had these kinds of thoughts. He was overcome by a sense of unfairness that seemed to stand before him like a concrete wall barring his way. He wanted to get round it, to see over it, but he couldn't.

Chapter Six

'How did it go?' Charlotte asked when Nick got back, though she could tell by his manner that the reunion with Paul had been a failure.

He flopped down on the hotel bed.

'It's been too long,' he said wearily. 'If only Marion had let him come over and see us in the States.'

'How is Marion?' Charlotte felt bound to ask and was indeed curious.

'Oh, she's still got her nursery school. She seems okay. She hasn't really changed.'

Inexplicably, this was a relief to Charlotte, though why she should be glad that Marion had remained unchanged was a mystery hidden somewhere within her own vanity.

'What's Paul like?' she asked.

'Tall and spotty. No personality.' Nick answered.

'Oh come on! He was probably nervous. It'll be better when we've got our own place and he can come and stay,' Charlotte comforted, 'I've called one or two estate agents today. There are two houses in Cambridge I've arranged to go and see.' She was feeling rather pleased with her day. The houses in question sounded promising and the old bug for bricks and mortar had stirred in her as a palliative to the deeper feelings of unrest.

'I'm going on Monday. I'll combine it with seeing Audrey.' This was said in order to make it clear to Nick that she did not expect him to go with her. She could have viewed the houses on Sunday but the properties she'd selected were smaller than he might expect. She had not fully admitted it to herself, but they were of a size to accommodate herself and Vicky at a manageable level.

Nick did not respond. Equally, there was a reality he had not yet faced.

'I thought we might go out tonight. See a film. Have a meal somewhere,' he said, steering his thoughts away from the dismal sense of panic that had accompanied the events of the day and now Charlotte talking about property in Cambridge.

'That would be nice,' she responded. 'What shall we see?' The idea appealed because a film would negate the need for conversation even though there was more to discuss now than at any time in their marriage.

They'd stopped talking for about six months now. The long hours of discussion, late into the night, always about the business, had become so boring to Charlotte that latterly she'd not even bothered with the pretence of listening. But Nick had carried on, talking at her, ranting on about the inefficiency of his staff, seemingly oblivious of her lack of interest. He'd stopped these sessions when Fortress against Fat had started to go seriously wrong. He'd closed in on his problems and grown silent and preoccupied in a manner that was no longer aggressive. He was bewildered at what was happening: unable to accept the failure. In fact he was quite terrified.

The degree to which he and Charlotte had ceased communicating was most strongly demonstrated by her being completely unaware of how close they were to insolvency.

He'd bought a newspaper, the same one he'd supplied with so many stories years ago when his ambition had been in journalism and he'd wanted so badly to get to Fleet Street. He swiftly turned the pages.

'Here we are. What do you fancy?' he said, spreading out the entertainments page over the bed.

'I don't know. What do you prefer?'

'No, I asked you. Why do you always have to answer with a question,' he said, suddenly becoming irritable.

'I don't always answer with a question,' she snapped back at him.

'You do! You don't know that you're doing it, that's the trouble. You can't make a decision.'

'Oh, for God's sake!'

'Look, choose a film, will you!'

'Here we go!'

'What do you mean "here we go"?'

Charlotte sighed. She really couldn't be bother with these tedious little squabbles, not any more. For the past few months she'd managed to maintain a superficial civility with Nick who'd been even more preoccupied with business than during the earlier part of their time together. She'd been resentful, even jealous of his work. She'd accused him of hastening the course of their affair, pushing her to make the choice between him and Dan, primarily because the initial energy involved in secret meetings, clandestine love, had reduced his business effort. He hadn't liked that accusation. It was too close to the truth. They'd had a big fight over that one, with Charlotte forcing the pace in order to top up the level of passion. But now, oh, she couldn't imagine summoning the enthusiasm for that sort of thing. She'd hung on to a pretence of it for quite a while, hoping the feelings might become real again, but they were way beyond that first intensity and excitement and she'd been relieved, if not exactly glad, that Nick's attention had become so very elsewhere. It had occurred to her that he'd found someone else and this had hurt, but not because she had any love left for him, it was merely pride.

She wasn't yet ready to start questioning why she remained with him, though this was probably pride as well. It suited her to come back to England as part of a successful partnership: it was how she wanted it to appear to her friends, her mother.

'Do you want to see a film, or don't you?' Nick demanded, unpleasantly.

'We might as well,' she said, thinking to add that a film would be preferable to a boring and probably boorish evening over the supper table.

She scanned the list of films in the paper and decided they should go to the new Clint Eastwood: a story about a detached stranger riding into town appealed to her mood.

On Monday morning she got up early and caught the train from London to Cambridge. She'd telephoned her old friend, Audrey, on Friday and had been quite nervous about it. She'd not spoken to her since the split with Dan and was not certain Audrey would want to see her. She was a strong churchgoer and had always voiced her disapproval of other couples they both knew who'd failed to stay together for the sake of their children.

But Audrey was, and always had been, a good sort, in fact a thoroughly acceptable example of a real Christian. She was bigoted, but that was part of her charm. Most of all she was kind and had probably been the only buffer between Charlotte and insanity during the dreadful two years when post-natal depression had been such a leaden weight and life had no joy, not even the new life of Vicky.

'Charlotte? Charlotte!', Audrey had responded when she answered the telephone on Friday. 'I can't believe it! All this time!'

Of course nothing would have changed in Audrey's life. A rock remained a rock, and Audrey was as solid and reliable as granite. The prospect of seeing her again was not entrancing but comforting. The impetus was to find out about Dan.

On the train Charlotte now allowed herself to dwell on thoughts of her former husband, the poignant, dangerous thoughts that had filled and widened the rift between her and Nick. She knew it was possible these thoughts were enchanted, that it was only the distance of time blurring the misery of a stale relationship and re-focusing on an image of Dan that was her own concocted composite of the bits she wanted to remember.

She thought about the house where she'd lived with Dan and wondered about seeing it again – her house but no longer open to her. It was still Dan's home though she knew he'd taken a flat in London soon after becoming an MP and perhaps he'd let the house near Cambridge, perhaps there were strangers living there now. This thought produced a coldness within her, an unpleasant sensation that had to do with irretrievability.

Audrey was waiting at the station, her arm like a flagpole in a gale as the train drew in.

'I was worried you might not recognise me,' she said, clasping Charlotte in a bear hug. 'Oh, it's so good to see you again. Isn't Vicky with you? I thought you'd bring her. The children are terribly excited.'

'Vicky's still in America – with Frances,' Charlotte explained, adding the bit about Frances because she didn't want

Audrey to suppose she might have left Vicky alone. She remembered now that Audrey had always had this effect on her, the heightened awareness of her own shortcomings. Why had she thought of her as comforting?

'How are you?' she asked, holding Charlotte at arm's length now and inspecting her with an expression of exaggerated solicitude as if she'd only recently emerged from some harrowing experience.

'I'm fine,' Charlotte told her. 'Really fine.'

'And so thin!'

Charlotte smiled. She liked her thinness and having been unable to eat after the row about nothing on Saturday night she'd decided to go without food on Sunday as well. She had, she realised, wanted to feel thin when she met Audrey again: Audrey of the batch baking, home-made biscuits and bottled fruit.

Audrey had thick, greying hair cut in a straight line on a level with her chin. Her face was slightly ruddy in complexion and the only make-up she used was red lipstick. Her large frame had only ever been clothed in the style she wore now, ample Laura Ashley skirts, hand-knitted jumpers and an anorak. What could be seen of her legs showed thickly ribbed tights stuck in flat brown lace-ups. Charlotte couldn't exactly explain why, but Audrey looked like a home-made biscuit herself, big and misshapen but wholesomely appetising and full of goodness.

'Come on,' she said, energetically. 'Let's get back to the house and have some elevenses.'

'I'm dying to hear all about America,' she said as they drove out of Cambridge in the Morris Minor Traveller she'd had at least a decade. 'But first you must tell me what you want to do today. Did I hear you right about looking at some houses? Are you really back for good?'

'I've got two to see this afternoon.'

'How exciting!'

Audrey and James and their three children lived in a converted village school. James was a likable know-all, and like Charlotte, a graphic designer by profession. He had a studio in the upper part of the house and worked there with two assistants (maybe more now).

42

'Here we are!' Audrey said unnecessarily as they pulled up outside the Gothic front door that was never used.

They got out of the Traveller and Charlotte followed Audrey round the side of the building to the glass panelled lean-to that had been built over the back door. One of the panes was smashed.

'That's our very own football hooligan,' said Audrey with long-suffering and that underlying pride peculiar to mothers of rumbustious sons.

Charlotte peered beyond the broken glass and remembered the last time she'd passed through Audrey's back kitchen with its rows of cobwebby gumboots and wall pegs heaped with old anoraks. It had been with Dan, during the last few days they were together. They'd gone there for Sunday lunch. Audrey and James hadn't known that it was all about to fall apart and there'd been a lot of talk about another couple who'd recently parted and the effect it was having on the child of the marriage. Audrey had been very disapproving; was she still, beneath the effusive welcome?

The main part of Audrey's kitchen was a monument to self-sufficiency. Shelves and shelves of the famed bottled fruit lined the walls, a basket of vegetables, freshly dug from the garden, stood by the sink, with crumbs of chalky mud hanging from the roots. Two loaves of home-baked bread were on top of the Aga, and from a great number of hooks ranged along the Welsh dresser dangled an assortment of hand thrown pottery mugs.

'Nothing's changed,' Charlotte murmured.

'Sorry?' Audrey said.

'Nothing's changed. It's all just as it was the last time I was here.'

Audrey's colour deepened a little as she too remembered the last time. Was it the next day or the day after that she'd found out Charlotte was leaving Dan? She remembered how unsettling it had been, coming so soon after the other couple she and James knew. It had made her look at her own, somewhat argumentative marriage and wonder whether James ever cast an eye elsewhere.

Never one to pass over what was uppermost in her thoughts, she now looked at Charlotte and asked whether she'd seen

Dan since coming back.

'He doesn't even know I'm in the country,' Charlotte told her, slightly taken aback by the directness of the question, but relieved it had been Audrey and not herself who'd started talking about Dan.

'Have you seen him lately?' she asked.

Audrey sat down at her scrubbed pine table.

'Not for a long time,' she said, pausing, wondering whether to go on, or perhaps Charlotte already knew about the wretched business earlier in the year? 'Not since the court case,' she added.

Charlotte didn't know. Her eyes gave her away, widening, staring as she slithered on to the chair the other side of the table.

'What court case?' she asked.

'Oh dear,' Audrey said. 'Still, it's all over now, though it was very unpleasant at the time.'

'Tell me please!' Charlotte insisted, impatiently.

Audrey thought for a moment, a little put out by the way Charlotte had just spoken to her; after all, it wasn't as if she'd any claim on Dan any more.

'It was a rape case,' she said, somewhat bluntly.

'My God!' Charlotte exclaimed, the palms of her hands falling flat on the table.

'Not Dan, of course not Dan,' Audrey hastened to explain.

'Who then? And why was he involved?' Charlotte demanded, a cold flush running through her.

'It's complicated,' Audrey continued, hesitantly. She felt a bit sly, or rather, that she might be appearing so, and this made her uncomfortable with herself as well as with Charlotte who was exhibiting the territorial expression of the former wife.

'A girl had been living at Dan's house, James and I met her last Christmas. Oh, she was extremely nice, a solicitor.' Audrey stood up in order to occupy her hands with some other activity while she related the story. Why had she used the word living and not staying and insisted how extremely nice Mickey was? She didn't much like herself at the moment. She felt confused and inexplicably resentful towards Charlotte. She and James had liked Mickey and even though she was so much younger than Dan they'd hoped something might come of the relationship, perhaps for themselves as well as for him, because they'd missed being friends as couples: it hadn't been the same when Dan had come to dinner by himself, there'd been the sadness, the residue of Charlotte.

'Of course Dan wasn't there much of the time. Mickey – that's the girl's name – she was, well, a sort of lodger at the house, I think. Anyway, she was there alone when it happened. A man broke in. It was rumoured that she knew him, or had known him. Then there was the court case and, oh, it was all rather nasty. People said unkind things and the full facts never got reported because they can't print much about those sorts of cases any more. Dan had a run in with the local Tories. Some of them wanted him to resign his seat in the Commons because of the possible scandal, but really the only scandalous bit was the way he was treated.'

'What were the unkind things that were said?' Charlotte asked.

'Oh, silly nonsense,' Audrey said dismissively, reaching for two of the pottery mugs. But she couldn't resist saying it, who could?

'A *ménage à trois*, but people are prepared to believe anything of that sort if a politician is involved,' she added, somehow compounding the allegation even though this was not what she'd intended.

'I see,' Charlotte said quietly.

'Oh, you don't!' Audrey said anxiously, putting down the mugs, facing Charlotte squarely. 'None of us really knows exactly what was going on but I can't believe anything like that of Dan, can you?'

'No,' Charlotte conceded, bleakly. 'No, I can't.'

'I wish I hadn't said anything now,' Audrey continued. 'It's spoilt our day, hasn't it?'

Distressing, perhaps as everything else she'd said had been, this last comment was the most disturbing, revealing that Audrey had perceived too much, more than Charlotte was yet prepared to admit to herself. The knowledge that Dan had possibly found someone else burnt in her. She felt jealous and despairing and wretchedly unjustified in having such feelings. They were no longer her right.

Chapter Seven

Dan's weekend with his daughter had gone well. Vicky's pleasure in seeing him had been unbounded and two days was too short a time for her to start exhibiting the sulky aggression that was beginning to concern the school.

On Sunday evening he drove her back in Frances' car.

'I'll bring your bag in,' he said, parking outside the school and reaching over to the back seat for Vicky's weekend case. He wanted to prolong their being together, to see the places where she lived and slept so he could picture her in these surroundings until they were both back inEngland and he'd be able to see her on a regular basis. He'd speak to Charlotte as soon as possible to find out her plans, but he had decided to take a firmer stand than before: if necessary he would go to the courts and ask for formal access. He wanted Vicky to have a home with him as well as with her mother.

'No, it's all right, I'll manage. Anyway, it's not allowed,' she answered him, sixth sense telling her it might be unwise to permit him access to those who had found her out.

'I really think I should come in,' he persisted. 'It's going to seem a bit strange if I don't.'

'I can't see why,' Vicky said, affecting a little petulence.

'Vicky, I've come all this way. I can't just drop you off as if it's an everyday thing.'

'But none of the other kids' parents come in. I'd feel like a baby. Daddy please!' she pleaded, and of course he gave in, just as he always had to Charlotte.

He felt uneasy about it as he drove off. It was a feeling he'd not known for several years, but came back to him now as if it had been Charlotte who'd got the better of him. The issue was not large, but it was a question of what was right and what was wrong, and Vicky, like her mother, had succeeded in manipulating him to act against his will. It revived a sense of weakness in himself he'd not had cause to examine since Charlotte's departure. It was meeting his past and remembering the shortcomings that had cut into his self-esteem. It was a jab at the scar, a sharp reminder of failure.

Frances drove him to San Francisco airport. Traffic on the Bay Bridge was more than usually heavy and he only just made the flight. All the years they'd known one another in England they'd never so much as touched, but at the departure gate they kissed each other's cheeks in the effusive manner of America. Momentarily they were awkward because neither was naturally demonstrative and the gesture held sincere regard plus an element of apology for misunderstandings of the past. Each had resented the other's role in Charlotte's life.

'Vicky can phone you weekends from our house,' Frances proffered as Dan moved away.

'Yes. That would be nice,' he called back to her. 'Thanks. Thanks for everything.'

It was early evening in New York when Dan got in to La Guardia. He rang Mickey and suggested they meet in Manhattan. Winter was well on the way and the air as cold and damp as in London as he got out of the cab on Lexington. He walked a couple of blocks, steam rising from the streets at every manhole, and above, the New York fog dripping down against the flat-faced buildings. It felt very enclosed, a city of nightmare proportions, a pastiche of hell, though maybe it was just his mood. He was looking forward to the evening with Mickey but now preoccupied by thoughts of his daughter: it seemed entirely wrong that she should be separated by such vast distances from both her parents, but there was more to it than that. It was a combination of the way Charlotte had so completely excluded him from decisions involving Vicky, a sense of ineffectuality in himself to have allowed it to happen, and Vicky's vulnerability. She was like Charlotte in every way, but most of all in this. Her eyes had darted about when she'd pleaded with him not to come into the school, this manner of her insistence triggering so vivid a memory of her mother, and

47

yet it was not until this moment he remembered how steeped in ulterior motive Charlotte had been on such occasions, deceiving him every time simply because deception was her way, almost for its own sake. Some people were like that, but it was never easy to recognise and admit it in someone loved. And ulterior motive, especially for its own sake, indicated a disturbed inner life, an imbalance in the drives and emotions. It amounted to dissatisfaction at the least, despair at the worst.

Had he been a more impetuous man Dan might well have turned on his heel in the midst of this worrying train of thought and gone straight back to San Francisco, but practicality held him down, clod-like, the ballast in a life that rarely deviated from sane and reasoned action. Only twice had he freed himself from this weight, the first when he'd bullied (his view) Charlotte into marrying him, and the second so very recently when he'd crossed the Atlantic on a wing and a prayer, a foolish middle-aged Romeo, an old dog with a vain notion. Dan's self-regard had never been strong.

He'd reached Maude's, the Edwardian style bar attached to the hotel favoured by Europeans. It was a place where a woman could sit alone without feeling uncomfortable, and Dan, being the sort of man he was, had naturally taken this into consideration when arranging to meet Mickey. His preference would have been to have collected her from the office in Brooklyn, but she'd been alone in New York for months . . . just as Vicky had been at her school. A small wave of irritation and sadness buffeted him, a mildly self-pitying sense of redundancy.

Maude's was a very brown place, dark and heavy and richly warm, an attempt at the old gin palaces of south-east London, destroyed in the sixties, recreated in the eighties, a seedy style reassessed as chic through the vision of nouveau nostalgia. Mickey was sitting at a table for two, her head framed against a large mirror elaborately engraved with an old-fashioned advertisement for brown ale. Dan saw her before she noticed him and for a moment experienced that sense of division peculiar to such situations, seeing and not being seen. A tall young waiter had approached the table. Mickey's face tilted up, smiling. The waiter inclined his head nearer. Words were exchanged. More smiling. Dan edged past a group of men gazing at a large flat screen video over the bar. The sound of American football roared at him and the group of men, like a stray piece of jigsaw from the pictured crowd, responded with a sigh and a groan: their side wasn't winning and there was nothing they could do about it.

Dan reached the table where Mickey and the waiter were still engaged in conversation.

'Dan!' she exclaimed in greeting and pleasure.

The waiter turned. Was there surprise in his expression? Did he think it inexplicable, a waste of youth, a most unlikely alliance? Would he be thinking this man must have money, it's the only explanation?

'What can I get you sir?'

Dan had sat down and Mickey taken hold of his hand in an uncharacteristically overt gesture of possession. The scene continued: the youthful waiter now left in no doubt as to the nature of the relationship, Mickey, eyes bright, excited, nervous, Dan, seeing too clearly how the tableau was flawed, the casting wrong. He felt very tired then, his worries, near paranoia, suddenly too overblown to be allowed any more expansion in his thoughts. Enough was enough. Mentally, he reset himself.

'Sir?' the waiter repeated, receding, no longer more than a bringer of drinks.

'How did it go?' Mickey asked when he'd gone.

'Fine, though I was sorry you weren't there. Vicky was . . . ' he paused, searching for the right adjective and failing to find anything that could adequately describe the way Vicky had been. 'I think you will like each other,' he chose instead.

'And Charlotte, how is she?'

'She wasn't there. She's gone back to live in the UK. Vicky will be joining her at the end of the school term.'

'You didn't know? She hadn't told you?'

'No. It was rather a surprise. Her friend Frances, you know, the one married to an American, is looking after Vicky at weekends.'

'All this way. . .' Mickey said. 'Do you suppose Charlotte would have let you know.' She had pieced together her own picture of Charlotte. She imagined her to be a tall, intimidating sort of person, cold and unpredictable. She thought of her as self-possessed and single-minded, a woman who always got her own way. It was an image of a rival, because she'd always understood that Dan had loved his wife more than she, Mickey, would ever expect him to love her. After all, their relationship had been founded on low expectations: they were sort of trying one another out were they not?

'We're not enemies,' Dan said, but as if the idea was new to him. 'I'm sure she'll be in touch when we get back.'

They were due to return to London in a few days' time, to go to a christening. They planned to attend the event together, though it was Mickey who'd been invited, she was to be godmother. They'd thought to spend ten days there, enough time for Dan to sort out business and political commitments, leaving him free for an extended holiday in America, though really it was to be the trying one another out time. And Mickey, who'd already been in New York some months, was due the time back home to see her family.

Of course, it was all a great deal more complicated than this. The child to be christened belonged to Mickey's friend Josephine who for more than a year had been living with Mickey's estranged husband, David. The situation was bizarre, perhaps untenable. To have been allotted the spiritual and not the physical role seemed a peculiar yet irresistible twist of fate, and to have refused would have seemed as churlish and bad-loserish as turning down a consolation prize. It was not as if Josephine had stolen David from her. David had thrown her out for other reasons, though the child, Josephine's baby, had been conceived before all that.

To the outside eye nobody emerged with much credit from so messy an affair, but it seemed to Mickey incumbent upon all of them that Giles Alexander, five months old, should in no way suffer because he was the incidental issue from all the mistakes and misunderstandings.

Josephine and David had not stayed together and perhaps this made it somewhat easier for Mickey, who was not entirely without normal human jealousy despite her own culpability. She'd thought herself still in love with her husband at the time the baby was born, which coincided with her going to America; and soon afterwards David had written to her, tentative words and phrases that hinted at a reconciliation, but nothing had come of them. It was too late.

So she was to attend the christening with Dan, who knew both David and Josephine, and who sat beside her now, looking tired and old and worried, and whose hand she was still holding as if trying to prove a point.

'Let's go back to the apartment,' she said. 'I'll make something there. I don't feel like eating out.'

They finished their drinks and Dan paid, absent-mindedly considerably overtipping the waiter who only then observed and allotted the grey-haired Englishman sugar daddy status. They always did it, the older guys, big money, small balls: it was an acceptably comforting thought for somebody with the opposite set of proportions.

'Can we walk for a bit,' Mickey said when they were outside. 'I love New York when it's like this – sort of subterranean.' She linked her arm into Dan's. He knew exactly what she meant and was pleased she seemed so untroubled and hopeful even though the city still oppressed him.

But he was wrong in thinking her carefree. Her pattern for the future had been vague and unstructured until now. She thought she had been prepared just to let things happen, but things that included Dan, Dan in New York. She didn't want to go back to England, not long term; too much had gone wrong for her there. She'd thought maybe Dan felt the same, though it was early days. Unwittingly, she'd conjured up a blurred but possibly blissful future existence removed by both time and geography from the horrible past. The notion had been a warm one, a pocket of comfort and joy that had made food taste good again, music sound uplifting, New York, no matter how dark, misty and grey, seem a brave, invigorating place to be. And now, all of a sudden, the feeling had begun to change. Vague hope had turned to chilling uncertainty: how could Dan contemplate a future in America while his daughter was about to return to England.

'It's not as warm as I thought,' she said, out loud.

'Come on, we'll get a cab,' Dan said, his own thoughts having been travelling in a similar transatlantic direction.

Later that night, after Mickey had scrambled eggs that tasted bland and blanket-like they took off their clothes and made an effort to be lovers. Each was very careful of the other, remembering too clearly the long time they had liked one another as friends, perhaps too long for this latter day transition. Neither could really look at the other, only close their eyes and accept the tentative touch of hands guided more by theory than practice. It was revision of zones discovered on other bodies, an exercise fraught with involuntary comparison.

Dan, whose naked flesh had seemed passable in the hotel bedroom of a few days earlier, was now struggling to summon sufficient self-love for it to feel right, for the act itself to be non gross.

Something had gone wrong, been lost, and Mickey's nakedness made her seem strangely unfamiliar. Perhaps it had been a mistake to attempt to turn it into a ritual. Before, they'd made love in bed, under cover, in the dark, whereas this time they'd started in the apartment's living room, with the light on and nothing in the impersonal, predominantly beige surroundings to soften a contour, smother a shiver. Maybe it would have been easier if they'd not wanted to love one another so badly.

Later into the night Mickey dreamt of the rape. It was getting on for a year now since it had happened but the memory was hideously precise and clear, more so than it had been at the time, as if only now was she able to focus the detail.

Arthur, the strange, intoxicating little man whom she'd thought homosexual, but who had become her lover and caused the destruction of her marriage to David, entered the stage of her sleeping mind like the genie from the lamp; suddenly he was there, smiling, leering, coaxing. Mickey shrank from him but was mesmerised, fixed in terror by those hugely round, almost opaque eyes. The index finger of his left hand seemed to expand and grow and then metamorphose into a sort of dagger that glinted and started to vibrate as if an electric current was being passed through it. It became hugely threatening, advancing towards her, wagging admonishingly, and then it began to stab at her, though the first few strikes were hardly felt. Maybe it was all a joke, a cruel little tease of the sort so beloved by Arthur. A tickle here. A tickle there! But no joke. Not funny at all.

The finger, the dagger, Arthur's raping phallus, Mickey felt it now as if her body was being seared in two. She tried to scream but no sound came because there was no air to gulp in to fuel the cry. She was being smothered, an enormously heavy mass of softness being pressed over her face. Then abruptly it stopped and she was up and running, though for every stride she gained, the distance to escape became that bit longer. She tripped and tumbled down a flight of stairs and then she was running the length of the drive outside Dan's house, the tall, densely planted trees bending and swaying towards her, a wind as cold as ice whipping round her naked body.

The police were there at the end of the drive, forming a row of disapproval across her path. Guilty! Guilty! You're the guilty one.

But I'm not. He came to me unbidden.

Genies never come unbidden.

He tried to kill me! Don't you understand?

But he didn't, did he!

I'm not sure.

Attention seeker.

She woke up and gasped in continuing terror at the realisation of another body in the bed. She went for the side lamp, her fingers fumbling for the switch.

The light on, Dan stirred and woke too, levering himself up into a sitting position. He saw her distress and reached out his hand to touch her shoulder. She flinched away from him.

'Mickey?' he said with concern.

She got out of the bed, snatching for her dressing gown as if her exposure might be seen by him as indecent.

'A nightmare,' she murmured, knotting the gown's cord into her waist. She sat back on the bed and pulled her fingers through her hair. 'I've always been prone to them,' she added, not wanting to have to relate the sexually sordid contents still stored in her head, though Dan had been the one person she'd been able to tell about Arthur. She never thought anyone else would be able to understand – the captivating cleverness of insanity – its near contagious effect. She felt half-mad now. Dan touched her again and she felt as if she'd been singed. It had been all right before, when she'd talked to him as her friend and employer and the man who had let her stay in his house after David had told her to go. It had been easy then when touching went unnoticed because it was without significance. Friends could touch without threat. Lovers expected more. Fingers probing and seeking, greedy for arousal no matter how cold and dry the flesh they crept over. Mickey, her back turned against Dan, shivered with revulsion. In that moment she hated him so very vehemently and without cause, a surge of bitterness rising in her to the point where she felt quite rigid with spite. God, if he touched her now she'd shatter completely and cut him to bits. Hate! Hate! I hate you! she seemed to be yelling insanely inside her head; and of course, it was herself that she hated: nobody else could come anywhere near being so loathsome.

Chapter Eight

'What are you doing today?' Nick asked.

'Going to Cambridge again,' Charlotte answered him, adding, 'there's so much to be arranged,' as if she already had cause for guilt, need of excuse.

He paused in the bathroom doorway, apparently studying the tiled floor.

'If you don't see anything worth buying have a look at rented stuff. It's costing an arm and a leg to go on staying here,' he said.

He advanced a few steps into the bathroom then turning, calling back to her: 'And do you think you could find a launderette or something, getting the hotel to wash everything is rather extravagant.'

It seemed to Charlotte, brittle and bad-tempered first thing in the morning, that this accusation of extravagance was being directed entirely against her.

'I suppose your idea of a launderette is me washing everything by hand,' she snapped.

'That wasn't what I said.'

'It's what you meant.'

'Have it your own way.'

She roused herself from the bed in a frenzy of imagined affront made more unacceptable by the frustration of having to concoct these little abrasions and failing to understand why. Her mouth contained that thick, liverish bitterness, the residue of too much to drink the previous night, and cause for yet more unfocused resentment in the general direction of Nick.

'You'd be the first to complain if my hands got all

washer-womany she accused the back of his neck. He was leaning over the basin, brushing his teeth in that pedantic, over vigorous way of his. Irritation, stemming from this and then inflating to encompass everything that he was, made her turn away and retreat to the bedroom. When he could speak again he shouted: 'Why don't you take your foul temper back to bed,' and slammed the connecting door to keep her at bay.

A year ago, maybe longer, she might have flown to the barricade and hammered on it with her fists until his temper was such that he flung the door open, his eyes narrowed in anger, every muscle in his body taut and ready to get at her. But that sort of behaviour no longer convinced either of them. They'd gone sour on one another; they really couldn't be bothered with lust any more.

Charlotte moved over to the wardrobe to choose what she would wear for the day. She planned to meet Audrey again but more particularly she wanted to speak to James in the hope he might be able to put some work her way. During the years in America, she'd worked spasmodically, finding it difficult at first to get anything in her line. At one point she'd even considered waitressing, which in the States wasn't at all the low grade occupation it was in Britain. But Nick had told her not to be so stupid: they were rolling in money and how would it look to their friends if she turned up at their table in a white pinny?

That had caused one of those narrowed eyes, violence threatening rows.

'How dare you try and tell me what I can do and what I can't. How dare you!' she'd screamed at him.

'You're my wife!'

'So what!'

'You wouldn't be here if you weren't.'

'I wouldn't be out of work if I wasn't here.'

'You're bloody ungrateful.'

'I didn't know that gratitude was part of marriage.'

'Oh shut up.'

'How would you like it if I tried to tell you what sort of job you should have?'

'You're just a stupid bitch!'.

'You always resort to insult when you're losing an argument.'

How she hated him when he called her names. It wasn't the unpleasant words that made her bristle and burn with indignation, it was that she'd married a man not quite as clever as her but who thought himself her equal, even her superior.

In their last year in America she had managed to find work that satisfied both of them. She'd been doing a few hours a week in one of the small art galleries across the Bay in Sausalito. She was no more than a glorified shop assistant, but the owner of the gallery also had a public relations agency in Manhattan and had asked her if she'd undertake one or two freelance jobs in graphic design. After that she got more work via a Fortress Against Fat client who Nick introduced her to at a party. He'd wanted a cover designed for his company's annual report and from there it snowballed in a pin money sort of way, because although the designs were good, it was Charlotte's low charges that brought in the commissions.

She ran her hand along the row of hanging sleeves in the hotel wardrobe and picked out a business-like suit that might help James to view her as a potential colleague rather than his wife's wayward friend. The bathroom door opened and Nick emerged, run out of steam, fully dressed, ready for the day.

'I'll see you tonight', he said. 'You might as well forget about the launderette.'

She turned from the wardrobe, head up, victorious; she didn't give him much quarter these days. It was the mean streak in her.

He caught her expression.

'I'll make enquiries myself,' he added. 'Have a nice day.'

He'd gone and the victory, which could only have been hollow, altered to defeat. She could imagine what would happen next: he'd find a launderette and so would she, and they'd squabble over which one was better. It was all so relentlessly demeaning. She didn't like herself one bit.

To restore the balance a little she decided to ring her mother before leaving for Cambridge. It was providence. A good deed rewarded.

'Oh Lottie, what a relief you've telephoned. I couldn't remember the name of the hotel. It was on the tip of my tongue but I just couldn't think of it. I told him I was a silly old fool and that I'd probably remember it as soon as we'd finished

57

talking. Oh, it was so nice to have a chat with him, and you'll never guess, but I should think you two must have just about gone past one another in the air. Think of that!'

'Mother, what are you talking about?'

'Dan, of course. He flew to America the same time you were coming back.'

Charlotte felt a wave of nausea. She'd missed him.

'Dan rang you from America?'

'No, no. From Cambridge.'

'But I thought you just said. . .'

'It was only a short visit. He's back home now and he wants to get in touch with you.' She said this in a tone of blinkered hope and promise, as if Charlotte was a teenager about to embark on first love.

'Why did he go to America?' Charlotte asked, although it was already in her mind that he could have been going there to see her. The possibility was tantalising, its attraction making it more believable than was sensible, but then why shouldn't he want to see her? He had loved her a lot.

'Oh, I didn't like to ask him,' Mother answered, allowing the continuance of optimistic uncertainty.

Had it been otherwise, Charlotte might have remembered that never during the years she had been married to Dan and before that when they were children, could she have thought of a single occasion when he'd done anything unplanned, un-announced, incautious.

'You will telephone him, won't you, dear?'

'Yes, Mother, of course I will.'

When the call was over Charlotte remained still and quiet for a moment or two. She felt excited and nervous. It seemed like a touch from the hand of fate. She decided then that she wouldn't ring Dan but instead she would go to the house, especially as she was travelling to Cambridge anyway. This course of action would spin out the optimism, and besides, she wanted so badly to see him, not just to hear his voice over a telephone line. And there was the house. She wanted to be inside it again, to see how it felt. . .

'I've found the place. Look. Dan, look.' She'd folded back the page of the local newspaper and handed it across the breakfast table.

'Doesn't it seem perfect – exactly what we've been hoping to find?' she'd said, watching intently for his reaction to the postage stamp size photograph in the estate agent's advertisement.

She'd waited, breath drawn. It mattered so much, moving, making a change, doing something to set a new course.

'The one next to it looks more likely,' he'd said, without looking up from the page.

She'd felt a heavy lump of disappointment sink into her and from it that sharp irritation she was finding increasingly difficult to control.

'Let me see,' she said, spikily, snatching the paper from him. 'Which one do you mean?'

'On the left.'

The lump expanded.

'But it's nothing like the sort of thing we want. For a start, it's new and in a quiet cul de sac which means an estate. It's horrid. I hate it. I'd rather stay where we are.'

Dan looked at her with his kindly, long-suffering, vaguely troubled expression which made her feel like a worrisome child and perhaps encouraged her to behave as such. She used words like hate and horrid too readily because she wasn't prepared to be thwarted and hadn't the patience to argue her case in more reasonable language. More to the point, Dan let her get away with this awful behaviour perhaps perceiving that the fight was more within herself than with him.

'We'll look at both,' he said, and as she had already set her mind against any other house but the one she'd chosen, she readily agreed to this apparent compromise.

Her moods at that time had swung from elation to deflation with very little in between. Years later this was to be written about in women's magazines as one of the primary symptoms of stress, less recognised a decade earlier as being anything other than immaturity. The onset of misery had come at about the time she married Dan, maybe a little before, but not because of him, and much as she had wanted to blame him then, she'd never been able to summon more than irritation, and only that because none of it was his fault – because he couldn't be held to blame. It was really to do with the same restlessness that had plagued her all her life. Marrying Dan had meant giving up art college which was too far away from their first home together; and giving up art college had meant the beginning of unstructured time because at the start of the marriage she'd not been able to find a job.

The little terraced house in Cambridge had provided a temporary solution for a year, maybe eighteen months. She and Dan had set about modernisation and with this activity had come the first swing to elation. While Dan was out at work she spent her days painstakingly rubbing down woodwork, leaving not the slightest blemish of old paint even though it was unnecessary to go this far. She had a compulsion to make everything perfect, even the bits that couldn't be seen, because the greater the task the more rewardingly her time was filled. And then, one day, it was all done and she sat at the pristinely stripped and sealed pine breakfast table and felt the pendulum inside her swing down. Moving was the only answer. Starting again, which meant the new house had to be old, only she couldn't explain this to Dan because to do so meant admitting the hollow truth to herself. If he made even the suggestion of questioning her shallow scheme she became spiky and irritable because part of her relied on him knowing it all and under-standing the signals that meant it was too close to the bone for examination or explanation. Some day, when she was ready, she would get herself out and take a good hard look at the person whom she disliked so greatly, but no date was fixed, and meanwhile, the camouflage of activity had to go on. It was like deciding to give up a bad habit – but not yet.

Of course they bought the house, and Charlotte, aware of Dan's reservations about the purchase, was over bright in her manner and enthused to an almost nauseating degree about each little new discovery in the form of its architecture, the contents of its overrun garden and the view on a fine day. The long-suffering half smile seemed to settle permanently into Dan's face. He was working long hours at that time and would come home too exhausted to take any great interest in Char-lotte's constantly changing ideas for improving the house, which really needed very little doing to it, apart from the garden.

Not so long after moving in Charlotte's elation went, suddenly and completely and unexpectedly. Nothing to look forward to, that's how it felt. All day she tried to think up forms of frenetic activity, but the sense of futility that came with the deflation defeated each idea. Bricks and mortar had had their day and there she was, ensconced in what suddenly seemed like a prison.

The house was isolated, a point Dan had guardedly made at the outset.

'Do you think I want to live on an estate and have lots of mumsy friends?' she threw at him. 'Tupperware parties and coffee mornings and listening to endless sagas about potty training!'

He didn't respond. He never did when she accidently made mention of something related to babies. Having a child was what he wanted and maybe what she wanted too, but the cow-like capitulation to such an undertaking, the poignancy of making him so happy, was beyond her means. It had quickly become a matter of silent contention. He wouldn't push her because he already suffered knowing that he'd done this once in marrying her, which made him too careful of her moods, too caring altogether, making her more mean-hearted than she really was.

She contained her despair for some weeks, too proud and frightened to risk a told-you-so from Dan, although she should have known she could rely on him not to do that. Facing up to it herself was the problem, the ultimate one in the layer of problems she'd created, each feeding off the others but always coming back to the core, which was dissatisfaction with the person she had turned out to be.

Then Dan came home with a holiday brochure full of people with carefree smiles and very white teeth – people leaping out of the brightly painted pages to bite her. He handed it to her like a box of chocolates; like a treat to make her feel better.

It was October, the holiday season over. He'd come to her in the kitchen which was hot and steamy from a vat of plums she'd gathered from the garden earlier in the day and was now simmering on the way to jam.

'What do you think?' he said. 'We could go to somewhere hot the week after next. Have a bit of a break. Get away from it all.'

'Get away from what? Do you think I need to get away. Do you think it will make any difference?' It came out on a cold, even tone, which made the questions unavoidable.

Any difference to what? Dan might have asked, because they had not talked about any of it. Instead, he picked up the brochure from the draining board where she'd put it aside, and plunged it into the vat of bubbling plums.

This was one of only a very few times that Dan did something singularly indelible. For a moment they both stared at the vat.

'For Christ's sake! I've spent all day . . . ' she darted forward and snatched out the wilting pages, flinging them into the sink, the jolly holiday-makers, their faces now plum red.

'Why did you do it?' she said, her back turned to him as she ran cold water over the pages.

'It seemed like a good idea at the time,' he said.

He'd moved close up to her and she felt his hands slide round her waist. It was a bold move because they didn't touch each other very much, they'd never got into the habit; and now it felt sort of awkward. A little scene had been created which they were not accustomed to handle. Other people carried on in this way all the time (didn't they?) but it was generally too overt for the tentative territory of their relationship.

She didn't attempt to move away from him, partly because she was trapped against the sink but also because there was the feeling that the scene had to be worked through and that it had the potential to be a turning point.

'Why are you so patient with me?' she mumbled. It was easier than it might have been, because she wasn't having to look him in the face and see all that goodness and kindness and caring which made the truly horrid part of her want to hurt him.

'I thought I'd just been fairly impatient,' he said.

'Momentarily and sort of staged.'

'It was puerile and I'm sorry if I've spoiled your plums.'

'They're your plums too,' she said, feeling and sounding horribly, disgustingly, deliciously meek.

Don't back off too much now, she thought, or I'll alter in a flash.

'I wish you'd talk about it,' he said next, his tone heavier.

'That's the trouble – there's nothing to talk about,' she said, sighing in order to shift the sudden lump of self-pity lodged in her throat. 'There's not a single worthwhile thing in my life – nothing worth discussing.' For once she was unaware of her cruelty to him, and as they were still standing in the same attitude she didn't see the pain in his face.

'What do you think would be worthwhile?' he asked her after a slight pause.

'Oh, I don't know, just being something, doing something with a purpose. It's all right for you: you've got your career. I'm not even qualified to type letters.'

'Is that the sort of thing you want?'

'No – oh, I tell you, I don't know. I wish I did.'

'Perhaps you should get a job, anything, just to get you out of the house. You shouldn't be alone all day.'

'I don't want a job just for the sake of having one and not being alone,' she murmured. 'It would just be avoiding the issue.'

Dan's hands fell away from her. He could be tenacious in reasoned, logical argument, after all that was his vocation, but the contrary, self-defeating nature of depression baffled him. He did not suffer in this way. Often he was unhappy, or rather, not happy, but this was quite different from the affliction suffered by Charlotte.

He moved towards the stove and began idly to twist the wooden spoon that had been left plunged in the vat of fruit.

'Don't you think making jam is worth something?' he said.

'No I don't.'

'What's more worthwhile – sitting at a desk all day dealing with silly squabbles that don't achieve anything, or making something that adds to the quality of life?'

'Don't patronise me, please.' She was too miserable to be angry, only pathetic.

'I don't think I am. I don't mean to. I just happen to think quality of life is important. It's what people in our position strive for.'

'People in our position?'

'Who don't have to worry about the basics.'

'Which we would if you weren't out there doing something worthwhile.'

'Isn't it worth something to you that I'd be miserable without you? Can't there be times in life when just living is sufficiently worthwhile. You are my quality of life, Lottie.'

'So, I exist for you.'

'Firstly for yourself.'

'Maybe that's the problem: I'm too selfish and that's why I'm miserable.'

'We're all selfish,' he said, as if he was thinking of a particular selfishness in himself. 'I'm sorry, it was a bit extreme to call you my quality of life. I didn't mean to make you sound like an adjunct. To be honest, most of the time I've known you, even when we were children, it's seemed more like the other way round.'

'Please, don't say things like that. Don't give me the upper hand, I'll only misuse it.'

'I'm not sure that's something either of us can change – the balance of power.'

'If that's what you really think, how can you stand it?'

'It's not something I've considered to be a matter of choice.'

'You mean you've never thought of ditching me?'

'No.' He didn't ask the obvious rejoinder, but that was because the balance was against him, as it had always been. He couldn't risk an honest reply from her or the torture of disbelieving the sort of response he wanted.

She knew as much, but at the age she was then there was only frustration in that knowledge. The potential for misery was entirely within herself but at that time she was still floundering about searching for outside cause and blame, demeaning herself with the unthought-out assumption that a shift in the balance, to be with someone who had the upper hand, could solve her problem. It had taken all the intervening years to accept responsibility properly for herself and to see the value in living with someone who was reasonable and patient, and gentle and kind; maybe even to understand about making jam and quality of life.

This focusing on to pockets of memory was something new. Dan had been a warm glow over the past few months, there in the corner of her mind where she had placed him, like a piece of comfort; but until now she had been unable to recapture what it had been like day to day, sharing life with him. Perhaps this was because it had been so much easier with Dan than with Nick; she may have been troubled within herself, but marriage to Dan was peace and understanding whereas being with Nick was largely war and bull-headedness.

The last time she'd seen Dan (really seen him and been with him as opposed to the brief and stilted hellos and how-are-you's that went with the collection and return of Vicky each Sunday pre-America) had been the day of the divorce.

In contradiction to the event, the day had been warm and sunny, late in the year, Indian summerish: a perfect day. How had she felt? Elated because something so huge was happening? Probably. At first, anyway. The passion thing with Nick was still running high then; the question as to whether she liked or disliked him hadn't been considered.

The building where the marriage to Dan was about to end looked very much like the place she'd gone to take her driving test. Only everyone fails, she'd thought, almost whimsically, as she mounted the stone stairs to the first floor.

The waiting room was bleak as could be. Metal-framed chairs with canvas seats were lined up against two facing walls so the protagonists in each marriage could glower at one another. That was how it seemed set to be but not how it was. Charlotte was a little early and Dan had not yet arrived. She paused just inside the long, narrow room and surveyed the half dozen or so other people already waiting. Nobody was looking at anybody else. They were people with heads bowed or eyes averted to the ceiling; people who'd finished with the fighting and conceded defeat. Maybe some were bitter, others relieved, whichever, she wondered whether the tense joyless-ness of their little gathering had hit them as hard as it did her in that moment. Instinctively, she yearned for Dan, just for a split second, out of habit. It was all loneliness and failure and vaguely sordid in this room. Being stiff-lipped and civilised was the etiquette of the place whereas weeping and wailing might have been more appropriate.

Charlotte felt very strange or perhaps just out of place. She was drawn to search for the misery in the other people's faces, it was a natural curiosity, but, like them, she found she couldn't look. Were any of these people married to one another or were they all like her, one half, waiting? Nobody was sitting next to anybody, but they wouldn't, would they – not now.

Then Dan came in and without hesitation took the seat next to her. They greeted one another in whispers, as people do in waiting rooms. They smiled at one another.

'Sorry I'm late,' he murmured.

'No, I was early.'

'Are you all right?'

'Fine. And you?'

Crazy.

The door at the far end of the room opened and a woman clutching a large white handkerchief emerged. Those waiting moved uneasily in their seats. Nobody wanted a scene, some-one else's scene that might touch too closely on the scenario of their own. The woman sniffed and went into a huddle with another woman, older, probably her mother, and a young woman in black, lawyerish clothing. A moment later a man came through the same doorway, his hands plunged in his trouser pockets, his demeanor defiant, embarrassed, guilty.

'Lovell,' a small man in a black gown called out.

'That's us,' Dan said, and Charlotte was grateful to be able to register irritation at this unnecessary observation.

They stood up and proceeded towards the doorway into the courtroom which was not unlike a nonconformist church. Pew-like seating led up to a large desk which stood on a raised platform. Behind it sat a man whose features Charlotte could not now remember. She and Dan took their places, side by side, close up at first and then each moved slightly away as if it was unseemly for any part of their bodies to touch at this juncture.

Questions were asked, their exact phrasing now lost. It was made clear that the sole interest of the court was Vicky and not her parents, deemed beyond hope. The court needed to be satisfied that every provision had been agreed and would be made for the child of the marriage and that unless this was satisfactory, a decree nisi would not be granted. The word adultery was heard. Nick was mentioned. Irretrievable was said. Charlotte felt like a criminal – and a liar.

She tried to hang on to that moment of irritation she'd felt in the waiting room. It was necessary in order to remain calm and convincing while Vicky was discussed as if she belonged to some vast amorphous body and not to them; and while cold and direct enquiries were made as to the certainty of the marriage being over.

There was a point when she wondered whether it would be hugely difficult or the easiest thing in the world to capitulate, to say that it was all a mistake, and thank you very much and sorry for wasting their time. There was even a point when she was convinced that Dan was holding his breath just waiting for her to say the word so they could go home and carry on as if nothing had happened. It was like the marriage service in reverse and getting to the bit where the vicar asks if anyone knows of any just cause or impediment.

While all this was going on in her head words were coming out of her mouth that seemed to have been programmed in from another part of her being that was remote from the immediate emotions. No, she said, plainly and clearly, there was no possibility of a reconciliation.

Outside, on the sunlit pavement, they paused by the door as if each was wondering what next because surely it couldn't end so abruptly, with so little ceremony.

'Lunch?' Dan said. He looked pale, and beads of perspiration showed on his forehead.

'Where shall we go?'

'There's a restaurant round the corner. French. I believe it's quite good.'

They started walking.

'This is very civilised,' she said.

'It is,' he responded, and these two words somehow conveyed the mountain of hurt.

They continued in silence. She began to think that it had been a mistake agreeing to lunch. Maybe it was uncivilised to be too civilised. They weren't that sophisticated and their marriage had been too real for a sudden transition to friendship.

The restaurant was light and spacious, small tables with crisp white cloths, polished silver cutlery. it was only just after midday and few of the tables were occupied. Unidentifiable violin music filtered from the walls.

They studied the menu. How could they eat?

A wine list was brought.

'Champagne?' Dan said, their eyes meeting at last. What have you done? Do you know what you're doing? He didn't have to say it.

'It gives me a headache,' she replied, thinly.

'I know,' he sighed. 'I know.'

She searched for some neutral topic of conversation, something that wouldn't touch on their shared past or their separate future, but the possibilities were too banal for the occasion.

'What will you do?' she asked, plunging in.

He sighed again and she understood that it was inordinately difficult for him, this lunch, this urbane finale.

'What can I do,' he said, rhetorically. 'I'll see Vicky as often as you'll let me. . .'

'As often as you like,' she broke in.

'You say that now, but you'll want some sort of structure; once a week, once a month – I don't know.'

'Does it have to be like that?' she said, stupidly.

'How else can it be?' he said, a little impatiently. 'I've got to build a new life as well, you know.'

Of course he had, but his saying it affected her in a way she could hardly bear. The feeling was utterly selfish and possessive, and she'd no right, but in that moment she was jealous of his future, the new life which excluded her.

The food came, and somehow they fell into the sort of conversation they might have had over countless meals in the past. They'd each gone too near the edge of tolerance to have continued in the earlier vein. Now they talked in more non-specific terms round the notion of structure, though God knows how they managed it.

'Structure sounds like routine to me,' she said at some point.

'And that's bad?'

'You know I'm terrified of routine.'

'I think there have been times when you've been terrified only because you wouldn't allow yourself routine.'

'I need to think about that one.'

'You have to build the structure out of the routine. There's no other way.'

68

'You're always so sure of these things.'

'Dogmatic, you mean.'

'No, I'd never accuse you of that. I'm the opinionated one.'

He smiled and put a piece of steak in his mouth. Charlotte did the same and then found it difficult to swallow: they were eating and talking and it was all quite natural and normal and enjoyable, only, of course it wasn't, of course not.

'Is structure simply a matter of filling time, then?' she asked, to keep it going.

'At its lowest.'

'And at its highest?'

'At its highest I suppose it's more abstract. People go to church because it forms part of a structure but some actually *believe* as well. We go to work for structure and to support structure and sometimes it's even enjoyable.'

'Do you want my potatoes?' she said, already transfering them to his plate.

He paused only a moment, but it was long enough for her to register the trespass. An hour earlier she had forever forfeited the right to put her unwanted potatoes on his plate. It was a poignant, painful, singular moment, and it severed them to a far greater degree than anything else that had happened that morning.

'I'm going on,' he said, 'aren't I?'

'No. I like to hear you pontificate. I always have.'

'I don't sound too pompous, do I?'

'Only a bit.'

'Only a bit,' he echoed, gently, appreciatively. 'Would you like a pud?'

'We could look at the menu.'

And, of course, there were plums.

'Do you remember,' they both began at once. The shared past. How would they live without it?

Sitting on the train to Cambridge more than three years later, the memory was sharp but edited. Conveniently, Charlotte had left out the over-riding factor of that time, her being passionately in love with Nick. Now it seemed clear, with hindsight, that all she'd wanted had been a bit of time out from the marriage, her real life, the proper existence that felt preordained. It was monstrous of her to expect it, but surely Dan would understand.

Chapter Nine

Charlotte arrived at Cambridge station mid morning and took a taxi to the city centre. Most of the estate agents were in the same road. Nick's suggestion that they find somewhere to rent was now more appealing than it had been first thing that morning; already, despite the beginnings of caution that had filtered through the intoxicating hope, she was halfway towards the reinstallation of herself and Vicky in the house that belonged to Dan but still felt like her property, as perhaps did Dan himself.

She avoided the agencies from which she'd taken details of houses to buy, she was in too impatient a mood to have to waste time explaining, inventing, changes of plan.

By lunch time she'd agreed to take the lease on a basement flat in Bateman Street. It was too small but garrety in an upside down sort of way that suited her sense of transition.

She had lunch at Eaden Lilley, though she could hardly eat a thing and preferred that her stomach felt flat for the rest of the day. She walked along to the Market Square and took a taxi out to the village where Audrey and James lived.

As the car stopped outside the coverted school house Audrey appeared from round the back, green wellied, one of the familiar shabby anoraks buttoned round her like boiler lagging. A small, but sharp puncture began a degree of deflation in Charlotte's balloon of optimism. The sight of Audrey reminded her of the conversation they'd had only a few days earlier. How could she have so completely disregarded what Audrey had said? But the relapse was only momentary. Surely the conclusion had been inconclusive: the *ménage à trois* nonsense, the suggestion that Dan and the girl . . . she put it out of her mind, at least, she did her best to do so.

Audrey was her usual welcoming self though a little over solicitous, evidently mindful of their last conversation. This made Charlotte feel a bit like an invalid or someone who'd had a recent bereavement.

'What about the houses? Have you made a decision?' Audrey asked when they were inside.

'I think I might have found something but it's neither of the ones I looked at before,' Charlotte said. She wasn't anxious to tell Audrey about the basement flat in Bateman Street. Audrey would want to see it and then she'd start speculating in all sorts of directions, most obviously that there was a shortage of money, which, of course there wasn't. She could imagine James and Audrey discussing it, Audrey telling him to be charitable: poor Charlotte, she's obviously down to her last bean. You'd better give her some work. She needs the money. This fantasy dialogue made her pride shudder.

'Is James about?' she asked, 'I wanted to have a word with him if he's not too busy.'

'Yes, he's in the studio. All by himself today but I know he'll be happy to see you; he gave me no end of stick the other day for letting you go before he got back.' Her kindly, clean-living face spread into a beam of relief. 'Actually, it suits me quite well that you want to have a chat with James. I can leave you with him for a couple of hours. I don't think I told you the other day, but I'm producing at the moment.'

Fortunately, Charlotte knew this to be the language of theatre. That bright, obsessional sparkle had lit in Audrey's eyes. She was heavily into amateur dramatics and how could Charlotte ever forget her friend's legs in fishnet tights? She remembered with mean accuracy going to see Audrey as Prince Charming: it was shortly after Vicky was born and she'd felt as fat as hell herself, but the sight of Audrey's legs made her feel a bit better.

'We're doing *Cabaret* just before Christmas,' she revealed.

'Bit of a change from the old panto.' Charlotte could see that Audrey was enraptured by the production, its daring and ambition, flying in the face of tradition; though hadn't Lisa Minelli worn fishnet tights in the film version?

71

'There's a wardrobe session this afternoon and I feel I have to show my face,' Audrey continued, as James appeared.

'Charlotte!' He stopped in the kitchen doorway, as if taking in a spectacle. Like Audrey, he'd gained weight, middle age spread. He'd grown a beard, which was grey and very un-Jameslike (Charlotte seemed to remember he'd once made a loud and bigoted pronouncement about men who grew beards). He didn't appear as tall as in memory but he was the same solid presence, a man to be reckoned with and someone of whom Charlotte had been a little in awe. She supposed it was his positive, slightly stern approach to life, the gruff good-natured steamroller type whose approval somehow mattered.

'How are you then?' he said, advancing into the room, clasping hold of her shoulders and placing a kiss on her cheek.

'I'm fine, and you?'

'Never better. Never better.'

'James. I've got to go out, Cynthia's, the costumes, but it's worked out quite well because Charlotte would like to talk to you. A bit of manly advice, maybe,' she smiled encouragingly at Charlotte who was inwardly cringing at this obvious misconception of her reason for wanting to speak to James. Both were looking at her in this kindly fashion now, the pair of do-gooders that they were. She remembered then how insufferable they could be.

'Well now,' he said, like a Catholic priest about to hear her confession. They were alone, upstairs in the airy studio with its white melamine drawing boards and angle-poise lamps. Charlotte already felt at a disadvantage because James had put her in a low-level seat while he perched on one of the high stools favoured by graphics people.

'Actually, I wanted to talk to you about work,' she said, and it sounded wretchedly blunt and to the point.

'Oh, I see.' He seemed surprised, maybe even disappointed. 'I thought perhaps . . . '

'Of course we've progressed a lot over the last few years. It's all a great deal more technical these days. I always said it would go that way and I think I can say we're as up to the minute as any other studio, probably ahead of many. It's a very competitive market you know, and you're only as good as your last piece of work. Poster paints in the kitchen – we still get people coming in looking for work, their portfolios only memorable for the smell of stale chip fat.' He said all this in the most kindly tone, smiling, a little sorrowfully at the last bit. 'It's a very competitive market, very competitive indeed,' he repeated. 'Technology is the watchword these days,' he added, meaninglessly. 'But if you'd like to show me what you've been doing.'

Charlotte glanced round the studio again and opened her handbag. She hesitated a moment and then drew out the video cassette she'd made in America.

'If you have a spare minute,' she said, handing the tape to him.

He looked mystified.

'It's my portfolio,' she explained.

His expression had changed completely. He was put out, caught out, denied the gratifying role of father-confessor, and now constructive critic.

'Audrey and I don't have a television,' he said, flatly.

'I'd quite forgotten,' Charlotte said. She badly wanted to laugh but remembered in time that James took himself extremely seriously.

She gazed at the neat cassette case on her lap and thought, I've delayed long enough. I can't wait here another minute. I must see Dan.

'I'll leave the tape with you. Perhaps you could borrow a set or something,' she said, standing up.

'I can't promise anything,' James cautioned. 'It's a very competitive market, very competitive indeed.' That was another thing she'd forgotten, the way he kept on repeating what he had said. What a boring old fart he had become, she thought, or maybe he'd always been that way but as a younger man it had seemed more acceptable because all of them were more opinionated then.

'You're not leaving?' he said, attempting to re-establish the tone of concerned and kindly friend.

'I must. I've another appointment,' she told him. 'Please apologise to Audrey for me.' How stiff and formal they had become. Some friends you could meet again after years apart and take up just where you'd left off, that particular understanding and easiness unbroken. It had always been like that with Frances. Charlotte felt a little sad that it was so irrevocably lost with James and Audrey, though perhaps they'd never known one another's true natures: it could happen with friendships between couples.

The taxi took an agonising half an hour to come and pick her up from the old schoolhouse. James asked nice questions, the answers to which he paid no attention. Then he talked about his three children, the boy who was being privately educated and the girls who weren't, and how well the boy was doing, captain of the school bridge team, quite virtuoso on the tuba, and how helpful the girls were at home. He kissed Charlotte again just before she left and it was vaguely unpleasant. He waved from the door.

She assumed without any doubt that Dan must have seen the same limitations in their erstwhile friends, and she quite relished the prospect of tearing them apart with him. She knew how horrid she was, but then so did Dan: he'd married her at her very worst. God, when she thought back on it! He'd always been solidly there; seen as a bit of a joke, something of a lap dog type by her friends at art school. And she'd used him, shamelessly really. He'd paid for the abortion of the college lecturer's child and married her straight afterwards even though she hadn't even pretended to love him. And all those years they were together, strange how greatly time contracted in memory – it seemed like a loose month. She couldn't remember the detail at all, the small, day-to-day things of living together. All she had was a growing sense of loss and regret which had come to focus on Dan as its source. She wanted him back or perhaps it would merely be a matter of establishing that she had never really lost him. She craved the contentment that had been on offer before, the possibility of peace of mind; an end to arguments, rows, the exhausting business of forever having to defend, the demeaning process of thinking up words that would hurt.

The taxi had turned into the lane that led to the house, her house, Dan's house, the home where Vicky should be growing up. They'd called it Little Lakeside because there was a pond in the garden and Dan's parents' home was Lakeside.

She felt slightly light-headed. Her hands were cold but damp and they had begun to tremble. Any minute now and she'd see him again. She was quite certain he would be there, he had never not been where she wanted him.

The taxi stopped at the end of the drive. A black Mercedes was parked further up, in front of the house. The light was beginning to go and it had started to drizzle. A wintry wind whipped through the trees, their lower branches tilting and swaying across the gravel-covered driveway. Tufts of grass were showing through the stones, a sign of neglect. The heels of Charlotte's shoes, bought from Macy's designer section, sank between these stones and she remembered how other pairs had been ruined along the hundred yards or so between the lane and the front door of the house. The detail did come back, the trivial and unimportant.

The smell of the house now came to her as she stopped by the weathered oak door, that particular musty wood smell, accentuated by the damp air. She breathed it in, the past evoked so strongly that she lifted her bag and for a moment she was about to search for a key.

The mistake upset her. It made her feel cold and more nervous, and for an instant, horribly bereft. She rang the bell.

Movement sounds came from within the house and then the door opened and Dan was looking at her.

There was a pause, while she searched his face. He seemed only a little surprised then a small frown settled across his features: perhaps she had no right to expect pleasure in his expression.

'Come in,' he said, without having spoken her name. He'd hardly altered. Or had he? He still looked sad and tired. Was that gratifying?

'Dan.' She smiled at him and would have liked to have done that civilised, sophisticated thing, kissing one's former husband. But she couldn't. It all mattered too much for any carelessness or posturing.

They went through to the drawing room where absolutely nothing had changed, all the same furniture, arranged in exactly the same manner: indicative of a clinging to the past? Like Mother? Her focus went back to Dan. He was watching her with a steady, perceptive gaze, as if he knew what had just passed through her mind.

'Can I sit down?' she asked, with a rather coy formality she didn't like at all. She didn't know how to be with him and yet he'd always been the one person with whom she'd felt most herself, whether she'd liked that self or not. She'd always been easy with him, confident because he was so constant. And now she felt the opposite of all that. If she wasn't careful she'd flounder.

She'd sat down without waiting for his permission, and, of course, she'd chosen the gold sofa with the silk tassles at the corners and the high back and sides. It was the sofa passed on to them by his parents, the one on which they'd made love before they were married, and left little stains they'd rubbed at with handkerchiefs. She put her hand against one of the cushions and it felt cold. The whole room was chilly, the fire unlit, the feeling that came from absence of use.

'Mother said you wanted to see me,' she said, smiling again at the middle-aged man with the grey hair and well-cut suit, though she didn't see him like that: interposed was the image in her memory, the close-up view that saw the person and disregarded the inevitably changed exterior.

'Yes.' he said. He had remained standing.

'It's been a long time,' she said, falling into the refuge of cliché.

'Yes, it has,' he said.

'It's rather cold in here,' she said, looking at the dull, grey hearth.

'I haven't been in long,' he said. 'I only got back from New York yesterday and I've been out all day today. The house hasn't had time to warm up.'

'Perhaps if you lit the fire. . . '

'I don't spend much time in this room,' he informed her.

She couldn't think how she was going to break through his formality. He seemed almost angry with her. She couldn't countenance indifference. She had to be producing some sort of emotion.

'Funny you going to the States just as I left,' she said then.

'Is it?' he said. He hadn't moved at all. He was still standing, about six feet away from where she sat and to one side more than facing her so that she had to keep turning her head to speak to him.

76

And then it all came out, the unexpected fury.

'Just what do you think you are doing, coming back to England, leaving Vicky in California, not telling me your plans concerning her?'

'I didn't think . . . ' she was near to being dumbfounded.

He cut her short: 'I'm never sure with you – perhaps you didn't think – perhaps you did.'

'What do you mean?' she asked, the beginning of anger rising in her along with the sense of guilt she always felt at any hint of criticism where her care of Vicky was concerned.

'I think you know,' he said, turning away from her.

She might have known he wouldn't argue it out.

'I don't,' she insisted.

'How do you think I felt,' he continued, his back to her. 'Flying across America and finding Vicky by herself.'

'She isn't by herself,' she countered, indignantly. 'If you've been there you know very well that Frances is keeping an eye on her.'

'You should have kept me informed. I only found out where she was by guesswork.'

'So that's it. You feel you were made to look foolish,' she shouted at him, just like she yelled at Nick when she was in the wrong.

He turned, his expression cold with dislike. 'You do have a way of putting things,' he said.

'Is this why you wanted to see me?' she demanded.

'A telephone call would have sufficed,' he said.

'Well, you know now. Vicky will be back here by Christmas,' she said, hating the pompous sound in his voice, wishing she could strike at him in some way and finding how with the next mean accusation.

'How come, if you were so concerned, you didn't bring her back with you?'

He didn't answer. There wasn't the chance. The door from the back hallway opened and a slim, dark-haired woman, young, pale and as tired-looking as Dan, came into the room. She paused when she saw Charlotte and then looked to Dan, questioning.

'I'm sorry. I didn't realise . . . ' she began, retreating.

'Mickey, this is Charlotte,' Dan halted her, seemingly wanting her to stay.

77

'How do you do,' Charlotte said, icily.

Mickey smiled, slightly, then the expression dropped from her face and she looked only blank and sort of wrung out.

'I think Charlotte is leaving now,' Dan said.

'Yes. I've got to catch a train back to London,' she said, rising from the sofa.

'Only I'll have to ring for a taxi,' she added. She felt utterly wretched. Surely this was the most hollow moment in her life. The vaguely formed hope that had grown into a warm and glowing sense of certainty over the last few hours, was quite wiped away by the dislike so clearly displayed in Dan's eyes, and now this girl, about whom she'd known but whom she'd chosen to disregard. The two of them stood there, looking at her, the unwelcome intruder in their chilly little set-up.

'I'll drive you to the station,' Dan said.

Charlotte accepted this as the lesser of the two impossible situations, the other being that she might have to wait some time for the taxi.

She went out to the car without speaking to Mickey again. What a miserable, insipid-looking person, she thought, trying to pull herself out of the slough of despond.

The silent trip to the station took ten minutes and it wasn't that they had nothing to say to one another, but too much. The atmosphere in the car was so tense Charlotte had to concentrate to keep her breathing even. She didn't want him to know she was upset, but of course he knew. In fact the electricity between them had never been greater though this did not occur to either. Charlotte's sense of displacement was very nearly overwhelming.

When they reached the station she got straight out of the car. Her judgement was diminished by the state she was in and she slammed the car door much harder than she'd intended. She felt a fool. She'd exposed too much of how she felt. Dan and that wretched girl would have a field day. A hand touched her arm.

'It's only fair to warn you,' Dan was saying. 'I intend applying for formal access to Vicky. If necessary, in court.'

A car horn sounded loudly and she looked beyond him to where he had left the Mercedes, blocking the road.

'You're in the way,' she said.

'Yes', he answered, looking at her very hard. 'I am!'

Chapter Ten

It seemed to Mickey wholly consistent with everything else in her life which had started out well and then turned round on her that the christening of Josephine's baby should be taking place in the same church where she and David were married. But she was far too self-effacing to see it as a deliberate piece of cruelty by either Josephine or David. It was, after all, quite natural that his son should be christened in the parish church. Even so, now that the day had come it was a great deal harder to bear than she'd imagined when Josephine's letter had arrived in New York, asking her to be the child's godmother.

The service was due to begin in five minutes. It was to be one of those small, private christenings, unconnected with the regular services of the day, slotted into the early afternoon. The vicar hurried in from the vestry. He'd probably come straight from his lunch table. He put his hand to his mouth to cover a yawn or a touch of indigestion. He was, of course, the same clergyman who had performed the marriage ceremony.

Mickey fell to wondering what he might think of the transposition now before him, the couple he had married little more than three years ago, and now the child to be christened: a not unexpected order of events, but how often did a guest of the wedding emerge as the mother of the issue? She checked herself in this line of thought: it didn't do any good to dwell on what might have been.

There were three other people in the pews apart from Dan and herself. An elderly-looking woman wearing a large black hat with a grey feather was sitting the other side of the aisle, and, in the row behind her, an aristocratic-looking couple who were neither young nor old and who Mickey guessed were the impecunious noblefolk whose stately home was where Josephine had her flat and the job that consisted of little more than selling lavender bags to the monied hoi polloi.

As yet there was no sign of David, Josephine, or the baby, then the huge sound of small lungs broke into the churchy silence. Mickey resisted the urge to turn and look. She'd not seen David for months and didn't know how she would feel when the moment came. She hoped it wouldn't be like Dan's meeting with Charlotte, all the passion still there, taking them unawares.

The vicar asked those present to leave their pews and follow him to the back of the church. Mickey now saw that Josephine and the baby were alone. Was she relieved or disappointed? Josephine smiled. They'd spoken over the telephone the previous day, neither mentioning David.

The baby looked like nobody, just a baby with an angry red face.

The service began. The vicar had an incongruous electric kettle, recently boiled, from which he poured steamy holy water into the ancient stone font. The screaming, bucking baby was placed in Mickey's godmotherly arms and instantly subsided, his small blue eyes fixing upon her with a sudden and curious intensity.

When it was done the vicar shook hands with everyone and didn't appear to remember Mickey. It was as if her marriage to David had never happened.

Outside the church Josephine's hat blew off and her abundant red hair flew up and round her face.

'Oh, shit!' she said in her deep, educated voice. Nobody looked surprised.

Dan retrieved the hat and Josephine gave him an odd look that seemed unconnected with the moment.

'Come along,' she said to the group in general. 'Let's get back before Giles starts bawling again.'

They were to have a small party in the library of the stately home. Peter, the present earl, led the route in an elderly Morris that appeared to have a clutch problem. Josephine went with the woman who wore the grey feather, her mother, and Mickey and Dan followed on with Peter's long-nosed wife whose name was Laurela.

'So that you don't get lost,' she said.

'Do you have any children?' she asked with conversational uninterest as they drove along.

Things were explained.

'Of course, you're our Member,' Laurela exclaimed with discovery. Her manner was sort of vague, aristocratically fay.

'Yes,' Dan said. Only the year before he'd been asked by the family to do something about death duties. Josephine had been their emissary. Peter and Laurela were holidaying in the Bahamas at the time.

Mickey was wondering whether David might appear at the party. Dan was remembering the evening spent with Josephine. It seemed like the first thought he'd had over the past few days that did not involve Charlotte, though the memory ran on and of course she was there. He'd taken Josephine to bed, just that one occasion, but it hadn't worked. He'd thought then that casual sexual encounters might go some way to assuage the continuing sense of loss but it had been rather the reverse, most particularly, he remembered, with Josephine, herself in love with someone else.

It seemed impossible that the strong dislike he now felt for his former wife could have any connection with love. The marriage ending had left him on a lonely plateau of unfinished emotion, from which he'd begun to retreat with Mickey. It disturbed him now that he'd been so angry with Charlotte. The decision to regularise his access to Vicky (though he preferred to think of it as her access to him) had been made, he thought, for her benefit; but when he'd told Charlotte his intention it had felt and sounded like a threat. He'd wanted to hurt her and it appalled him that at last he'd fallen into the classic situation of using his child as a weapon. He'd seen it so often as a solicitor, listened to so many tales of woe and injustice from aggrieved husbands and wives attempting to justify their entirely selfish manipulation of custody proceedings. He'd been so determined that Vicky should not be the subject of any such wrangle but maybe he should not have allowed it to be at any cost. Maybe he'd been wrong in that.

They'd turned off the road and past the lodge cottages either side of the main gateway that led into the long drive up to the house. Grassy meadows spanned to the horizon as the narrow roadway curved off and through the arch of the stable block into the yard where the Morris had must emitted a final spurt of blue smoke.

The earl seemed oblivious to such signs of mechanical trauma. He got out of the car and slammed the door in much the same way he might have slapped the rump of a horse.

'Come into the hice,' he said, like Prince Charles.

The library was a very brown room, its leather-bound volumes covering the walls almost to the ceiling.

'It's the only room we can keep warm,' Laurela said to Dan. 'I think it's the books, you know. Insulation.'

Dan smiled. There wasn't a great deal more to be said about books in this context.

Across the room Josephine, the baby now asleep in his carry cot, had that trespassing look about her, Mickey thought. It was the same, slightly anxious but purposeful demeanour she'd adopted in the past when something had to be said, something, no doubt, that was going to be upsetting. It had been like that when Mickey had finally extricated herself from the wretched affair with Arthur and gone home full of hope for a fresh start and a baby with David. But Josephone was already there, with that look, and it was too late because David had found out about Arthur. And Josephine, at other times so fulsomely self-accusing, had offered pity more than apology. She'd been trespassing then, but with a sort of licence, because she'd never hidden that she loved David, and Mickey was so full of guilt herself, it was impossible for her to say anything.

Of course she hadn't known, then, about Josephine's baby. In fact she didn't find out until the day he was born six months later, and by then too much time had elapsed and the gulf with David become too great for any counter-recriminations. And really, the failure of the marriage had nothing to do with Josephine, nor Arthur. It simply hadn't worked: they'd been lonely with one another. Nevertheless, the baby had been hard to take at first because the maternal urge had been so strong in Mickey just before, and she couldn't help feeling, well, cheated, she supposed.

It had become easier as far as that was concerned. The problem was quite different now. She glanced to the other end of the room where Dan was engaged in conversation with Peter.

'Mickey,' Josephine had begun then paused, her lips pressing together against the fragile phrase she sought. Then she let go: 'Oh, Mickey, there's so much I want to talk to you about but you've been away such a long time I can't remember how to be when I'm with you.'

At this Mickey registered the inner recognition she too had forgotten. It was Josephine's beguiling way to thrust this disarming sort of candour at the very few people she was prepared to tolerate.

'I can tell you, I've had the most ghastly miserable time in recent months. There's absolutely nobody left round here worth bothering to know. I got so desperate at one time I even started taking Giles to the baby clinic just so I could find someone to have an argument with.'

'And did you?' Mickey asked, feeling warmer.

'Not a hope. My dear, I just couldn't get through the mindless barrier they put up at those places. This dolt of a woman doctor, wrote out a prescription I thought was for Giles' bum rash, but when I took it to the pharmacy it was Valium for me! What do you think of him?' she continued without pause. 'Giles, I mean. Don't you think he's well, you know, all the infantile superlatives?' The anxious look had returned.

'He's lovely,' Mickey managed to say.

'And you really don't mind all this mumbo jumbo godmother business?' still the anxious insistence.

'No, I think it's . . . '

'Civilised? Maybe too civilised? God, Mickey, you're the only friend I've got. I'm afraid there just wasn't anyone else.'

'Civilised doesn't really seem quite the right word, but something like that.'

'I'm so pleased about you and Dan, really,' she jumped on.

Mickey wanted to qualify this but knew it would be inadvisable, after all, nothing had been decided, not yet.

'I thought David might have been here,' she said, by way of steering the conversation in another direction and at the same time trying to achieve the impression of easy enquiry about her former husband.

83

'I didn't invite him,' Josephine said, drawing in her breath and looking stoical.

'Of course, I would have liked him to be here. I even would have liked him to be Giles' godfather, but I didn't want him to think I might be laying a trap.' Her manner was quite different when she talked about David: the brashness went, she was almost wistful.

'But surely . . . ' Mickey began.

'Surely nothing,' Josephine interrupted. 'All the time I was with him it was surely nothing. He still wanted you.'

Adrenalin rose in Mickey's chest. Even now? she thought, but with more curiosity than emotion. It seemed he could still produce a physiological response in her. And how cruel it was that only when it no longer mattered, she should discover that David had been wanting her when she'd been just about out of her mind with wanting him.

'What I meant was because of Giles,' she said.

Josephine gave her a questioning look.

'I mean, it's not as if he's without a sense of responsibility,' Mickey continued, awkwardly.

'My God!' Josephine murmured, understanding appearing in her face. 'You think David is Giles' father. Of course you do! Oh Mickey, I'd no idea. Why didn't you say? No, of course you didn't. What could you have said!'

'But you and David?' Mickey said in a confused tone.

'Never while you and he were still together,' she answered, 'Oh Mickey, how could you think that?'

Giles Alexander had woken in his carry cot and started making intermittent grizzling sounds.

'He's revving up for a howl. He does cry a lot.' Josephine said, casting a haunted look in the direction of the noise. 'Look, I think I'll take him outside for a few minutes, give him a bit of fresh air. Do you want to come?' It was more than an invitation, it was a plea.

'Of course,' Mickey said. She would have agreed to anything Josephine asked of her at that moment.

The baby was lifted from his cot and swaddled in a blanket. Mickey followed them out of the library and through several shrouded stately rooms, the baby, his small, staring eyes fixed on her over his mother's shoulder. The noises had stopped. He had that intent look of seeing a great deal more than he could possibly comprehend.

They came to a narrow half-glazed side door that opened out on to a stony pathway leading into a part of the grounds where the remaining bushes of a maze had been tortuously clipped in an attempt at topiary.

'I like it here,' Josephine said. 'It's a right old mess, like me. Oh God, I do have this way of sounding pitiable, don't I, but this place is so unthreatening, I mean, it's such a failure itself.'

To Mickey it was merely a place where the wind was blowing and there was no warmth. The top of one of the bushes had been cut into the shape of a christmas pudding but surely it couldn't be meant to be that. The baby was still staring at her.

'Itzy witzy, itzy witzy woo,' Josephine cooed against his ear. 'It gets you like this, you know,' she said to Mickey, 'but I feel more sane since I've had him, despite the depression, I suppose it's having somebody else to think about besides oneself.'

This Mickey could understand. She'd closed in on herself since the nightmares had become a frequent torment. It was as if she was protecting her own madness and in the process locking herself away from the possibility of recovery within the sort of relationship she could have with Dan. Quickly she cut off further thought in this direction. So far she had survived the intimate requirements, the play acting bit in the bedroom when you were with someone who assumed reciprocal desire. God, how she wished to be left alone but at the same time was terrified of what might happen if she relinquished the normality on offer with Dan.

'Dear little person,' Josephine was saying to her baby. She looked at Mickey, her expression ever so slightly malicious.

'You know, I thought you might have had an inkling,' she said. 'But there again, it never occurred to me that you thought David was Giles' father.'

A gust of wind side-swiped the christmas pudding.

'What else was I to think?' Mickey said. 'You moved in with him as soon as I moved out.' She didn't mean it to sound like accusation.

'But you were my dearest friend. You still are. Work it out. If Giles was David's we'd have been at it while you and he were

85

still together. If that's what you thought you must have loathed me.'

Mickey felt horribly uncomfortable with this conversation. Josephine was now displaying hurt indignation.

'As I'd already transgressed myself I didn't feel in a very strong position to loathe anyone.' She used formal-sounding, distancing words when she spoke of the affair she'd had with Arthur. It was so difficult now to relate to how she'd felt at the time, how she could ever had allowed herself to become entangled with such insanity. She'd been like Giles, a staring, mesmerised innocent; and like the baby, she'd been incapable of comprehension. Arthur, clever as could be and mad as a hatter. Even when she'd gone to see him in prison, after she'd turned him into a rapist (had she? she hadn't thought of it like that before), it had seemed as if he was still the one that understood it all while she was more confused than ever.

Dan had saved her. Dear Dan. Oh, she must make it work with him. She must!

'Dan is Giles' father.'

'Please,' Mickey began. 'I know you're upset with me.'

'Oh, for goodness sake! He is. I'm not the sort to tell lies, you know that. Too much honesty's always been my problem.'

They stopped their meandering stroll around the skeletal maze. Of course Dan was the baby's father. Of course he was.

'Work it out,' Josephine said and Mickey, so passive and non-violent, could have hit her for saying this again. She didn't want to work it out but memory had been triggered: Josephine coming to see her, a year ago, maybe a little more, marking Dan out of ten. She'd been indignant then as well, Josephine often was. Dan had upset her, caused some offence, though it was difficult to imagine Dan capable of any unkindness. What had he done?

'Surely you remember me coming to see you after it happened,' Josephine was saying.

'Yes, I do now, but I hadn't . . . ' Mickey was about to say worked it out.

'It was only the once,' Josephine had continued. 'I envy you, as always,' she added.

God, how vile she could be when she lost control of her bitterness.

86

'He called me his wife's name. I'll never forget that.' She had a mean, ill-disguised expression of triumph all over her face.

Now that the memory pressed into her thoughts Mickey tried to recapture all of it in an attempt to make some sense of not having even suspected the obvious. Had she dismissed it as bravado? Had she found it so impossible then to envisage Dan as anyone's lover? Or was it just that she'd been too engrossed in her own affair with Arthur? Too much had been happening at that time. Everything had seemed unreal.

'Perhaps you didn't believe me. I know people have always liked to think that I make things up.' Her expression changed then: the triumph fell away and vulnerability returned.

'Oh, I shouldn't have said anything. I shouldn't have told you, but I thought maybe you knew.' She looked desolate. 'He's never said anything?'

Mickey shook her head. She was trying to imagine how Dan would react because she was quite certain he had no idea of his role in all this.

'I thought not, and you must promise not to tell him,' Josephine said in a dramatically resolute tone.

'Does that mean you want me to?' Mickey responded, bleakly and unkindly. 'I think he should be told.'

'You mean that he's not the sort of man to shirk his responsibilities,' Josephine echoed Mickey's thoughts. 'No, you mustn't tell him. Promise. I don't want that sort of involvement. A duty job. Besides, Dan is yours now, and I'm pleased for you, really. I've got this bundle of fun,' she said, looking at the baby, 'and I don't want to share him.'

The wind had turned colder and the light was beginning to go.

'Let's go back in,' she said, 'Forget what I've said. Perhaps I did make it all up.'

Mickey was shivering when they got back to the library, although whether it was from the coldness of the wind or reaction to Josephine's burdensome secret, she couldn't be sure. How stupid it was the way people told each other to forget the unforgettable. Dan was still talking with Peter, and Mickey knew it was going to be difficult to look him in the eye. As soon as she saw him she felt the new barrier there would be between them.

Laurela approached them as they entered the room. Her mouth was smiling but her expression was otherwise baleful.

'Your mother isn't feeling very well,' she hissed at Josephine.

Mickey glanced beyond them and saw the remaining guest was well on the way to drunken oblivion.

'Oh, Mummy!' Josephine groaned.

'Can I help?' Mickey offered, almost grateful for the diversion.

'If you could just hold on to Giles,' Josephine said, handing over the baby. 'She gets so aggressive when she's like this. I'll take her upstairs and make her lie down. She'll pass out as soon as she's horizontal.'

There was a small scuffle over by the Dickens and then minus a shoe, the old lady was escorted out.

'Very tiresome, and so sad,' Laurela murmured to Mickey. 'Peter and I are just so pleased to be able to do what we can for poor JoJo. She's had such rotten luck one way and another. Let down badly. Anyway, we're so very grateful that you and Mr Lovell were able to spare the time to come today.' She sounded as if she was opening a garden fête, but it seemed the cue to leave. Dan and Peter had come across the room to them. The baby, still in Mickey's arms, still gazing intently into her face, suddenly jerked out a hand. Dan caught hold of it.

'Splendid little chap, isn't he,' Peter said. 'Such a pity he's, well,' he paused 'without a father.'

Dan nodded, still holding on to the tiny fist.

Here was the moment, Mickey thought. Dear God, such poignancy! She couldn't stand it.

'I think we ought to be going soon,' she said, swallowing a lump as hard as a marble.

Josephine came back and a few minutes later Dan and Mickey made to leave.

'Not a word!' Josephine whispered.

Mickey smiled thinly. Was this person really her friend, and if so, what sort of a friend was she to her in return? A melodramatic sensation of impending sacrifice lay heavily within her.

'Cheerio,' she said, getting into Dan's car.

'Keep in touch,' Josephine called after her.

'I'm glad you got us away,' Dan said as they turned down the drive. 'Intellectual socialists are such heavy going.'

'Are they? Socialists, I mean,' Mickey responded on auto-pilot.

'Red as red but still bellyaching like mad about death duties. I really got collared.'

'So did I,' Mickey said in wistful preoccupation.

That night Dan tried again to make love to her.

'What is it? What's wrong?' he asked as she lay stiff and dried up as a brittle twig.

'I'm sorry,' was all she could say, because to tell him that Josephine and baby Giles lay between them, just as they had between her and David, would be to break the promise, and she couldn't cope with any more guilt.

She lay awake for a long time, too cold and full of confusion to sleep or do anything about her predicament. She felt so terribly guilty, about all sorts of things, even about simply being.

'We've got to talk,' Dan said in the morning.

'Yes,' Mickey agreed, desolately.

'It's not going to work, is it?'

'No.'

Dan, sitting on the edge of the bed, next to where she lay, his grey hair, normally so neat and in place, dishevelled from a restless night, his eyes sorrowfully earnest. She could hardly bear to look at him. She knew nothing of love any more. It had been stamped out of her by the indifference of David, the violence of Arthur, the injustice to Josephine and her baby in which she was sworn to connive. An overwhelming sense of unworthiness had turned her to ice.

'There's nothing more to be said, then,' Dan decreed. That edge of bitterness and disappointment was in his voice, but in the next moment he leant forward and kissed her face.

'We'll go back to being friends,' he said with such an effort at kindness that she had to say something to try and convince him that it wasn't his fault, not in the least bit, that she couldn't love him.

'Oh Dan, I'm so sorry,' she said very quietly. It was in her mind to continue with an attempt at explanation but she knew it would sound only feeble and like an excuse, and if she told him

89

that love and sex seized her up, made her want to die, that its potency was too rich for the lily-livered creature she had become, he would doubtless wear that worried look of his for ever more and want to take her to a shrink, engage her in rehabilitation so gentle and wrapped in kind concern that her already abject condition might slip into a capitulating dependency that would trap them both in worse horrors.

'It's all right,' he said, the way people do when absolutely everything is not all right.

He gazed at her for a moment, as if taking a last look before closing a door. He stood up then and turned away from her. He left the room and some minutes later returned with a cup of tea which he placed on the bedside table by her. Was there comfort in the mundane? Perhaps.

Two days later Dan drove her to Heathrow and again watched her leave, only this time there was no seed of hope. They smiled and waved to one another and it crossed his mind that he might never see her again even though this was unlikely. More accurately, he would not see her in the same way when they met again: there would be that distance inevitable between people who have tried seriously to love one another and failed, because he didn't love her, not in that way. He knew it now because the sadness was no more than a flat kind of disappointment; it didn't have the sharp edges of pain he'd experienced before.

Chapter Eleven

On Monday night Nick didn't sleep. It was to be the last night Charlotte would be with him in the hotel as she was moving into the Cambridge flat the next day, while he went to the merchant bank, his only remaining hope for raising the cash he needed to get Fortress Against Fat going in the UK.

He didn't try to lie still in the ill-sprung hotel bed. He kept turning over, letting in the gust of cold air of which Charlotte normally complained. But she didn't wake and he wasn't sure what he'd hoped for if she had. In one way he was glad they would be apart for a few days until he joined her in the flat he'd not yet seen. The strain of being with her in the night, during the raw hours of insomnia when he was no longer able to manufacture any confidence, was proving more difficult than he'd imagined when he'd made the decision not to tell her how badly things were going. It had been pride and bloody-mindedness that had brought about this decision, and nothing to do with wanting to protect her from the worry. And now, he longed to pour it all out to her; to rant on about it, to have that release.

He'd let it go on too long, though. It was better that she didn't wake. How could he explain it all now, added to which, he thought it possible she might leave him if she discovered how close to bankruptcy he was. He had this low opinion of her staying power because she was so like him. Weakness turned her off. Pity wasn't in her nature. He felt all this with a sort of angry resentment which in someone else might have been more like self-pity.

By tomorrow night he might know the worst and he'd be in

the bed alone. He wondered whether he'd be able to continue the pretence if tomorrow's meeting failed: whether he could move to Cambridge and somehow ride it out. Fortunately, there'd been so little communication between him and Charlotte over the past few months that so unsatisfactory a course seemed possible.

He felt very alone. Charlotte was a pain, but like a gangrenous leg. He didn't want the amputation. They said you could still feel it, long after it had been chopped off, and there was always the thought, that it might have been saved. He turned over again and thought he must be near derangement to have dreamt up such a simile.

It seemed to him now that he hardly knew Charlotte other than as a person with whom to quarrel. There'd been the intense preliminary bit, the excessive intimacy that went with falling in love, although was it that, or just a huge lust for something new and different? Either way, it had distorted the people they really were, and when that phase had cooled there hadn't been time for the relationship to deepen at the less frantic tempo of everyday married life. He regretted this now, the undivided drive he had given to his business, but it was too late to change the emphasis of his life. Success meant everything to him and his vision had been too narrow to equate this with anything outside making money.

His appointment with the bank was early, as was the train Charlotte intended taking to Cambridge. They sniped at one another, briefly, over accusations of excessive time taken in the bathroom. Often, he knew, he started these pieces of meanness; it was a sort of habit, his irritability, like people who used bad language and half the time they didn't notice they were doing it. But she had begun it this morning. She'd been sharp and venomous for days. At one stage he'd actually enjoyed producing this cutting edge in her, that was if he had time, but it was different now. He realised, with some horror, that he would have preferred a little kindness from her, just for the moment.

She left before him. He would have liked a kiss but didn't get one. He fetched out the Cartier attaché case she'd bought for him the previous Christmas. It wasn't her style, but she deemed it his, smooth burgundy leather with lacquered brass clips. He wasn't sure about it any more.

He laid it on the unmade bed and opened it up to check through the papers he needed for the meeting. The glossy cover of the Fortress Against Fat business presentation lay on the top. It was a thick document, crammed with correctly added up rubbish, an expensive accountant's hypothesis for ideas that had already failed, yet he'd slung all his remaining energy into it during the days since returning to England. It had been put together in record time and God, he hoped it would do a convincing job! A single surge of optimism rose in him then died. With the vulgarity that went with despair it came into his mind that he might just as well have saved the additional funds he'd borrowed on his American Express Gold Card, the four thousand pounds it had cost in less than a week to produce such a catalogue of bullshit. Lavatory paper might have served better.

He smiled to himself at this pathetic puerility and flung shut the lid of the case. Four thousand pounds he'd spent, a thousand of them to the graphic artist who'd produced the cover design which looked like Dover Castle and relied too much on the quality of the Astralux paper. Charlotte could have done something far better, but of course he hadn't asked her.

He picked up the case, swallowed to wet the dryness of his throat, and set forth for the fateful meeting. In the lobby of the hotel he was stopped and asked if he was vacating the room. The question had been somehow pointed, a nervous glance between the receptionist and the hall porter when he'd answered no and that he'd be there at least another night.

In the taxi to the City he realised that the hotel must have seen Charlotte leaving with the luggage: they thought it was a runner. He wanted to laugh out loud. The idea had possibilities. The taxi became jammed in traffic and he found himself watching the meter, the immediate, instinctive concern. Six months, a year ago, he wouldn't have noticed, not the fare, only the time; but the last occasion he'd had such a meeting the bankers had come to him.

The meter reached five pounds outside the grey stone portal of the bank and he debated using this as a means of avoiding a tip to the driver. But when it came to the point he hadn't the confidence to carry it off and gave the man two fivers, hesitating a moment for some change then letting it go because his hands were shaking and he didn't want the fellow to see; or perhaps in the end it was just to have that feeling of superiority, though this didn't work and all he felt was foolish.

He went into the imposing building which at one time would have impressed but now intimidated. His throat was dry again, his hands sweating like armpits. He actually found it an effort to produce a sexual smile for the pretty girl behind the reception desk. She spoke his name into a telephone receiver. Things were being said from the other end. He waited. She listened. He watched.

'Mr Brown is very sorry . . . ' the rest of it, a collection of platitudinous excuses, amounted to the City of London telling him to bugger off. The faceless Mr Brown wasn't even prepared to reveal himself. Nick wondered how many other people had played their last card via this girl with her confident, eighteen or nineteen-year-old voice and uninterested pitiless eyes. It was a measure of his state of defeat that he didn't attempt to argue with her but merely turned away and went out into the street. This was only one bank, but it might as well have been the last. He had no heart, energy or enthusiasm left, only a dull sense of relief that he no longer had to manufacture these driving forces. There was no money left and no time to raise any more. His bankruptcy was complete.

He walked down the street until he came to a tube station, he didn't notice which one. It was years since he'd used the underground. He'd forgotten the huge gusts of wind pushed out of the tunnels by the trains, the endless advertisements for underwear alongside the escalators: was it thought by the advertisers there might be some subliminal connection between thermal vests and Y fronts and travel via the bowels of the earth? The notion remained with him, an inconsequential piece of inanity, but something else to think about.

He got off the tube at Liverpool Street and took a main-line train going to Cambridge. How quickly and automatically he'd returned to the ways of no money. He sat in a second class carriage which smelt of stale cigarette butts and commuter grime. A woman opposite him, with a large varicose vein bunching out of her calf, was reading *The Sun*.

What was he to do? Perhaps he could go back to journalism, though it was many years since he'd written a story, and he'd allowed his contacts with Fleet Street to lapse. Fleet Street! What hope, hadn't they all gone to Wapping? He didn't even know where Wapping was.

The train stopped at every station, making the journey seem interminable and after a while, pointless. He'd embarked upon it without any thought or purpose. He didn't want to see Charlotte, not yet. Instead he found himself heading for the house he'd bought for Marion and Paul, for all three of them at the time. He'd thought Marion would sell and move into something smaller after the divorce, maybe even go back to Birmingham. He was glad now that she hadn't, that the place and the people were still the same, only time and circumstance had altered and these were ever changeable.

It was a bitterly cold day. In London he hadn't noticed and didn't have a coat with him. He let the taxi go at the end of Marion's cul-de-sac, not thinking there might be the chance she wouldn't be home. Marion had always been there.

He rang the door bell. An icy wind sliced across the back of his neck. A completely unjustifiable sense of outrage rose in him. He'd paid for the damned house, hadn't he. He grabbed hold of the latch and wrenched at it. The door opened. It hadn't even been locked.

He hesitated a moment then stepped inside. The familiar smell, common to everywhere Marion had lived, pervaded the hallway. It was a fatty smell, the residue of home-cooked meals high on cholesterol. It was funny the way you didn't notice the smell of a house when you lived there, it was only when you came back after a time away, and yet it was instantly recognisable.

He breathed it in and found it oddly comforting and irritating at the same time. He closed the front door behind him and wandered through to the living room. Every chair pointed towards the television, and all of them were worn, tatty and stained. Marion had never bothered about such things, although at one time she'd made some effort, to please him or rather, not to displease. It must have been a relief to her, not having to worry or bother . . . He started. A sharp knocking sound had come from above, as if someone was banging

95

something on the floor upstairs.

Again he hesitated, thinking of the possibilities. Perhaps Marion was upstairs in bed, but at this hour of the day? And being the man he was, it then crossed his mind that she might not be alone. Outrage again, then he dismissed the idea, Marion had never been the type for daytime sex. The knocking was repeated. Burglars? If so, surely they must have heard him come in, but perhaps not.

He glanced round the room and grabbed hold of the only weapon-like object in sight, a Bavarian beer mug with a hinged pewter lid. He went back out to the hallway and crept up the stairs. He felt alarmed but not frightened. He wanted burglars. He wanted to be able to smash someone over the head, to wreak a violent relief-giving revenge.

He reached the door that led into the bedroom over the living room. A split second elapsed and in it he heard the sound of a cough, a terrible lung, deep rattle.

He opened the door and there in the bed was Marion's mother, the abundant hair that had been red as carrots now forming a tangly grey frame round a face that seemed to have aged twenty years in three, which was the last time he had seen Ruby.

'Oh, my God! Get out and come back in five minutes,' she shouted at him, then started choking again. But he didn't leave. He went over to her, the Bavarian mug dangling foolishly from his fingers. He put it down on the bedside table and stood by helplessly while she bent into a large white handkerchief.

He noticed her back, the exaggerated, hunched curve, the back of an old person, but Ruby was still in her fifties.

The coughing subsided, and she flopped back against the pile of pillows arranged sick-bed fashion.

'Oh, don't bother now,' she wheezed, meeting his eyes, 'You've seen me at my worst. You'll just have to take me as you find me, though I've never been any good without my make-up.'

Still he hadn't said anything.

'But then it was always a bit more than skin-deep with us, eh Nick?' she added, her mouth spreading into a grin like a basking shark.

'Ruby,' he said in a low, slow voice, responding in spite of his revulsion. 'I thought you were burglars.'

'I might say I thought you were the same. Are we both disappointed? Oh, don't answer that one. I'm bored out of my mind lying here all day. Anything for a bit of excitement, but I suppose you'll do.'

'Nice of you to say so.'

'Oh, don't be coy with me!'

'Coy, I don't think that's quite my style.'

'Oh, I can think of a time : . . ' she trailed off, wickedly. Her eyes hadn't changed. They were the only bit of her that hadn't, just as suggestive and knowing and evil as they'd always been.

'What are you doing here?' he enquired.

'I'm being looked after,' she sighed. 'Never get old, Nick. Throw yourself off a cliff or under a bus before you get like this.'

'What's wrong Ruby?' he asked.

'Dear, oh dear, I've just realised that you sound like an American,' she said avoiding the question. 'Sit down Nick. I must say, you're the last person I expected to see, but it's a nice surprise. You're still a lovely man to look at. Come on, sit down and tell me all about everything. How's Lottie and that spoilt brat, Vicky? Or is that why you're here? Have you had enough of them?'

Nick sat down, but far enough away to gain some distance from that penetrating gaze.

'I see I'm right,' Ruby said when he didn't answer immediately.

'No, not really,' he said, knitting his fingers together.

'But something's up. You've got that whipped dog look about you. Has she got tired of you, is that it?'

'You're a meddlesome old bitch, Ruby,' he said.

'I thought it was a bit strange, you and her coming back here,' she persisted, unabashed. 'Things didn't work out for you in America? I guessed as much when Marion told me you were back.'

'I'm bankrupt, Ruby.' There, he'd said it. The words seemed to have come from nowhere and filled the room with a sudden stillness.

Ruby was silent for a moment.

'I shouldn't think Lady Muck's taken too kindly to it,' she said.

He was able to look at her now. It was oddly comforting to have found Ruby of all people to tell what had happened. It was rooted in the past, their abrasive candour. From the beginning they'd know one another for exactly the people they were. Ruby had looked at Nick and seen the mean-hearted ambition that inevitably would make her daughter miserable, but she'd done nothing to discourage the marriage. She'd wanted Nick in the family, at any cost. She'd wanted him from the first day Marion had brought him home, nearly twenty years ago, when poor old Frank was still alive. She'd even contemplated ditching Frank and going off with Nick herself, and she probably could have done it and what a team they'd have made! They were two of a kind.

On the wedding day she'd seen it would never last with Marion. She remembered dancing with Nick at the hotel where they'd gone for the reception, such as it was, only the family, theirs, because Nick had nobody, nobody he wanted to be bothered with. They'd danced long and slow and Marion had got upset. And Nick, so much younger then, hadn't fully understood how it was going to be, or hadn't accepted it. Frank, of course, had never noticed.

So it hadn't been such a big shock when Nick left Marion and went off with hoity-toity Charlotte. The only surprising thing was that the marriage had gone on for as long as it had. But for Ruby the split had been unbearable at the time. Nick had travelled up to Birmingham to tell her himself. She was past her best even then, and they'd both known it. She'd hated him for a bit, done what she could to spoil things for him with Lady Muck. But she wasn't that big a fool and after a few months she'd gone to see Charlotte and charmed her into friendship, looked after the brat. Nick, naturally enough, had been wary at first, but Ruby knew how to be irresistible, and wouldn't they always have that shared guilt over Marion?

It was, of course, the only thing they'd never discussed and never would, although it had occurred to Ruby that Charlotte knew. It was the way she'd looked at her on occasion, a sort of curiosity. Did women in harems sneak a look at one another in that way and with that thought? Ruby imagined so. But it was all right, because Charlotte liked her and must have known it was all in the past by then.

'Charlotte doesn't know,' Nick said.

Ruby's heart lifted at the thought of all the trouble to come. It was something to get her teeth into, something to follow, even take a hand in. It had to be fate that had brought Nick back to her at such a moment, though she'd yet to discover what he was doing here, with both Marion and Paul out. Still, she wasn't one to question fate too closely.

'Are you going to tell her?'

'I should have said something months ago, when things went bad in the States.'

'She's no idea, then?'

'You're loving this, aren't you?' he said, still holding her gaze.

Ruby smiled.

'Yes and no. I'm not one to enjoy other people's successes. I'd rather a bit of disaster, but perhaps that's only because I've never achieved much myself and I always felt I should have done.'

'I didn't know you had ambitions.'

'Of course you did! I think I could have done rather well on the stage.'

'I'm sure you could. Why didn't you try?'

'Never had the opportunity, or the education. I was far too interested in boys when I was a girl, but I had a lot of success there. Oh, I had such a lot of fun, broke so many hearts.'

'I've never asked you why you married Frank?'

'Had to dear. In those days it wasn't quite the thing to be an unmarried mother, not like now. Frank wasn't too bad, not when he was younger. He worshipped me, you know, and that was nice. It made me feel good when nothing else was happening.'

'Nothing else?'

'You know what I mean.'

'Naughty old Ruby.'

'Naughty yourself.'

'Didn't you ever fall in love?'

'I think you asked me that once before.'

'Did I? I can't remember.'

'It was when you told me you were leaving Marion. "Haven't you ever fallen in love Ruby?" you said.'

'I don't remember it.'

'No I don't suppose you would,' she said, an edge of bitterness in her voice.

'Come on, Ruby. Don't go mean on me. I'm the lowest I've ever been, you don't have to make me feel any worse.'

Ruby paused, pressing her lips together. A moment ago she'd been all ready to hammer him into the ground, and serve him right for resurrecting that old wound. She'd rattled his bars on occasion in the past, told him a few home truths when Marion had had Paul and he'd behaved like the rotten bastard he was. But what was the point any more, besides which, she wasn't in that strong a position, stuck in bed. He could get up and leave and never come back, but if she played it right he'd come again and again until he got back on his feet, and by the look of him that might not happen for quite a while. She'd seen him defeated before, when he'd chucked up newspapers and started that advertising business of his and it hadn't gone too well, not to begin with. That was when he and Marion had had to give up their place and come and live with her and Frank. Happy days!

'Tell me all about it, then,' she said. 'Now everything, mind. I want to know the lot.'

An hour later he had told her a great deal about making and losing a fortune in America. Of course, this wasn't what she wanted to hear, but it was better to let him get it off his chest, all the indignation and feeling sorry for himself.

Once of twice he'd mentioned someone called Frances, a woman friend of Charlotte. Ruby wanted to hear more about her and she was certain there was more. She wanted the gratification of knowing he'd cheated on Charlotte, her of the grand passion – she who had lured him away from Marion and herself, and, of course, Paul, poor boy, with his spots and lanky limpness. And she wanted to know about Vicky, but only to find out if Nick had any affection for the other woman's child. She did so hope not. Paul was a disappointment, no looks, not much in the way of personality, but she was fond of him and didn't want him usurped.

She interrupted.

'What was Charlotte doing while all this was going on?'

'Spending the money,' he answered, bitterly, because he'd

worked himself up into a mood of aggression.

'And what about the child?'

'Vicky?'

'Who else? Or are there others you haven't told me about?'

'Shut up Ruby!' he said, unpleasantly, but she was glad to see him angry again. This was more like old times. Perhaps he wasn't finished after all.

'Vicky,' he continued, 'was, and still is, set up in an expensive private school.'

He shouldn't have told her that. He knew as soon as he'd said it. He'd told her far too much, but none of the rest of it could make any difference to the future. He'd never been happy about Vicky getting an expensive education while Paul had nothing.

He saw the same thought in Ruby's eyes, and wanted to tell her he'd thought of doing the same for Paul but couldn't see it working with Marion bringing him up. But how could he say that? There were limits, even in what he said to Ruby.

She'd closed her eyes now, holding in her own anger, remembering that she didn't want to drive him away.

'Are you all right?' he asked, thinking she might be in pain and realising he hadn't given her a chance to tell him what was wrong with her.

'I'm sorry,' he said, and it was a sort of all encompassing apology he hoped she'd understand. The old girl had a way of getting to him. He'd missed her, he realised with something like a revelation.

She'd opened her eyes agin.

'What is it, Ruby?' he asked, suddenly fearing the worst. It was a spontaneous and unselfish concern; the first of its kind for longer than he could have remembered.

'It's Big C,' she said, being of the generation that still hovered round euphemism for cancer.

He swallowed and felt the chill of the disease strike at his own heart.

'How long have you had it?' he asked, rather than how long had she got.

'Years probably,' she answered, wearily. She really didn't like to talk about it, as if by doing so she encouraged its progress, but it was as well he knew. He might even feel a little sorry for her. A touch of pity could be a useful, manipulative tool.

The disease had only recently been diagnosed, but for years she'd had thoughts about it, the little nigglings. She'd heard that people could think themselves into cancer but who could tell? She reckoned it started with things like needing a cigarette to go to the lavatory and not thinking of it as something you'd have to keep on with. The oddest thing had been the way she felt when the doctor told her what she'd got. Knowing for sure had stopped the worry. She'd thought about not telling anyone, being stoical, but she couldn't keep it to herself, and because the worry had gone she was able to sound brave and accepting. It made her feel special, elevated. There were bad bouts of pain but she had drugs to ease that, wonderful drugs, artist's materials they were. She had incredible half-waking fantasies, dreams that seemed so real and maybe pointed to there being something afterwards. In one of them she'd met Gracie Fields of all people. It was a lovely woodland setting, all softly lit, hazy the way it can be in among the trees when the sun's trying to get through. There was Gracie, in a nice yellow dress (she'd never dreamt in colour before) and a sweet, approachable smile on her face. She was old, of course, her hair white as cotton wool. They'd had a little chat, about nothing in particular, just polite conversation. She wanted to ask Gracie, as delicately as she could, whether she wasn't dead, but it was awkward to come out with such a personal question and she had sort of known Gracie would be evasive about it.

Nick was looking at her with that sad, not knowing what to say expression she'd seen in others. He was a lovely man, even if he was losing his hair. Perhaps she'd have a nice dream about him next time round with the pain-killers.

She came out of this small reverie at the sound of the front door being opened downstairs. Marion must be home from her little school which, thank God, she didn't run from the house any more: all those toddlers, yelling and bawling and biting one another, what a nightmare that would have been for a dying woman, for any woman. Marion had always had masochistic tendencies.

Ruby wriggled back into her pillows and prepared herself for the interesting little meeting that was about to take place.

She was damn certain Marion didn't know about Nick being here.

He glanced over his shoulder at the closed door. The sound of Marion's footsteps coming up the stairs filled the room and dictated a conspiracy of silence between the former in-laws, adversaries and briefly, lovers.

The door opened. Ruby smiled. There was still enjoyment to be had out of this world.

Chapter Twelve

The basement flat in Bateman Street really was claustrophobically small. Previous occupants had been students in their second and third years at the university, single people oblivious of the limitations of a 1950s Ascot water heater, a cooker with only two working rings, and a power point for round-pinned plugs.

Charlotte, carried away on impulsive haste the previous week, had descended into the flat that morning and seen the stark reality. The shabby furnishings compounded the gloom of the below street level rooms and she'd sat down in a sudden state of despair. She dreaded Nick's arrival. Surely he'd think she'd gone out of her head to have taken such a place; perhaps he'd even guess at the reason for her choice. The flat had two single beds. Nowhere was really spacious enough for a double.

She imagined him turning up, probably at the weekend, and insisting they go and stay at the Garden House Hotel. That morning she very nearly abandoned the basement herself before he had a chance to see it.

The whole thing was like a bad dream, especially after the opulence of their apartment in San Francisco, but she must grasp hold of the optimism she'd built up, scramble back on to that raft of future promise. It had listed quite a bit, tipped her over the edge, when Dan had been so cold and full of dislike but she'd manage to cling on. There had to be hope, and logically she wouldn't expect immediate progress with Dan

She spent the morning cleaning the flat, finding sticky corners with years of built-up grime. At midday she went out and bought groceries to stock the kitchen, although she couldn't imagine eating in the place. She also bought bed linen, all her own stuff still being in store, and three frilly cushions from Laura Ashley so there could be just something new and nice in her basement.

In the afternoon she got an early edition of the Cambridge Evening News, but it was the wrong day for jobs and there was little more than part-time posts for artisan occupations.

She sat at a mean-sized table, the newspaper spread out in front of her, and thought what next? Mid afternoon in a provincial city with nothing to do. She thought of Nick, having his high-powered meeting in London; of Vicky, so very far away; and Dan, what was he doing at this moment? She thought of them all and it seemed to her that none of them could possibly be thinking of her. In a sense she'd divorced herself from each one of them. There was nobody she could relate to, nobody who really cared how she might be spending her afternoon. To have pin-pointed her isolation in this way brought forth a self-pitying sob, so strong and involuntary that it actually hurt her chest. She couldn't bear to sit still a moment longer.

In an outward manifestation of the restlessness of her mind, she moved about the tiny flat, almost unaware of what she was doing. This inner restlessness had always been her curse: it had made her dissatisfied with so much in her life that might have offered the calm she thought she saw in others and envied. Of course, all such thoughts in her present state of flux related to her longing for a return to Dan; presently just out of reach and possibly lost forever, though she couldn't allow herself to think this.

If only she hadn't met Nick, she thought to herself now. If only. If only. Looking back and through the distortion of an imagined love, she felt certain she would never have left Dan if Nick had not been there, offering an alternative that, with hindsight, amounted to no more than the attraction of change, something different for difference sake. And here she was, in her mid thirties, with no way of life at all. The one in America had been no more than an interlude, vibrant and glitzy at times, but superficial. She'd loved the Americans, but she didn't really understand them; the dinner parties where they'd talk about the nature of their souls, reaching for the intense and meaningful and reducing it all to nothing with their excess of artful artlessness. Nick had found these occasions tedious and in time so had she, although initially she'd thought this was the sort of thing she'd always wanted. But self-exploration could be a disappointment and perhaps that was the trouble with Americans.

Charlotte was bored. She'd hung all sorts of dire miseries round this simple fact in the course of her agitated afternoon, and being the sort of person she was, it was just as likely she'd have felt the same in any other situation, given an hour or so of unallocated time. She was intelligent enough to think of this herself and to use it to lift her spirit a little and try to think more positive thoughts. The flat was not forever, whatever happened. It wasn't as if she really needed to be there now: Nick had money, plenty of it, and the law would give her a good slice, although she preferred not to plan along that line. She'd never been able to think that what was Nick's was hers, not in the way she had with Dan, with whom she'd started out relatively poor.

This train of thought led her to Frances, who years and years ago had lived in Cambridge, but as part of the university community, not the town's, the two being as far removed from one another as blacks and whites in South Africa. Frances had been cross with her all those years ago. It had been a winter afternoon but it couldn't have been that cold, because they'd sat on the slope of grass that ran along the river bank by the Backs near Kings. It had been shortly before she married Dan, and as she remembered, Frances had more or less told her not to, but instead to sort herself out, make something of her own life. That was because marrying Dan at that time meant giving up her college course, not because he'd actually told her to, but there was no alternative as his new job meant moving away, and she had neither the avant-garde imagination nor maturity to consider marrying but not living together until it was convenient to both.

Surely it was up to each and every person to make a life for themselves that did not totally depend upon a marriage partner, Frances had said to her in so many words, most probably in her never unkind way which nonetheless, unfailingly struck the bullseye of defencelessness.

It was just a pity it had taken Charlotte so long to reach this inevitable conclusion herself. Even in America, where in the last few months she'd been getting it together in terms of a career, she'd not even considered remaining there in her own right.

She went out again, down the street to a telephone box where she called James. Had he been able to look at her video? She expected a negative answer, but had prepared herself to this, and whatever he said, she planned on retrieving the tape in the morning.

'Yes,' he told her, after the usual ingratiating, chauvinistic tones of his greeting. 'I did manage to glance at it.'

Exasperation, that most infectious of emotions she'd caught from living with Nick, rose in her. How could you 'glance' at a video tape!

'I do rather need it back,' she said. 'Would it be alright if I came over and collected it tomorrow morning.'

'Where are you?'

'In Cambridge. I moved into the flat today.'

'All by yourself?'

'Nick's still in London,' she said.

'You should have told us. Auders,' she heard him shout away from the receiver, 'Charlotte's been moving house today – all by herself.'

'Is it alright if I come and fetch the tape?'

'Audrey says you're very naughty not letting her know. She'd have come over and given you a hand.'

'Really James, there was nothing much to be done. It's only somewhere temporary,' she said, alarmed at the possibility of her old friends seeing the flat. It was enough that they already seemed to view her with pity when hadn't she thought to create a quite different impression?

It was agreed that she would call round for elevenses in the morning. She replaced the receiver and remained a few more seconds in the kiosk. She couldn't face going back to that basement, not straight away. Instead she went to the end of the street and out into Hills Road. She walked on, towards the centre of the city, but with the aimless, self-concious step of one without direction or purpose. She'd remember this afternoon, always. It would stay with her like a caution, even when

107

in time, her life might be quite different.

After a few minutes, in which it had started to rain, she went past a car hire place. Her pace slowed, she hesitated, then turned back and went into the office where a man in greasy overalls was eating a sandwich. This reminded her that she had not eaten all day, but food no longer occupied much of her thought. Fortress Against Fat had made most meals psychologically indigestible, until she'd reached the point of losing interest as well as appetite.

The car she hired was small, ordinary, and inconspicuous, and took her straight out of Cambridge, along the old familiar route she'd driven so many times without conscious thought. It took about twenty minutes to reach the village, and as before, the light was beginning to go. At the road junction by the corner of the village green she halted and for the briefest of moments shut her eyes. She imagined that Vicky was in the car, but not this car, and that they were on their way home for tea and later listening to Radio Four while she prepared supper for Dan and herself.

A car horn sounded from behind, snapping her back to the present. She turned into the High Street. It was all exactly as it had always been. There was never anyone about. That was a memory to sharpen her focus on the past, when Vicky was a baby and she'd felt so trapped and lonely at home all day while it seemed that everyone else left the village during daylight hours in order to pursue interesting and purposeful occupations. There lay the roots of her restlessness at that time, the growing sense of life passing her by. The boredom and depression, how she'd let it take hold of her, until there was no joy to be found in anything. She knew now, or at least she thought she did, that none of it had been Dan's fault, that the problem had lain entirely within herself. If only she'd allowed a little more time though it was easy to think this in retrospect, to forget the intensity of despair, though wasn't she approaching a similar state now. Similar, but different. It wasn't a blind search for escape, not this time.

She'd left the High Street and turned into the lane. She slowed the car as the roof of the house came into view. Her heart had begun to pound unevenly, as if she was trespassing, which, in a way, she was.

Her house, but not hers. The sense of displacement over-whelmed her this time. She drove past the end of the driveway and on down the lane a short distance until she came to the gateway that led to the fields behind the house. She turned off the road and switched off the engine and side lights. The sudden stillness and silence intensified the engulfing sense of loss. She could see the house clearly from where she'd stopped, the garden she'd created, the rustic summerhouse where Vicky and Audrey's little boy had played mothers and fathers for hours on end, while Audrey went off doing Meals on Wheels and teaching Asian women English and all sorts of worthy activities for which Charlotte could not summon an ounce of interest, any more than she had for the wealthy women of California and their obsessive concern with fat and eclectic exploration of methods for its removal.

Such a long way to go, she thought, beginning to shiver now that the car's heat was going. All that way to find out that she'd been running away from herself, not Dan.

There were no signs that anyone was in the house. No lights were on and it was nearly five o'clock and the evening drawing in. There was no car in the drive, but she hadn't expected Dan to be there at this time. Even so, when she stepped out of the car she closed the door quietly, and went to the gate that led into the fields so that she could approach the house from the back and thus avoid the alarming crunch of gravel underfoot if she'd gone round the front.

Being furtive didn't suit her, but she couldn't help it. A bold, proprietorial approach was more than she could muster.

Her feet were soaking, her high-heeled shoes caked with mud from the ploughed field she'd had to circumnavigate to reach the meadow where once she'd kept a donkey who'd loved Dan and not her. She unfastened the smaller gate that stood in the hedgerow bordering the division between rough ground and garden. The back of the house lay ahead, just a few yards of lawn to cross and she'd be at the kitchen window.

She stopped then, by the gate. What on earth was she doing! This was complete madness. She left the gate swinging loose and started retracing her steps. It was now nearly dark. Never in all the years she'd lived with Dan in the house had she taken the route she was walking now: there had never been the need.

109

Access to the meadow was simple and straightforward via the garden. She felt utterly foolish staggering along through the mud.

A rustling wind had got into the trees, so that she didn't hear the car coming as she reached the last stretch of hedgerow that ran the length of the property. She saw the lights first, the headlamp beams swinging round as the car turned into the driveway.

She crouched down and heard the car door open then the treading footsteps on the gravel, but going away from the house, back towards the road. Clear of the crunching stones, she then heard the sharper sound of steps on tarmac, advancing down the lane and towards the field entrance where she'd left the hire car.

She saw Dan stop by it, bend and peer inside through the passenger side window. Nobody came down their lane, not to stop.

She was shivering so much now that it seemed impossible he wouldn't sense her presence. Of course he must be suspicious of an unknown car parked off the road and with a clear view of the house. He was a politician, a public figure and prey to crackpots, terrorists, and the secret people whose job it was to observe the private lives of such as him.

He'll call the police, Charlotte thought, hysterically. And if he doesn't do so straight away, he'll note the number plate and they'll trace it back to me.

Dan had moved away from the car and come up to the gate. Surely he would see her, and suddenly this was what she wanted and yet couldn't make happen: it had to be him finding her, not she him.

She waited, in an agony of hope and yet feeling so ridiculous she'd no idea how she would explain herself when the moment came. Then she saw him turn away, and it was as if he had seen her but chosen not to. She felt quite stunned, as if he'd slapped her face, though worse than that because slaps didn't come from indifference.

She heard the footfalls replayed in reverse then she saw the lights going on in the house and the curtains being drawn, shutting her out.

Only then did she understand the true nature of vulnerabil-

110

ity. At times, particularly when she was much younger, she thought herself exposed, but never in the way she was now. Vulnerability was not being found out when you wanted to be. It was realisation that a secret pride from which you had taken succour for the greater part of your life, did not exist any more.

She moved on, so cold now that the immediate physical need for warmth propelled her towards the car. She didn't look back at the house, to see if a curtain had moved, her departure been watched. She drove away, back to the nasty little burrow she'd chosen for herself, and waiting in the street, looking equally cold and alone, stood Nick.

'I was just about to give you up,' he said as she got out of the car.

She waited for him to question where she had been, to comment on the state of her shoes and legs. It was a weary anticipation. She might even tell him the truth.

But he said nothing. Even after he'd followed her down the narrow stone steps to the basement door and they'd gone inside and could see one another properly, he said nothing, not even the expected reaction to the awfulness of their new home.

Each had their own preoccupations and perhaps accepted, with unquestioning relief, that the other was not predisposed to any sort of conversation or enquiry apart from the banal communication as to what they might eat.

Charlotte removed her shoes and went into the kitchen. She opened the cupboard she had stocked earlier in the day and gazed, unseeing at a row of tins. It was some while since she'd prepared a meal. More often than not they'd eaten out in America, that was when they'd made time to eat together. And now, she couldn't think what he might like, as if he was merely an acquaintance come to call, a person with whom she had only tenuous links.

He came to the doorway of the kitchen. She knew he was there but she didn't turn. She could feel his gaze on her and wondered then what he might be thinking, though she thought it didn't matter, that she didn't care. In spite of this, she was aware that her back had stiffened, ready now for his incredulity, the harsh words he would find to describe what she had done, or rather, failed to do in bringing them to this place.

'I'll go out and fetch some wine,' he said, turning away.

111

She heard the front door close after him and only then did it occur to her that something bad had happened for him.

Their relationship had dwindled to contact at extreme levels only. There was nothing in between any more, but had there ever been, or was it just that the extremes which had once been vibrant and exciting had become no more than tiresome and unpleasant. Passionate rows became bitter quarrels. Intensity of feeling switched from desire to dislike.

When he returned with the wine she had managed to produce a meal and they sat at the small table, either side, facing one another but not looking, each with their own concerns. There was no radio, television, or any other means of filling the silence, so that eventually Charlotte had to speak. It had crossed her mind that he might be playing some sort of game with her, that all this silence was a huge piece of sarcasm.

'I know what you must be thinking,' she began defensively.

He looked up from his plate, evidently keen to hear what she knew of his thoughts.

'But I thought it would be better to move in here, as a stop gap,' she put in, unnerved now by his gaze. 'Better than throwing money away on hotels,' she continued, unable to find any other justification that could make any sense.

Why didn't he speak? She couldn't bear this punishing silence from him; as if her day hadn't been bad enough, when all he'd had to put up with was a business meeting which evidently hadn't gone his way.

She pushed back her chair and stood up to clear away the plates.

He followed her into the kitchen and then she felt his hand on her shoulder.

'It's not too bad here,' he said, clearing his throat.

'Oh, come on!' she half exclaimed, twisting round.

He pulled her to him, and it was so unexpected that she flopped against him as if suddenly without strength.

'Let's go to bed,' he murmured against her ear.

She was quite bewildered by his meekness but still wary. Maybe his suspicions extended beyond the infidelity that was only in her mind. Perhaps this invitation of his was more test than desire. Whatever it was, she was in no mood to fight.

The bed was narrow but they were both thin. The room was

112

cold, but she was grateful for this as it made sense of her shivering. They made love in the dark and when it was over he kept his arms round her and after a pause that was long enough for it to have meaning, he said that he loved her, and it was impossible for her not to take some pleasure and comfort from this, though using sincerity as a weapon at this stage struck her as being curiously underhand. Perhaps he did love her but he'd certainly mislaid the feeling for the past couple of years. She lay awake in his arms, trying to work it out. Maybe he considered this squalid little place quaint and romantic. Could it be that it made her seem like his mistress again rather than his wife. Silly notions, all of them. At least there hadn't been a row. She wouldn't have had the stamina for that, not tonight.

Nick woke at about three, the inadequacy of the bedding exposing him to the cold air. Gently, he retrieved some covering from the side where Charlotte lay sleeping.

He remained awake for some while, thinking about the future, trying to come up with something, anything that he could do quickly to regain a decent level of income. Dipping into despair, he imagined having to go on the dole, but would he be eligible even for that? He'd not paid UK taxes for three years. His thoughts gravitated further, to Ruby and how instantly she'd noted his defeat and revelled in it, the festering old bitch, though it had been a relief to be with someone who knew the worst. The pair of them were finished. He still had sufficient arrogance to equate his business failure with Ruby's terminal illness, and her being at Marion's a piece of fate designed to ease his own dejection.

A turning point? Was it that? Marion, of course, had been flustered, a little hostile (as much as she dared) finding him at the house. He'd left soon after she returned, not wanting to provide explanations to two wives in the same day when he wasn't prepared for either; and it was still a mystery to him why he'd gone there at all. He wondered whether Ruby would say anything. She thought she knew it all but she'd been wrong about Charlotte – and so had he. How had she known? He'd not had to say a word. This place said it all.

Chapter Thirteen

Charlotte and Nick's temporary reunion in misunderstood relief continued in the morning. They were careful and considerate of one another, smiling when their eyes met, as polite as they would be to strangers.

At half past ten Charlotte set out in the hired car for elevenses with James. She left Nick at the flat without asking him what he planned for the day, such was their habit of indifference.

James wasn't there when she arrived, and Audrey came to the door with a pair of earphones clamped round her head and a Walkman slung over her shoulder, looking hardly less incongruous than if she'd donned a Mohican hairdo.

'No, I haven't entered my second childhood,' she said, slipping the earphones down round her neck. 'It's the production – *Cabaret*, you know.'

'Yes, of course.'

Audrey, normally such a bastion of calm capability, seemed vaguely aggitated.

'Somebody's dropped out at the last minute,' she said. 'Can you believe it! Oh, I knew it was all going too smoothly.'

'What are you going to do?' Charlotte enquired, following her into the kitchen.

'I'm going over the lines myself,' she said, indicating the Walkman. 'I should know them all off by heart as I'm producing the thing, but I don't. I can see it's all going to be a complete fiasco. There's simply no one else to step into this part,' she added with dramatic resignation.

'Is James here?' Charlotte asked.

'No, but he'll be back soon. How did your move go? You should have given me a call. I'd love to have helped.'

'There was nothing to it really. It's furnished and . . . '

'I've had a thought,' Audrey interrupted her. 'What about you taking over the part. Oh, it's the answer,' she continued, suddenly joyous. 'Why didn't I think of it before. You'd be perfect.'

'But I've never done anything before, not since I was at school,' Charlotte protested.

'Nonsense! You're a born actress.'

'But isn't there singing and dancing in it? I can't sing!'

'Doesn't matter. This part hasn't got any solos.'

Charlotte could see it was useless to argue. Drama was Audrey's thing and she championed it as if it was one of her children. Of course she had no intention of taking the part but for the time being she wanted Audrey firmly on her side. Fat old Audrey, who was a good enough friend but who Charlotte had always suspected might equally be a formidable adversary.

'That's settled then. You can borrow this thing or would you prefer a script?'

'What do you mean I'm a born actress?' Charlotte demanded with mock indignation.

'Oh you are. You're marvellous.'

'Thank you, but I'm not sure whether it's a compliment.'

'Take it as such,' Audrey assured her and went on to explain in enthusiastic detail all sorts of totally boring aspects of THE PRODUCTION, while she poured coffee into the hand-thrown pottery mugs and sliced up a cake that brought calories to the eyes.

Sitting, listening, Charlotte came to realise there was no real common ground between them, not without young children about; and even then it had been no more than the camaraderie of troops in the same trench. Audrey didn't really listen, that was it. She was affable, conversational, but she mostly travelled in straight lines, largely ignoring the scenery and incapable of grasping the abstract concept. That was what was so depressing about her and why the friendship had never seemed special in the way it was with Frances.

Audrey, a cake crumb adhering to her upper lip, was now

115

informing her that she was to attend rehearsal that evening at 7.00 pm sharp, the last word added in such a way as to suggest dire consequences should she be so inconsiderate to the rest of the cast as to arrive late.

James returned, apologetic, but not sounding particularly sincere about it. He smelt strongly of pipe as he bent and unnecessarily kissed Charlotte's cheek. There'd never been all this kissing before, when she was married to Dan. It seemed a sort of pitying gesture, as if she was a woman let down. It didn't bode well for the ensuing discussion.

'You two go upstairs to the studio. I know you've got business to talk about,' Audrey said.

'Yes,' Charlotte agreed, rising from her chair, smiling at James in what she hoped was a winning fashion.

He returned this, holding the exchange just a moment over long.

Charlotte followed him upstairs to the big windowful room, the studio, and once again there was no one else there, and on closer examination, none of the little signs that might have indicated this being the work place of others. The drawing boards, except for the one at which James went and sat, had very much the appearance of being spare.

'Well now,' James began. 'All settled in are we?'

Had he always been like this?

'Oh yes, thank you.'

'Come over here and see what I'm working on at the moment,' he invited her. She moved nearer to the drawing board. A somewhat pedestrian design for a brochure to sell motor accessories was spread out. James began to tell her about it, pointing out the basic requirements for the design as if she knew nothing of such matters. Worse, he did all this with his face rather close to hers, the pipe smell, she realised, had turned a little rank in his beard.

'You see, I wanted the eye to go straight to this area then move round the page,' he was saying.

'Yes, I see. James, my video. What do you think?'

'Not bad. Not bad at all,' he said.

'Oh come on. It's good. It's damn good. I need work, James, and I think you could do with a worker. I'd only expect to be paid for what I do. I'm not looking for a salary, just a chance to

116

get going over here,' she blurted it all out and immediately regretted her candour but James looked less surprised than she might have expected.

'Im glad you're being so honest,' he said unshakeably patronising. 'I think, possibly, we could come to an arrangement.'

He'd stood up and put his arm round her shoulder. It didn't feel right, but insufficiently wrong for her to remove herself from him. It was the same sort of situation she'd experienced long ago on a train, when a man sitting next to her had rested the back of his hand against her thigh all the way from Oakleigh Park to King's Cross and she'd just sat there not wanting to make a fuss in case nothing was meant, but when she'd got out she'd run the length of the platform to the ticket barrier and felt furious and indignant the rest of the day.

And now James was the man on the train. His arm stiffened, propelling her round, against his chest. His head veered towards her but his mouth missed hers as she jerked sideways, crashing into the drawing board. It remained upright, but she was now pinned against it face down with James on top of her, his beard rustling in her ear.

'For God's sake, Audrey's downstairs,' she hissed

The pressure of his weight eased, then he moved off her. He let out the most feeble laugh.

'Good job she didn't come up, she might have got the wrong idea,' he said. 'She might have thought we were up to no good, especially with your reputation.' The laugh again.

Charlotte was not one for the quick riposte, she was more of the slow fester. It was the man on the train syndrome repeated. She'd let it pass, say nothing, hope it would go away, pretend it was all a mistake, but burn up inside because it was unfair and beastly and if she tried to make a fuss there'd be lots of mud, most of it sticking to her.

'May I have my video, please?' she said, very evenly, sidestepping away from him.

'Of course. Of course. You didn't hurt yourself, did you, clumsy of me, slipping off the stool like that.' He was unbelievable! She'd never have guessed he could be like this, he of the hand-knitted jumpers, a fireside man of the slippers and pipe variety; the family man with stuffed-shirt opinions on lowering moral standards, the person who she and Dan had thought of as a rather endearing bigot. It was like the Archers going pornographic.

The inside burning was making her overreact, albeit in silence. And she couldn't escape, not yet, not with Audrey downstairs baking biscuits or whatever she was doing. She couldn't face her, not straight away.

Her life seemed to have slipped out of balance into Hieronymus Bosch type hideous horrors wherein comfortable old friends had become slimy predators; the house that had been her home no longer accessible but still tantalisingly there, in view, with her stuck in a moat of mud, her feet and legs sucked in and held down while the man in the house lived and breathed unaware, unconcerned; he who had loved her and by some terrible mistake she'd stabbed in the heart. Perhaps the real and original Dan, the Dan of a decade past, no longer existed. Wounded, warped and changed, he was someone else she didn't know, someone known now to other people, another woman.

I've changed, she might have said to herself and anyone else who cared to listen, and yet it came as such a shock to find that everyone else had been shedding skins, adjusting attitudes, tilting from bad to good and good to bad.

Bloody life! she wanted to shout. She'd even have stamped her feet if they hadn't been so leaden and glutinously in the mire.

'No, I didn't hurt myself,' she said, and never, it seemed in that moment of clarity, had she told a greater lie.

James restored himself by becoming pompous.

'This job I've been showing you,' he said, turning to scrutinise the now rumpled pieces of artwork on the drawing board. 'There's very stiff competition for this sort of work. One needs a thoroughly sound track record as well as creativity.'

'Of course,' Charlotte concurred. She was in a much more difficult position now. She was, in effect, compromised. She no longer wanted work from James but if she backed off, did less than plead, she would be destroying the pretence that his foray into sexual harassment had been no more than slipping from a stool.

A smile, which felt dreadfully simpering, set over her teeth. It was good manners, a habit hard to break; the wretched rule

118

of not making a fuss. But for whose sake? Could it be Audrey, for whom she cared not a jot? James, so truly odious, or just herself, not wanting the bother and unpleasantness? Probably the latter. The smile hardened. It was more acceptable to be doing it for oneself.

Downstairs in the kitchen Audrey was holding a rolling pin. 'All OK?' she said, looking up from her table of dough. 'I thought I heard something collapse.'

'Nothing serious, just the drawing board. You remember I said it was unstable,' James said, moving past Charlotte to his wife.

He put his arm round her ample shoulders and planted a kiss on her peachy cheek. Audrey, who was still rolling, wore an expression of tender complacency. Both then looked at Charlotte, their twinkling eyes saying 'We're all right, how about you – not so happily married as us, we think. A rickety drawing board is not even a pinprick to us.'

Was the whole of life pretence unless one exhibited constant misery, frustration and despair, Charlotte wondered, watching this little display of solidarity. It was so easy to believe that other people had got it right: the sort of people you never really knew. They were the couples you saw in restaurants with their children, having a lovely jolly time together; the couples on holiday who sat at a table near to yours and whose conversation never seemed to lapse.

They were also the people who took part in plays, Charlotte discovered that evening.

Audrey was frightful at the rehearsal, so much so Charlotte worried that James might have told her a distorted version of the drawing board scene; but she had no experience of amateur dramatics in the raw, the sudden change of character, even among those not in the cast. Audrey seemed continuously at the point of exasperation. She bellowed at everyone, accusing them of not knowing their lines, of turning their backs to the audience, of mumbling, being wooden, of acting like the middle-class English people they were rather than the decadent pre-war Berliners they were supposed to be. She was in her element bullying everyone and getting away with it because it was what they all expected – they loved it, all that make-believe, the pretence that it was real pretence, real

119

theatre and not an agglomeration consisting of the Womens' Institute breakaway drama group, the remainder of the Toc H minstrels band, plus a few Rover Scouts who'd got a taste for acting after taking part in the Gang Show. It was real with Audrey's tongue lashing them and when they got it right she didn't stint on the praise.

Allowances were made for Charlotte, and everyone was friendly to her, but it was a different world they inhabited, one wherein the decent thing was done, marriages were worked at, parent/teacher associations were a part of life, everyone had hobbies and some of them even still went to church, C of E, or Methodist. These people were the green and pleasant land of England, as indigenous a tribe as one could find. Of course, they did the occasional naughty thing, like making passes at old friends, but they didn't let it destroy their lives.

During the coffee break an affably expressed man who turned out to be the stage manager struck up conversation.

'New to the area, are you?' he enquired of Charlotte.

'Yes,' she told him, rather than No, I used to be married to your MP.

He told her that he and his wife took it in turns to be involved in these productions. Last year Mrs Affable had been Cinderella. They had to work it like that because the children were too young to leave at home by themselves. Charlotte thought of Vicky in America. She'd have to telephone the school. She'd said she wouldn't, so as not to upset Vicky, but such restraint was proving impossible: she needed to hear her daughter's voice. Several times over the past few days she'd had heart-stopping thoughts about Vicky, the unfounded nightmare fears of a mother guilt-ridden by too much separation from her child. It had been a difficult enough decision, this coming back to England ahead of Vicky, but made many times worse since Dan's anger over the way she'd arranged things.

The stage manager was telling her about an alteration he planned to the set. He was anxious about it. Could it be done in time? Lucky person, Charlotte thought, to have the luxury of so simple a concern.

Later, back in Bateman Street, Nick told her he would be flying to San Francisco the following morning and didn't know how long he'd be gone. She accepted this without question. It had been such a relief that he hadn't said anything untoward about the flat but she was still uneasy with him there. It seemed that both of them were still avoiding the issue because it wasn't convenient or, in Nick's case, she thought because he couldn't spare the time; though maybe there was still something there. It had been in their sexual encounter of the previous night, a sort of vulnerability in him that was surprising even now. It had to do with the driving insecurity that had brought him business success. It explained him to her in a way she was certain no one else, his first wife, miscellaneous other women (most, if not all, before her time of course) had ever known him. Perhaps she deluded herself, but she couldn't really think so. Her insufferable pride made it inconceivable that she had not been the love of his life; but then that was the antidote to her own insecurity. He might not care very much any more but he had for a time, and it had been like winning a prize.

So the moment hadn't come and perhaps it wouldn't be in the manner she'd imagined, a decisive parting. They'd drift into a lingering separation made easier by geographical distance. It crossed her mind that his plane ticket might be one way but she wasn't going to ask.

That night they slept in separate beds as there was no comfort in sharing a single, and the shallow reservoir of passion that had brought them together the previous night was now quite drained.

Charlotte couldn't sleep. She kept thinking of Vicky and Dan, as if she'd now lost them both. She couldn't come to terms with either loss because she'd done the leaving. It was like self-mutilation, the actions of a sick mind, but she couldn't even take refuge in surrender to insecurity.

At two o'clock she got up, put a coat over her nightdress and left the flat. It had started to rain by the time she reached the phone box she'd used the previous day to call James. She took her purse from her bag and mercifully it was full of coins, though she'd no idea how many she'd need to make a call to California. She lifted the receiver in the dank-smelling kiosk, it was cold in there as well, one of the panes of glass had been smashed. She dialled the operator and gave him Vicky's school's number. It would be about tea time over there. She emptied most of her purse into the coin box and waited for the connection, trying to conjure up a picture in her mind of the setting from which Vicky would be speaking, the elegant interior of the boarding house, creamy, Californian colour. A cold gust of wind blew rain into the kiosk where the glass was missing.

The connection was made. The American voice saying the name of the school, then that Vicky would have to be fetched from somewhere Charlotte didn't quite catch. The line went on to hold. Come on! Come on! The money in the box marked time.

If I don't speak to her. If I don't hear her voice. . .

'Mummy!'

Click. No more time.

'Please,' Charlotte said to the operator a moment later. 'I've no more change. They kept me waiting such a long time I didn't manage to speak to my daughter.' What did she expect, another chance without paying for it?

'I'm sorry, madam.'

The rain was now pelting down. A puddle had begun to form in the stale grime of the kiosk floor. Charlotte pushed open the door and made a dash for it along the street, perhaps Nick would have some coins.

Back in the flat she threw off the rain-soaked coat and crept into the bedroom. She'd no intention of waking him and having to explain this bout of maternal paranoia. She went through the pockets of his clothing but there was nothing except a wallet full of credit cards. At last she retreated to her bed. There was nothing else to do. Oh, Vicky!

She pulled the covers up round her and tried to find comfort in the thought that before very long Vicky would be sleeping in the bed across the room where Nick presently lay. This, though, was on the basis of a rather large assumption, but one that, with a sudden and involuntary wave of panic, she understood to be two-way.

It explained Nick's behaviour of the previous day. She'd set her own trap: Nick had no need to be critical of this place she'd chosen to live because it no longer concerned him. The idea grew and took hold of her. It made sense. It was the only explanation. He'd planned it all – brought her back to England

122

so that he could dump her and return to America alone. No wonder he'd been so strange and tentative and tender the night before. It had been the finale.

Charlotte quaked. Nobody had ever left her. The bedrock of her self-esteem cracked wide and in a place hitherto uncharted.

Chapter Fourteen

When Paul heard that his father had been at the house but hadn't waited to see him he felt as if his chest had filled up with cement.

Ruby told him when he got in from school. He went in to see her, as he had every afternoon since she'd been with them. It was the first thing he did when he came home. Ruby and he were special. He could say what he liked to her in a way he couldn't imagine telling things to his mother. This was how it seemed, although Ruby always did most of the talking, telling him about life with a capital L, because she'd really lived had Rube though Paul didn't know that most of it was down to an outsize personality and wishful thinking.

And there she was this afternoon, propped up on her pillows, looking smug and coy and patting the side of the bed for him to come and sit beside her.

'You'll never guess who came bursting into my room today,' she said, 'such a surprise it was.'

'Who?'

'Your father!'

After that she went into a sort of reverie about fate and her and Nick being special friends, over and over, as if she'd lost her marbles, until Marion shouted up the stairs that his tea was ready.

Fishfingers and chips. God, why couldn't she do him a salad. His spots were really bad again. Sometimes when he squeezed them it seemed like congealed cooking fat coming out. He couldn't eat anyway, not this evening. He felt tight all over, heavy but restless. He didn't know what to do with himself.

'Why did . . . ' he hesitated over the reference to his father, unable to call him anything that sounded as if he had rights. ' . . . he come here today?'

'I don't know,' Marion answered. 'Don't you want your tea?'

'I'm not hungry. Didn't you see him, then?'

'Yes.'

'And?'

'If you don't like those sort of fishfingers I won't get them again. Sainsbury's have got a new type. I nearly bought them but I wasn't sure you'd like . . . ' she trailed off then started on another piece of banality, muttering stuff about homework and an early night as if she didn't know it was nearly the end of term and half the teachers were on strike anyway.

Paul gave up. He knew it was a waste of time pushing her. She'd never talked to him about Nick. Taboo subject, like Rube's cancer. He'd no idea what exactly had gone wrong with his parents' marriage. Boredom, he supposed, fishfingers instead of salad.

Paul had become expert himself at being bored. He'd cultivated an outward attitude of teenage sloth that consisted of clumsy movement, a down-turned mouth and a general disregard for everything and everyone, with two exceptions, his grandmother and Stacey Middleton. With Marion in particular he exaggerated this lazy belligerence. He knew it upset her but somehow this made him do it all the more. It was as if he wanted her to suffer and worry, like she always had, over everything. He hated himself for it but he couldn't help it. He was carrying on where his father had left off.

Every thought he had came back to his father. He scraped back his chair and stood up.

'I'll put something over it and leave it in the oven,' Marion said. 'You'll probably want it later.'

He went upstairs to his room. He could have done with a heart-to-heart with Ruby, but suddenly she seemed like the enemy. He flopped down on his bed and stared at the Paddington Bear lampshade that had hung over him every night for as long as he could remember. He'd rebelled against it at one stage, but it had come back into favour during his kitsch junk phase. It was just a lampshade now, and of no interest.

Nothing much interested him at present. His room was a mess. The wall was marked where he'd taken down the Driller Killer poster. The collection of key rings he'd started when he was thirteen, lay in a dusty heap on the windowsill. Several model aeroplanes were ranged along the top of the wardrobe but they looked as if they'd been bombarded by the Luftwaffe, with bits fallen off, fuselages collapsed. Paul closed his eyes. The trouble was that none of it mattered. He just didn't care. The little things in life that had provided small pockets of joy, the delight in acquisition, the careful treasuring, it had all gone, and there was nothing else. He thought hard, trying to decide whether this non-sensation of indifference was the result of losing interest in the trivia that had hitherto dominated his life or if it was the other way round: was the difference cause or effect?

This introspection began to make him feel sick. His head ached because he hadn't eaten. He sat up with a jerk and swung his long, thin legs round on to the floor. A few minutes later he was heading down the road towards the town centre. The tightness was still in him, the feeling like he had when Stacey let him kiss her and put his tongue in her mouth, leading him on, revving him up, and then saying no as she had on the last few occasions they'd grappled together in dark places.

'Leave it out!' she snarled at him.

He pleaded with her, a mistake. Why wouldn't she let him when she had in the past?

'Because you look as if you've got the pox. They put me off they do, all those plookers on your face. You've probably got them all over,' she told him.

'I don't know why you let me do anything, then.'

'Neither do I,' she said, in that stroppy voice of hers.

'Stace, it's only 'cos you won't let me,' he continued. 'It's lack of sex that causes acne.'

'How d'you work that one out?' she scoffed.

'It is,' he answered her earnestly. 'I read it somewhere.'

'Some people believe anything they read in books,' she said. 'It's probably all that brain work's given you the pox.'

It was useless arguing with her. The more illogical she became the more certain it was she would win, though argument had nothing much to do with it; it was love that defeated him, at least, he thought it was still that. He loved her but she

126

didn't him and therefore she couldn't lose.

He hadn't arranged to meet her tonight but most evenings she and her friends spent a while loitering in the park or round by the library which was opposite the town's gathering place for low life, the King George Inn.

He turned into the shopping precinct and as usual it was deserted. The Christmas lights were up and most of the shops had festive displays in their windows. He crossed the empty car park. At the entrance to the park he paused. There was not a soul about, no sounds, no movement. He felt like the lone character in a film about germ warfare or evacuation of the earth. Having spurned his own tea, it hadn't crossed his mind that everyone else was having theirs, that he was half an hour earlier than usual entering the park.

Christ, he felt explosive!

He walked on, past the benches and bushes. Nobody. He would have welcomed even insults, the coarse, chanting chorus of the gang girls.

Ahead of him, in the centre of the park, a huge Christmas tree, presented to the town by its Scandinavian twin, stood newly dug in, its branches decked out with coloured lights. Just for a moment he experienced a spontaneous, childlike delight at the sight of the tree, then, 'Bloody Christmas,' he murmured under his breath, rejecting the comfort and joy.

'Bloody Christmas!' he was suddenly shouting and running towards the tree. He leapt up, grabbing at one of the lower branches. The tree listed towards him, shedding its needles into his hair. He ran backwards, gazing up at the top, steeple-like branch. He felt like a lumberjack. Then he ran at it again, leaping high, his hand outstretched.

There was a deep cracking sound and, almost in slow motion, the tree came right over, its branches splaying out across the path. The coloured lights followed, bouncing and shattering on the paving stones.

Paul stood back, transfixed. He felt high as a kite. His heart was pounding, his breathing now panting. He ran round the felled tree and broken glass, jumping on a bulb that was still intact, then off he went, the notion of being caught catching up with him. He ran like the devil, back the way he had come, past the bushes and benches, the places where he'd explored Stacey

Middleton, pleaded and begged with her, all the time thinking himself to be a superior being, taking a peculiar twisted joy from the abjuration of intellect in the vain hope of a moments tenderness from that smutty-mouthed pea-brain.

He stopped for breath at the park gates, bending forward, his hands on his knees. The exhilaration subsided. God, what a crazy thing to have done. What a pathetically puerile piece of stupidity. He shook his head, pine needles flying out. He glanced down the road towards the library at the sound of a distant giggle. A bunch of kids coming up the street. He made a dash for the car park then forced himself to walk rather than run. He thought he heard someone shout his name but he didn't turn, not until he was home and closing his bedroom door. He wedged a chair under the handle, turned out the light and lay down on the bed. He was trembling now. He turned over and pushed his face into the pillow, weeping with the frustration and pointlessness of it all.

Chapter Fifteen

'Hi, Mommy, guess what, I'm in a play.'

'Guess what, so am I,' Charlotte told Vicky over the Trans-atlantic line, clear as next door.

Over the past fortnight things had considerably improved in Charlotte's near-collapsed state of wellbeing. She'd got a job, in a design studio in Cambridge, she'd fixed up a place for Vicky at a city school, and she hadn't spent an evening alone. Events had pulled her along so that it was only during the night hours in the basement bedroom she had time to brood over the uncertainty of the future, and mostly she was too tired to lie awake for long.

Cabaret had proved to be her temporary salvation. She'd got caught up in the production, losing herself in her part and generally finding the camaraderie of being in a cast more agreeable than she could have imagined. Everyone took it all very seriously and by the second week Charlotte was joining in their intricate discussions about the timing of a cue, this inflection or that for the delivery of a particular line. The first night was only days off and a rehearsal of some sort happened almost every evening, always including Charlotte who had such a lot of catching up to do.

The job came via Joe, the nice, earnest stage manager whose wife had been Cinderella. Saturday at the end of the first week was the one night off from rehearsal and Joe had invited Charlotte to have supper with him and his wife.

They lived in an ugly, isolated house outside Cambridge. It was 1930s style with a large patch of land to the rear on which they planned to grow many vegetables, keep chickens and geese, perhaps even a pig or a cow. They had dreams of self-sufficiency.

Joe's wife, Jean, looked the part she had played. Her hair hung about her head in an uncombed fashion that might or might not have been deliberate. Her face was small featured, pale and pretty without make-up, and she had an eager, lacking-in-confidence expression. Joe, who was tall and thin and bore a slight resemblance to Gregory Peck circa 1940, had opened the door to Charlotte and they were in the living room when Jean came through to greet her, wiping wet hands down the sides of her Clothkits skirt as she said hello and how ever so pleased she was Joe had invited Charlotte.

'Joe says you've been living in America,' she said. 'I've never been, but I'd really like to go there.'

Charlotte smiled in reply. Joe and Jean were suddenly recognisable as herself and Dan ten years ago. How desperately she'd wanted to go and see the country where it all happened, and like Jean, her world had been largely limited to what went on within a fifty foot radius of the kitchen.

The house they had only recently acquired and were evidently greatly pleased with what they saw as its potential. As far as Charlotte could see this was demolition for the land value: the house was hideous, but to Joe and Jean it was individual after their previous home on a large housing estate.

The evening was pleasant to begin with and through the meal, talking about the play and the house and America, cosy and undemanding. Jean sniped at Joe once or twice, putting him down in the way of the young married mother where life is temporarily subjugated to domestic demands. She had been a teacher and doubtless would be again. Joe was a project engineer with a local electronics company. More interestingly, his brother ran a design studio in Cambridge, and that was how Charlotte got her job.

The meal finished, they moved across the room, which once had been two, and sat down in the lounge end where an assortment of easy chairs stood on a piece of carpet that didn't quite cover paint-stained floorboards. A Victorian bedroom fireplace had recently been cemented into the chimney breast which had the ravaged look of DIY.

'I can't think why you wanted to come back,' Jean said over non-tannin, herbal tea.

'My husband wanted to come back for business reasons.'

'I don't suppose you had any say,' Jean said, glancing at Joe.

'Oh, I was ready to return,' Charlotte said. 'I feel that England is my natural habitat, if that makes any sense. I liked America, but I didn't feel at home there.' To her own ears this sounded like euphemism for I missed Dan, but these people didn't know she'd been married before and she'd stopped mentioning any of that to anyone new she met, although at one time she'd taken some delight, even pride, in letting people know. It had made her feel daring and racy and brave. People had said she must have had courage to have done what she had. Little did they know she'd just been desperate for a change, recklessly in search of escape; sufficiently so to go all the way to America with the wrong man in order to discover that it was only herself she'd been trying to avoid. That was how it seemed. She hadn't much liked herself, then, now or ever. Instinctively she'd always thought of herself as a phoney who'd equally instinctively be found out by the nice people, the good people, the Joes and the Jeans, the Audreys and the Jameses.

Nick, of course, was like her, and that was the trouble, they had found one another out. They knew each other for what they were, and hadn't bothered with the exhausting business of adopting and sustaining yet another persona in the way they did with other people in order to impress, entertain, gain respect.

In the company of people such as Joe and Jean, Charlotte heard herself being self-effacing, tolerant in her comments about others. She felt toned down with them, her character and personality painted in pastel shades. It was evident they saw her as slightly glamorous and worldly-wise and therefore she could afford to underplay herself. She wasn't any different from anyone else in wanting to be liked, even by those who ostensibly meant nothing to her, although maybe it was indicative of her present state of insecurity that she actually minded what this nice, insignificant couple thought of her.

Joe was a younger version of Dan, decent, hard-working and kind, and a little bewildered by his wife's spasmodic

aggression. Charlotte doubted whether he was as clever a
Dan, whether he had it in him to surprise and delight Jean with
an unexpected perception; but he was probably capable o
wise judgement, the soothing logic of the male mind of the
problem solving, printed circuit board variety.

Jean, no doubt, had need of this. She exhibited the small
signs of discontent that represented familiar, if half-forgotten
territory to Charlotte. Her eyes spoke the I envy you thoughts
her occasional sharpness with Joe had that edge of blame for
an unidentified melancholy. It was spasmodic, slight, perhaps
would never develop into the agitated despair Charlotte had
known and was reminded of now but with the added torment
of regret.

'Joe's going to Singapore after Christmas,' Jean informed
glancing a grudging look at her husband. 'Two months he'll b
gone.'

'You make it sound like a holiday. It is work, you know,' Joe
responded with a gently, apologetic smile.

'Life's one long holiday for you,' Jean retorted, adding a
hard little laugh for Charlotte's benefit.

'I don't think it's going to be much fun out there. I gather it's
terribly hot and humid,' Joe said in placatory denigration.

'I wouldn't be complaining about the climate if I had a
chance to go,' Jean said. 'I've got this terrible urge to travel.'
she continued, speaking now only to Charlotte, as if Joe had
evaporated.

'I just feel at times that life is passing me by, that all the
exciting possibilities are in the past and never really came to
anything. I don't suppose you know what I'm talking about,
don't really know what I mean myself. It's hard to put into
words. It's just the feeling of only living once and the weeks
rushing by and the whole world waiting to be explored an
here I am stuck in one place with the children, just the way m
mother was and Joe's mother was, and it'll probably be the
same for my daughter. I mean, I just can't help thinkin
sometimes – what's the point? It's just the continuation of the
race for continuation's sake. I mean, there's got to be more
hasn't there?'

'Amazing what it does to you, this tea,' Joe said with eviden
embarrassment at his wife's sudden outburst.

132

'Oh, shut up, Joe. He thinks I'm mad – post-natally de-pressed. I'm not. Gary's nearly four, for God's sake!' She stood up and went over to the dining table where the remains of supper were still spread about.

'I'm sorry if I've embarrassed anyone,' she said in a less frantic tone.

'Oh, please,' Charlotte spoke. 'It's better to say these things.'

'Is it?' Jean replied, flatly.

Joe stood up now and with an endearingly anxious expression approached his wife's back. He put an arm round her shoulder.

'Misery guts,' he murmured.

Jean put down the stack of plates she'd been gathering and turned to him.

'Sorry,' she said, abjectly, touching her forehead against his chin, then turning to look at Charlotte.

'Sorry,' she repeated.

'Please don't be,' Charlotte said, getting up herself now. 'Let me help with the washing up before I go.'

'Absolutely not. Joe always does it. And please don't go yet or I'll think that I've spoiled the evening.'

She was really quite childish, Charlotte decided, so intense. Stay, stay, whether you want to or not because you can't leave me feeling bad about myself. The face that had been Cin-derellarish appeared different now, pitiable in another way.

Charlotte saw her younger self so clearly in the vaguely distraught Jean that given Cognac instead of tea, she might then have told her about standing in the mud, hiding in the shadow of a hedge, glimpsing the might have been, should have been.

Joe had gone to the kitchen with the dishes.

'He doesn't understand,' Jean said, assuming the female conspiracy.

'No, but I think he tries to,' Charlotte answered her.

Jean gave her a look that seemed to question which side she was on.

'I really must go,' Charlotte said. Get a job, write a book, start something, sort yourself out. Don't blame Joe, he's only a bystander, she wanted to say, but of course, didn't. Waste of

133

breath. Frances had said it to her hadn't she? All those years ago.

Chapter Sixteen

'This is yet another example of declining moral standards. How much worse has it got to get before something is done, before the namby-pamby do-gooders stop blaming Society and see that the only answer is to bring back the birch.'

So it went on, signed at the bottom of the third page by Primrose Shaw-Footting. Who else! She of the windsock arms and barrel chest, a party member of the most ferocious right wing tendencies.

Dan put down the letter and picked up the local newspaper, its front page headline IS THIS THE SPIRIT OF GOODWILL ran across the top of a blown-up picture of a felled Christmas tree and a small bewildered-looking child standing by, holding an adult's hand.

The house was cold. Dan had spent the past two nights in London after late sittings in the Commons. He'd only just got back and in less than half an hour had to be out again, to Audrey's wretched play.

He left the rest of the post and went through to the kitchen where Marigold had left him a covered plate, ready to stick in the microwave. He lifted the cover. A chop and a few overcooked-looking sprouts, a dollop of instant mash. He didn't think he'd bother, though Marigold left him petulant notes if she found food in the bin. The woman was turning into a harridan, but he was stuck with her and her awful cooking. She was loyal and honest and that counted for a lot, having someone he could rely on to keep an eye on the place. She'd been decent to Mickey as well, but then she'd thought Mickey was going to become his wife.

'I thought there might have been wedding bells this Christmas, Mr Lovell,' she'd said.

Abandoning the chop, Dan left the kitchen and went upstairs to change. Had he really wanted to marry Mickey? He couldn't imagine it, not now. He hated the loneliness of the empty house, always most acute during those first few minutes when he returned in the evening, but the void was still that left by Charlotte and not Mickey. He was still sad, sometimes, even now, enraged, over what Charlotte had done to him. She'd spoilt his life, Vicky's childhood and perhaps more. There'd been a time, about a year after Charlotte had left, when he thought he'd come to terms with what had happened. His wife had fallen out of love with him. It was as simple as that. It explained everything and a philosophical acceptance of this fact was the only course open to him. But it hadn't worked, this reasoned, magnanimous conclusion. The bitterness had come back, the dull, ongoing sense of loss. It used up too much of him, so that even when he'd done that rash thing and flown to New York to see Mickey, it was only partly a new desire. At a deeper level it had been no more than another attempt to blot out the past.

In the bedroom, he changed his shirt and suit for something a little less formal. His attendance at Audrey's play was unofficial, but he was not particularly looking forward to the evening. People expected him to go to these local events when he was in the constituency. Often he had a job staying awake, especially at the end of the week. He'd have preferred an early night, a chance to go through the rest of the pile of letters downstairs.

He glanced in the dressing mirror, failed to notice how drab he looked in his weekend clothes and went downstairs again. With a few minutes to spare, he flipped through the stack of unopened envelopes and saw that one was from New York. He left it with the others and went out to the car.

Audrey was waiting in the main entrance to the hall. Her face relaxed into an expression of relief when she saw him.

'Dan. I'm so glad you could make it,' she said, greeting him with a kiss on the cheek. 'I know how busy you are.'

He followed her into the body of the hall where most of the seats were already occupied.

136

'I've saved a good place for you,' she said.

Dan could hear all the murmurings of recognition as he passed the rows of seats further back. He nodded to one or two familiar faces, shook hands with a tall, thin young man Audrey introduced as the stage manager. The lights dimmed. Audrey touched his shoulder. She'd been going to tell him something but the precurtain hush had descended. He took his seat next to the aisle and she hurried off to the back of the hall.

Ten minutes into the first act he knew what Audrey had managed to avoid telling him. Charlotte's appearance on the stage ensured that he would not have any trouble staying awake.

There were three curtain calls at the end. The show, Dan had hardly noticed, only Charlotte, every move, every word he'd hung on, his back pressed into his seat, as if he was up there on the stage himself, a raw beginner tiptoeing across a swaying tightrope. It hit him hard that she could still have this effect on him. Seeing her again, being angry with her over Vicky when she'd called at the house, it had revived the old feelings more than he'd realised. What a damned nuisance. He sat in his seat, his neck stiff, his face set in a frown, his hands clapping as if operated by clockwork.

Matthews, no doubt, would be here, he thought, and began preparing himself for one of those falsely polite exchanges necessary in such circumstances. It had to be pitched just right, not too friendly but with no trace of hostility, even though he couldn't stand the man and not just because he'd got Charlotte.

What a ludicrous state of affairs, to have to be polite and enquiring to a man he would have nothing to do with in other circumstances, but who he was required to put at ease for the sake of appearances, good form and continuing evidence of that most fatuous of attributes, magnanimity.

He hung back as everyone jostled towards the exits. Audrey would expect some sort of comment and congratulation; he might as well see the thing through, and with any luck this would allow time for Matthews and other relatives of the cast to make their way to the dressing rooms. Wasn't that the procedure? He didn't know a lot about theatre etiquette.

What happened next seemed to go beyond his control.

Somehow he became swept along with someone else's plan, though it was probably nothing that definite. Audrey triumphant, buoyed up on the heady climactic moment of her achievement as producer, insisted he join them for the after show party. James, shaking his hand with great vigour, concurred in this insistence. Like old times, it would be. They hadn't had a get together for how long? Crass euphoria. It was the show that did it, a run on of the suspension of reality, keeping everyone up there in the larger than life zone of dizzy make-believe – just for a little bit longer, before everything went back to dull normality. That was why they always had a party after the last performance. Too flat, too soon to go straight home to bed. And maybe the same applied to Dan. He was not so manoeuvrable as to have allowed James and Audrey's overbearing ebullience to carry him along against his will completely.

It crossed his mind that he was entering the realms of masochism, a trait he'd always considered to be self-indulgence and to be avoided as much as possible. But he was out in the cold and attracted by the fire, to see how close he could get without being burnt.

The party was being held at James and Audrey's school house. Dan had only been there once or twice since he and Charlotte had parted, but it was that last visit together that remained with him. It had been only days before she left. He'd already known she was going but whether she'd actually told him then he couldn't remember. The telling had been no more than confirmation of a departure that had happened in spirit some weeks before. He remembered the sour vitality of those last few weeks, being so aware of everything she did and said, looking for contradiction of his fears, hoping for a reprieve.

An hour into the party and he hadn't seen her. People had spread through the house and he wondered whether she was avoiding him after the hostility he'd shown her two or three weeks earlier when she'd come to see him. Or maybe she and Matthews had gone off somewhere else, gone back to London.

The young stage manager whom Audrey had introduced earlier, was talking to him about electronics, but Dan was speculating as to how Charlotte had managed to be in Audrey's show if she was still staying in London. Then across the room he saw her, coming from the kitchen, a glass in her hand, her blonde hair piled on the top of her head with one or two long wavy strands falling over her ears. She was wearing something pink that looked rather like a track suit.

Dan looked away. Damn it, his heart was pounding. She looked over the top, Californian. Not beautiful, she'd never been that, but noticeable, and thin. He hadn't realised how thin she had become.

He glanced at her again. She'd remained on the other side of the room, by the door. The party had divided into pockets of conversation but she was alone. He'd have to say something, quickly.

'Charlotte. Over here.' It was the stage manager who'd called to her.

Dan saw her hesitate, her gaze switch between him and his companion. Then she came towards them, a slight smile across her mouth.

'Joe,' she greeted the stage manager. Then 'Hello, Dan.' A measured, cautious acknowledgement.

'Oh, you know one another,' Joe said.

'Yes,' they said simultaneously, both leaving it at that.

'Look, can I fetch you a fill-up?' Joe said, proffering a hand for Dan's glass.

'Thank you,' he let the glass go, let Joe go. He didn't come back, perhaps he sensed the exclusion as people at parties do when they offer to fetch drinks.

'I thought you weren't here,' Dan said as the rest of the room receded. He knew at once that something had changed, that polite, stand-offish intercourse was not what was required. Charlotte had a very solitary aura about her. She was quiet and still. Her eyes were watery and the hand that held the glass had a visible tremor.

'Are you all right?' he said quietly, with concern.

'Not really,' she answered him.

'What is it?' he asked in a manner too gentle for their present roles in each other's lives.

'It's silly,' she said.

He saw her swallow.

'Vicky. It's Vicky,' she told him.

'Is something wrong?' he urged her, alarmed now.

139

'Oh, no. She's fine. I've just been speaking to her. From a call box. She's in a play. Did you know? It's this evening – this evening over there. I mean, the play is tonight over there. It's only the afternoon at the moment.' Charlotte said all this in a bleak tone, her hand trembling round her glass.

'Oh, Dan. I do miss her. I feel at times – times like now, as if I've lost a limb. Silly, isn't it. Really silly. I can't stop thinking of her in her play and me not there to see it.'

'Frances will be there, won't she. She'll go and watch,' Dan said soothingly.

'Oh, I expect so. I said it was silly.'

'Was Vicky upset?'

'No,' she answered, on a high, desperate note. 'She was full of it. Bubbling over.'

Dan let out a sigh.

'I'm sorry if I alarmed you,' Charlotte said.

But the sigh was only partly relief. It was also to do with the ache in his chest, confirming the old desire. And any minute Matthews would appear, instantly distancing her. He remembered that, how quickly she changed when Matthews was there. Alone with her, even now, there was still the intimacy, the response to a sigh, a look, the smallest gesture; but it would shut off as soon as Matthews was with her.

He glanced past her. People were beginning to leave the party, but James had just come into the room.

'Aha,' he said, approaching them. He was smiling too much. He was embarrassed. Of course he was.

'Well,' he said. He'd also had rather a lot to drink. 'Well, it's jolly nice to see you two together again. Like old times, isn't it. Just like old times.'

Buffoon. Had they really been such friends?

'Sorry. Auders will tell me off,' he added sheepishly. 'My goodness, you haven't got a drink,' he said to Dan, and went the same way as Joe.

'Was he always like that?' Dan said to Charlotte as they watched James weave his way to the kitchen.

'I didn't think so. He made a pass at me the other day.'

'You're joking! James?'

'Yes, good old James. I think he must be going through some sort of mid-life crisis.'

140

'He was always so disapproving of that sort of thing. Do you remember how he went on about that couple we knew?'

'Oh, I can't remember their names, but yes, all that stuff about animal behaviour, lack of control.'

'And he's turned out an old goat himself.'

They stopped. It wasn't funny. The situation was not funny. They were looking at one another and seeing that it was deadly earnest between them in that moment. A jointly-remembered past, there was nothing like it to swell the regret.

'I can't blame him,' Dan said, no smile now, because he did blame James, in fact he was filled with a sense of outrage to which he no longer had any right, though that wasn't at all how it felt. 'You look,' he paused, understatement had always been his way, 'you look very well.'

'Thank you,' Charlotte said, gazing down into her glass.

'Lottie.' She glanced up at the familiarity of his using this shortening of her name.

'I'm sorry about the other day – when you came to the house. I was concerned about Vicky.'

'Yes, and I've made it worse by getting in a state tonight.'

'No, I'm sure she's all right.'

'She'll be back here in a few more days. Back for good. I've got her into a school in Cambridge. I was going to ring and tell you.'

'In Cambridge?'

'I've taken a flat there. Bateman Street. It's only temporary, until I find somewhere to buy.'

'I thought you were staying in London.' He was frowning and in doing so giving the wrong impression of his thoughts.

'Don't worry,' Charlotte said, defensively. 'I won't make a nuisance of myself.'

It was going too fast for him. Why should she say this?

'It didn't occcur to me that you would. Charlotte, what's going on?'

'Going on?'

'Where's Matthews?' The question was pivotal. Inordinately difficult to ask at this juncture.

'In America.'

'I don't understand,' mentally he was trying to force himself to take a step back from her.

141

'Nick's gone back to America. Can we leave it at that. Please. Anyway, where's your friend Mickey Mouse? Oh, Dan, I'm sorry. I didn't mean to say that. I'm sorry. I'm sorry. It was bitchy and I'm not really like that, am I? I never was. Piggy and horrid, but not bitchy.'

'Piggy all right,' Dan said, and he couldn't help a smile. Many things had been piggy but it was a word he hadn't heard used for a long time.

'Piggy Charlotte,' he murmured, and she caught his look and smiled too.

Perhaps he was a masochist after all. Charlotte being piggy was one of the most intoxicating experiences he knew; years back, even before they were married, he'd responded to her worst characteristics, her sharp and cruel perceptions, the disregard for his feelings. It was partly because he knew her better than she'd ever understood. When she was rotten to him it wasn't from strength but weakness: things were wrong in her head, she was uncertain and vulnerable when she did her worst. Understanding this, especially when she failed to herself, had made him her punchbag; but the only thing to make any sense of it all was that he'd loved her so much.

That he was more comfortable with himself as victim than aggressor was part of it as well. Maybe that had been the problem with Mickey, so very much victim material herself. They'd been a pair of punchbags, but dangling side by side, still and inert.

Charlotte had dealt him the first body blow when she was still a teenager, a student at the college, though even before that there had been a few glancing shots, when they were little more than children, at the time when she'd been reacting to the untimely death of her father and had rebelled against everything to hand. That was when she'd stomped into his parents' home with foul language erupting from a mouth outlined in blood-red lipstick, blazing, uncertain eyes encircled by thick black smudgy stuff. Leather and chains to shock and defy as much as possible, as many as possible, including himself, a tweed-jacketed, card-carrying member of the Young Conservatives. She'd appalled him, and disturbed him; he'd thought then that he hated her, the more so when he looked at her and felt a sweet frustrating pang in his groin.

After that he'd lost contact with her for a year, maybe two, only hearing the murmurings of horror stories from his parents who still saw Charlotte's mother whom they'd known since before the war, before Charlotte, before him.

Meeting her again by chance, in a disco bar where sitting beside his soon to be erstwhile girlfriend, he'd been unable to take his eyes off a tall, slim girl in high boots and mini skirt, gyrating her hips to a dissatisfied Mick Jagger. He hadn't recognised her. It was caterpillar and butterfly stuff, and not just in the metamorphosis but in the wanting to catch hold and keep something that couldn't possibly last.

She'd drawn him into her crowd of friends, the eighteen-and nineteen-year-old students with their defy the world, arty, be-different-for-difference-sake ways. He'd not much cared for any of them, only her: he'd have shaved his head and joined Hare Krishna to be with her then, though he never had altered his own image, largely because he'd never been aware of having one. He was, just there. He was a just there person, he'd decided during that period when Charlotte had treated him with cavalier indifference, made bearable by the brief spaces of time they were alone, usually at the end of an evening with the crowd. Then she would let go the zany, anything goes mantle adopted for the benefit of her peers. Then she would be her real uncertain self, telling him all her hopes and fears, trembling with inexperience as he lay on top of her on his parents' sofa in the unlit drawing room only ten feet below where they slept, his mother and father, who still disapproved.

The other students hadn't mattered. He'd never felt anything but an outsider with them, but he was used to that, he felt the same with the Young Conservatives. He was bothered though, right away, by Chad, a lecturer at the art college, a degenerate Peter Pan with narrowed, knowing eyes and the ability to hold spellbound the naive and virgin territory of his students' hearts and minds.

Charlotte glowed in his presence, basking in his lascivious gaze. And expecting the body blow hadn't made it any easier to take. The thought of Charlotte, young and clean, with the odious Chad, had sickened him as much as it had made him jealous. He would like to have taken hold of the man's greasy head and smashed it against one of the rough beams in the olde worlde pub where the crowd met and where Chad held court.

It had got worse. The Chad thing hadn't lasted long, but Charlotte was pregnant, a pregnancy soon to be dissolved in an abortion clinic. How Dan had loathed that squalid, pitiable business, the dark side of love. And Charlotte, at a low ebb, had agreed to marry him.

In the months leading up to the wedding and beyond, he'd carried her along on his own unholy joy. At times he'd felt as if he was playing a game in which he was the only one that really wanted to play. His parents, decent folk that they were, had done their best to pretend an about face, to accept his choice and be happy for him if not with him. Perhaps they'd seen the way it would go, though they'd never said a bad word against Charlotte, even when the marriage was over. They were kindly, sensitive people who offered support rather than told-you-so criticism, but their sadness for him had been even harder to bear. They'd retired to Spain, so he seldom saw them, and sadness in a sunny climate was somehow more finite than in changeable conditions.

Dan had a wretchedly clear picture of how Charlotte viewed their history, how she must have viewed him: from unpre-possessing young man, dull and shockable but who could be told about a pregnancy of uncertain origin, through to dull, middle-aging husband who could be told about an affair, even asked to advise on its future. He wondered whether she'd ever cared how much her truthfulness hurt him. His mistake had always been in allowing her to be too certain of him. Matthews, no doubt, had played it better.

Chapter Seventeen

Sooner or later the credit card people were going to catch up with him, Nick thought towards the end of the second week in San Francisco.

On the basis of going down in style, he'd spent only one night in the dreary, mind-dulling motel he'd booked into on arrival, and switched to the Claremont Resort in Oakland, Frances' recommendation from way back. The Resort's elevated position with its magnificent view right across to the Bay area and the bridge, lifted him a little, made it all seem worth another try. But the days went by and nothing developed. He sat in his room and made countless telephone calls, to bankers, entrepreneurs, all the people who in the past had come to him for a slice of the action in Fortress Against Fat before its latterly lean days.

Nobody called back. They said they would, keeping him couped up in the room for hours on end, just in case.

The situation was getting to him. It seemed the Resort's staff, their hearts, minds and hands finely tuned to the extraction of tips, had begun to view him with suspicion. His paranoia grew by the day and recognising it as such didn't help.

Then someone did call him.

'Nick? Is that you, darling boy?' The unmistakable voice of Germaine Hartnell.

'I thought it was you in the lobby, but you got in that elevator so quick I couldn't be one hundred per cent, not one hundred,' she drawled down the line.

'Germaine?'

'Of course! Now don't tell me you're too busy to catch up on old times. What are you doing these days, now that you're such a big boy?' she continued in her deafening, pariah tone.

Germaine, queen of the fitness business in Southern California, blonde, bronzed and brazen and pushing sixty the last time Nick had seen her, four, five, was it six years ago, he couldn't remember exactly.

'What are you doing in Oakland?' he enquired of her before she could ask him the same question.

'Why, waiting for you to come down here and buy me a cocktail, Nicky boy.'

'Just give me five minutes, will you?'

'Sure thing, but no longer, mind.'

It was mid morning but Nick was not dressed. How quickly he'd slipped into the ways of defeat.

Ten minutes later he walked into the bar and there she was, looking no different, standing up so he'd notice the splendid preservation of her figure.

The vast mouth opened wide, exposing teeth that, like those of a horse, gave the game away.

'Nicky! Nicky! Nicky boy.' She embraced him, her heavy musk scent rising in his nostrils to sneezing point.

She stood back and looked at him.

'My, oh my, still pretty, darling,' she said, so loudly that the entire clientele of the long verandah bar must have heard, but in California nobody took any notice of volume. Expansiveness was as natural as the oranges on the trees.

They took a table by the window and cocktails came.

'Now I want to know what you're up to. I want to know everything,' Germaine decreed, preparing herself for the narrow-stemmed glass with a bowl as wide as a soup plate and a variety of debris sticking from it, a raft of cucumber spiked with a miniature paper umbrella, cherries, slices of lemon and a fat drinking straw round which she now closed her lips like a sea anemone.

'I'm just looking round. Having a bit of a break, really,' Nick told her, his eye straying beyond her face, bent over the cocktail, to the still firm flesh of her breast, visible above the immodest buttoning of her blouse.

'A holiday? And all alone?' Germaine made it sound more

like an opportunity than an astonishment.

'All alone,' Nick answered her. Over the past fortnight he'd contacted just about everyone he'd ever dealt with in business, all of them except Germaine, the wealthiest of the lot.

And maybe it hadn't been entirely a neglectful omission. He remembered very well the first time he'd come to America, years ago now. He was working for someone else then, another woman, an English friend of Germaine. It had been a surprise for him to discover the nature of his employer's old friend, who, for no better reason than assumption, he'd expected to be similar to the grey-suited, middle-aged spinster, who, if she ever had an interest in men kept it well hidden. Not Germaine. He'd returned home from the first visit boggle-eyed and exhausted to find Marion in hospital having Paul, and Ruby, demon-angry over what she rightly perceived to be his neglect of family responsibilities.

Maybe there was still a vestige of something decent in his own terms that had kept him from seeking out Germaine at this present juncture. In his slender code of ethics it was all right for women to find money aphrodisiac but such motivation for a man was unacceptable, demeaning.

Had he been the shallow slob the likes of which Charlotte's friend Frances, thought him to be, he might well have called Germaine for old times' sake.

'You're being very British, darling,' Germaine accused him now. 'I said I wanted to know everything.'

'There's not a lot to tell,' Nick said. 'You knew I was living over here for a while?'

'Don't I just! You never called me, but then I guess you were too busy, making your fortune. Fortress Against Fat! I love it, but you must be into something else these days.' The look in her eyes was a good deal sharper than her drawl.

'That's right. The Fortress came tumbling down; but how about you, Germaine, your business is still flourishing?'

'I make the odd buck,' she smiled broadly at this understatement. 'It's going good. A lot of it's franchised. We've got places in seventeen states and I've just come back from Tokyo.'

'You're opening over there?'

'Looks like it. And Amsterdam.'

The germ of a contingency plan had entered Nick's thoughts.

147

'But darling, you're having a holiday so no business talk. Tell me how long you're staying and whether you're gonna spare a few days to come down to L.A.?'

The Lord will provide, Nick, who had little or no religion in him, thought on the first small wave of optimism to come his way in several weeks.

Fortunately there were no spare seats on the flight Germaine was taking back to Los Angeles that evening, leaving the way clear for Nick to buy a low budget ticket for the following day. The last thing he wanted was for her to realise that state of his finances. He'd done the right thing, staying at the Claremont. Nobody on their last nickel stayed there.

At Burbank, Germaine's chauffeur was waiting for him, a brand new version of the Beverly Hills type white limo, throbbing in front of the main concourse. It bore him away in the style to which he'd aspired to become accustomed and had so nearly achieved.

Germaine still lived in the house he'd stayed at in the early seventies. It was a slightly smaller Claremont with its white stucco columns in the drawing room and predominance of pastel shades against which Germaine herself glistened like a gawdy gemstone in a delicate setting.

The obligatory cocktail was brought to him within a few minutes of arrival then he and Germaine sat down to lettuce soup and champagne.

'So nice!' Germaine declared. 'Lunch alone is hardly worth eating.'

'You still live alone?' Nick asked.

'At present. I've had a couple of husbands since the last time you came here, but I guess I'm not the marrying kind. My last husband was that boy who's made it so big in those preppy movies. He looks about sixteen on camera.'

'And how old is he?' Nick asked with the old journalistic curiosity about age and a degree of desire to humour his hostess.

'Oh a good seventeen,' Germaine joked with that sun-baked laugh of hers. 'He's in his thirties. Too old for me.'

They had a pleasant hour of inconsequential conversation after which Germaine invited him to accompany her to the dance studio off Rodeo Drive from whence her empire had sprung.

148

The car was waiting for them, though this time the chauffeur had a companion, a huge man with crew-cut hair and arms like an ape. He opened the rear door for them and then went round the car to take the front seat beside the driver.

'A bodyguard?' Nick murmured to Germaine.

'You can't be too careful these days. I look so damn rich,' she said. 'And Rodeo Drive is rich pickings.'

When the motor drew up outside the health club they waited for the bodyguard to let them out. Nick, appalled in his English way at the necessity for such precautions, glanced down the street, as if he might see people with guns and masked faces. Instead his gaze stopped on the window of the chocolate store, the same place where he'd bought a box for Ruby but not Marion. Had he ever given them to her? He couldn't remember that he had. It was so long ago. Strange the way he saw Ruby in his thoughts: not the grey-haired invalid but the flashy redhead who was either giving him the eye or tearing him to pieces with her razor-sharp tongue. Maybe being with Germaine heightened the memory: they were not dissimilar, both strong, bold women, both old enough to be his mother, and he'd fucked them both.

Germaine was smiling at him. If Ruby had the tongue then Germaine certainly had the teeth. He smiled back. Why not?

Later that night, after dinner, she asked him to stay on and spend Christmas with her. It was less than a week away. He didn't have anything pressing back home?

'No,' he answered. 'Nothing that can't wait.'

'I thought as much, darling. Your eye sockets are like empty bank vaults.'

'Is it that obvious?'

'Pretty much so.' She'd changed into a shimmering silky number, white, like everything she wore, to emphasise the tan.

'You'd be doing me a favour, staying here over Christmas,' she continued. 'There are at least a dozen parties to go to and it gets to be such a bore the way eligible men are thrust at me. With you there they'll make assumptions and I'll be able to relax. Besides, I guess you could do with a little time out yourself,' she went on, doing the kindness of selling him the invitation. 'Englishmen are still at a premium over here, y'know.'

In the space of a few sentences he'd been condemned, then given a short reprieve. He couldn't, wouldn't, ask Germaine to fund him, but he'd thought it possible she'd grant him the UK franchise which would enable him to raise the cash elsewhere. Not now, though. Not now she knew he was broke. Nobody, least of all the likes of Germaine, backed a loser. The pressure in his head eased. A few days, nearly a week of not having to maintain the pretence. It had the appeal of a painkiller to a man on the rack with the screw about to be given another turn: in this instance Christmas in England with Charlotte, who maybe had guessed but didn't know.

'All right,' he said. 'I'll stay.'

'That's settled then,' she said, clasping her hands together and rising from her white leather sofa.

She approached him, then bent and kissed him lightly on the mouth.

'The assumptions by the way, are strictly for the party-givers,' she said, moving away from him. 'I'm on a diet these days, if you get my meaning.'

The thought of making love to Germaine had been with him most of the evening but as a fulfilment of expectation rather than anything like desire. He'd forgotten what a mind-reader she was and now he was left uncertain as to the meaning behind her gentle brush-off. It was only in the past few weeks that Nick had experienced rejection, in any sphere of life.

'You stay down here if you want. Have another drink. I go to bed early these days,' she called back to him as she went to the door. Then: 'Hey, I didn't ask you if you'd got a wife back home?'

This was the first directly personal question she'd asked him.

'I'm not sure,' he answered her, glibly.

'Like that, is it. I know the feeling,' she sang out. 'Goodnight darling, I'll see you at breakfast.'

Nick poured himself another bourbon, and holding on to glass and bottle went back to his seat. He couldn't even phone her. She wasn't on the goddam phone. She didn't know where he was. Maybe she didn't care, or had made herself stop caring. Wouldn't he, in her place?

A hard case like Germaine. It didn't matter her knowing,

offering a bit of pity. Three, four years? He and Charlotte. Day and night. Married. What did it amount to? Too much or too little? Both. Surely she knew. That vile hovel she'd rented. No telephone. Overt absence of expenditure. Twisted it all round on him, hadn't she? Lined him up for the big confession. And to think he'd been grateful.

He tipped a large slug of the whiskey down his throat. The final victory, to be able to offer him pity. She must have been postively slavering for it. Was it the whiskey or this sudden, concocted resentment that burned in his chest. Whichever, neither was sufficient to obliterate the deeper burning.

Chapter Eighteen

Five days before Christmas the police called on Marion. She'd been in the kitchen, trying to think up a competition riddle. The prize was a set of garden furniture, white-formed plastic with plump yellow cushions.

'Mrs Matthews?' A woman officer, her expression grave. Beside her a huge constable with a barrel chest.

Marion nodded. Something terrible had happened. Paul. An accident.

'May we come in?'

She stood aside to let them pass.

'Mrs Matthews, is Paul at home?'

Relief ran through her like liquid mercury.

'No, I thought you'd come to tell me there had been an accident,' she smiled at the WPC who did not respond in kind.

'Mrs Matthews, we would like to speak to Paul. When do you expect him home?'

'I don't know,' she said.

The officers exchanged glances.

'Why do you want to speak to him?'

'It's in connection with our enquiries concerning vandalism to the Christmas tree in the park,' the constable said.

'I don't understand,' Marion said.

'I think we'll wait, if you don't mind,' the WPC said.

Marion, bewildered, took them through to the living room.

'I don't understand,' she said again.

'We'll wait until your son comes home,' the WPC told her.

Marion gazed from one to the other, uncertain what to do next.

'Would you like a cup of tea?' she asked.

'That would be very welcome.'

She moved towards the door then paused.

'Paul's not in trouble, is he? He's not that sort of boy, you know.'

'One with sugar, one without.'

Marion, her task decreed, continued to the kitchen.

Her hands were shaking as she filled the kettle. Sunshine or rain . . . she mouthed the incomplete competition riddle. One with sugar, one without. Where was Paul? Not out vandalising trees. Never.

Twenty minutes later Paul came in. His face gave him away the moment he saw the police. Red as a beetroot he went and knew it.

'We'd like you to come down to the station. Mrs Matthews, you may come with your son.'

'I'll have to tell my mother. She's upstairs. In bed. She's not too well.'

They waited downstairs, Paul and the police.

'Why did you do it, lad?' the constable probed.

'How do you know I did?' Paul replied, insolently.

'Because you're the only one who's not been seen round since. You see, we know the pattern. We've seen it all before. We know the names and addresses and family details of all the youngsters that hang about in the town centre at night. It might not be a bad idea if you was to pass on that little bit of information. There's not much we don't know about what goes on in this town.'

'You've no proof then?'

'Don't get clever with us, lad.'

Paul turned away from them. He wasn't going to say another word. They couldn't make him. He felt tragic. Misunderstood. The antihero of a poignant tale.

'Oh, Mum.' Marion sat snivelling on the edge of Ruby's sick bed. 'Why did he do it?'

'From what you say he hasn't admitted that he did. Mountain out of a molehill, if you ask me. Even if he did do it, so what? It's not such a wicked crime, is it? Just high spirits, and I don't mind telling you, Marion, I'm glad to see a bit of that in him – that is, if he did it. Where is he now anyway?'

153

'Gone out again. I couldn't stop him. Oh, I've failed him, Mum. I have.'

'Oh, for goodness sake! Why do you always have to bag all the guilt. What about his father?'

'I'm surprised to hear you say anything against Nick. I thought you always felt it was my fault he left us.'

'There you go again.'

'Well, you're so friendly to him,' Marion whimpered, accusingly.

'Only for your sake. I tell you, my girl, if you smartened yourself up a bit I reckon you could get him back.'

Marion stood up in a gesture of exasperation.

'Mother, we're divorced. He's married to someone else.'

'That didn't stop him before, when he was married to you.'

'Anyway, what makes you think he's at all interested?'

'You don't think he's started calling here to see me, do you?'

'I thought he came to see Paul.'

Ruby was watching her miserable daughter and thinking, with a degree of secret satisfaction, that Nick would come again to see her, not Marion. Never mind. If manipulation of others' lives was all that was left to her then she'd make the most of it. This sort of power had always been meat and drink to Ruby.

'Mum, what's going to happen to Paul?' Marion wailed.

'Oh, I should think they'll send him off to the colonies,' Ruby said, unkindly, still refusing to take the crime seriously. She thought back to the time when she was a girl and got caught stealing from Woolworth's. She hadn't cared. She hadn't even wanted the stuff she'd taken. It had just been something to do. A way of letting off steam. Fighting back. Shameless, she'd been called, and they were right about that. Guilt and shame had never troubled her.

'Seriously?' Marion pleaded.

'How should I know?'

'You don't think they'll send him to borstal?'

'I tell you, I don't know.' But Ruby did. For years she'd devoured newspaper reports of crime and punishment. She loved reading about rapists and murderers, drunken drivers and people who assaulted traffic wardens, and the reports of anonymous youths, too young to be named, who rampaged through puberty, stealing cars, joy-riding into the night in their desperate defiance of everyone and everything. People did much worse things than attack Christmas trees, and got off with a fine or what was termed a community service order, digging old people's gardens, that sort of thing. Ruby, safe and snug in her pillows, felt sorry for the boys and girls who had to pay their debt to society in this way. The goody-goody, caring judiciary that handed out such soul-salving penance were of the same breed that had put bromide in soldiers' tea. Neutralise, emasculate, straighten and narrow. Ruby had an abiding contempt for conversion to the good, reformed smokers, atheists who became evangelising Christians, boys with spirit who settled down with wet weekends like Marion. She sighed and closed her eyes.

'Mum are you all right?' Marion, her voice always so anxious.

Ruby, eyes still closed, nodded.

'You're not to worry about anything. Are you comfy?' Marion continued. Ruby could feel her close by, smell the frying fumes in her clothes. Why didn't she just go away, leave her alone?

'You have a little nap. I'll bring you something nice on a tray later on,' Marion went on appeasingly, still hanging on to all the blame.

Ruby kept everything closed, then the room went quiet and still. The pain in her side felt like a red hot brick lodged under her ribs. Think of something else. Think of something else! Nick, Oh Nick! The trick worked, producing a different sort of pain, a memorised longing. She'd played the little scene countless times in her thoughts. It had been the big moment in her life, the one and only time the whole thing had been for real.

In her mind's eye she saw herself as she had been then, in her prime as the Scottish schoolteacher had said in that film she'd seen on telly. Her hair had been red then, red and abundant, and her figure, though full, was the shape that men liked, not the flatness that was in fashion now, the look-alike lampposts with their negative backsides and fried-egg chests. And she hadn't felt old then, not a bit.

The scene began with her leaving the bed wherein lay

unconscious the lump of snoring blubber that was Frank. The youthful Ruby then moved across the room and out into the corridor of the house in Birmingham where she and Frank had lived for twenty years. Strange how there was never any sound in such reverie, only image and movement.

Along the corridor, past the room to which Marion had removed herself and the baby earlier that day, shutting out Nick. A few more steps, not to be taken too quickly, the scene had to build up. The door to the room where Nick slept alone. The pause. The shiver of expectation. And hadn't the door opened from inside? She thought so, because there was Nick, not in bed, but standing just a breath away, naked and waiting for her.

The door opened with untimely intrusion. Ruby's eyes flicked open.

'Mum, I forgot your pills,' Marion said, standing at the foot of the bed, the small brown bottle dangling from her fingers.

Ruby glared at her and saw her shrink back, involuntarily, out of habit.

'I won't take them,' she said fiercely.

Marion seemed to steel herself and came forward with the pills.

'Now don't be like that,' she said in a half-hearted attempt at sickroom discipline.

'Like what?' Ruby spat out defiantly.

'Difficult,' Marion answered, awkwardly, proffering two white tablets in her open palm.

Ruby eyed them for a split second then grabbed them and threw them at the window. Marion was trembling, retreating, as if the violence might extend to her.

'I don't want them,' Ruby tried to yell at her, but it came out like a pathetic wail.

Marion left the room, no doubt to phone the doctor, the nurse, the hospital, some welfare crutch. Ruby closed her eyes again. Tears, she could feel them blinding her picture. Oh God, how she wished she wasn't so old and decayed and disgusting. It wasn't fair, still to have the longing, to remember so clearly. The red-hot brick burnt in her side but the relief-giving pills were just out of reach.

156

Chapter Nineteen

For days now Charlotte had woken with the sensation of hope. Everything seemed to be going in the right direction: her job, the imminent return of Vicky, the burgeoning re-establishment of her relationship with Dan. The dinginess of the flat no longer affected her, its temporariness now in little doubt. She'd heard nothing from Nick since his departure nearly a month earlier, and maybe this rankled a little, though only because he had done the leaving. She hardly gave him a thought otherwise. She was glad to be free of him, of his aggressive bad temper and ceaseless talk of business, the aspects of their relatively short time together that swamped the other memories so conveniently in her present state of renewed love for Dan.

The day after the party she was exultant. I've got him! she almost sang out loud.

When everyone else had gone home, the four of them, Audrey and James, she and Dan, had sat down together and drifted into a do you remember session.

Audrey was still high on the aftermath of her production and James had drunk far too much, but the combined effect eased what might otherwise have been an awkward reunion between the four of them.

'You two should never have parted,' James declared at one point, pouring more brandy into his glass. 'Spoilt things for us, you know. We've never had such a good holiday since the time we all went to Scotland.'

'Oh, thank you very much, James,' Audrey said, indignant-ly. 'Am I such a dull old stick?'

'Not a bit of it, I'm just saying that we had a really good time, the four of us,' James continued. 'We did, didn't we?' he added, looking to Charlotte.

She smiled then glanced at Dan who was already watching her. Her mind was working clearly and quickly despite the lateness of the hour: he wouldn't carry on sitting there if he didn't like what was happening. She returned her smile to James. In her mind was the farcical pass he had made at her over the drawing board, she couldn't believe that he had always been like this, but maybe it was only her perception of him that had altered. She wondered whether he'd made advances to other women. Audrey had let herself go. The only effort she made was the red lipstick, presently no more than a faded narrow outline, the rest of it eaten away during the course of the party.

Charlotte was a mean observer. She'd noted such detail when she was overweight and unattractive herself, taking small scoops of comfort from the thick ankles and bulging hips of others; the size labels spied in friends' coats. It was an old habit, no longer needed but hard to break. Besides, it did no harm, and she'd come to terms with not liking herself very much.

'Can we help you clear things up?' she said to Audrey as inward amelioration. The 'we', she realised, had slipped out.

'Yes,' Dan concurred, 'We can't leave you to do it all.'

James appeared to have passed out.

'No, no,' Audrey protested. 'It can wait until the morning. The children will help.'

'Would you like a hand getting James to bed?' Dan offered.

They all three looked at him, rigid as a shop dummy in his state of oblivion.

'I'll take you up on that one,' Audrey said.

Between them they got him along the passageway to the bedroom end of the house. The shared activity, the physical closeness, was like electric current, their breathing heavy the panting as they guided the dead weight of James.

'It's time I went home,' Dan said when the job was done.

'Yes, it's very late,' Charlotte said, like a stilted echo. She didn't want to leave in case it broke the spell. Things seemed to be nearly but not quite.

Then Audrey, dear Audrey, said: 'We're having a few friends round for drinks on Christmas morning. Gluttons for punishment,' she laughed, nervously. 'If the two of you . . .'

Huge assumptions were being made in all directions. She looked from one to the other. 'That is if you've nothing else planned,' she added.

'Vicky will be here by then,' Charlotte said. She could hardly breathe.

'Oh, bring her along. Of course you must bring her along,' Audrey said over insistently, the delicacy of the situation finally getting to her.

'Goodnight Audrey and thank you for a most pleasant evening,' Dan was saying. 'And I'll certainly try and make it on Christmas morning.'

'Will you?' Charlotte asked him as they walked together towards their separate cars.

He paused at the side of the road.

'Lottie, this isn't a game, is it?'

She shook her head and wished she didn't have her own car parked along the lane.

'I have to be in London until just before Christmas.'

'I understand.'

'When is Vicky back?'

'Next weekend. Perhaps we could meet her together – at the airport?'

'No, not too fast,' he said, gently.

The night was clear and cold. Charlotte was freezing and impatient. She would have abandoned her car and gone with Dan right away if he'd asked, but it was a sort of game, only the rules were now tacitly his, a transposition she found both frustrating and intoxicating.

He'd said no more. They'd not kissed, not done anything the slightest bit careless. It was going to be difficult for them to touch in that way, capitulation on both sides, past atrocities unforgettable, lust inappropriate. When it happened it could be with nothing less than serious intent; there was far too much at stake for sex to be used as the usual interim testing ground.

The heaviness of the situation, the breathe-holding intensity between comment and reply, questions and answers, magnified observation of expression in the eyes, each small gesture of

the body – there was nothing else like it, nothing else s
precisely stored in memory, not another thing in life that mad
the day dawn more brightly.

Charlotte, always more euphoric on anticipation tha
attainment, drove to Heathrow on the Saturday before Chris
mas with a sense of goodwill to all, that had nothing to do wit
the festive season. The previous evening she'd decorated th
flat with sprigs of holly and curling strands of red ribbo
happily alone, but for the last time. Joe and Jean had invite
her to spend the evening with them but the mood of their hon
would not have suited her present frame of mind with i
optimistic focus on the future.

She didn't have to wait long at arrivals before Vicky's plar
landed and, as an unaccompanied child, she was broug
through customs ahead of the rest of the passengers, trailed l
a stewardess dragging a trolley laden with luggage and parcel

When she saw Charlotte she simply ran, swift as a dart, an
flung her arms round her mother's waist, burying her face
Charlotte's jacket.

'There, Hun. We said she'd be here,' the stewardess sai
catching up.

Vicky seemed to have grown and narrowed in the short tin
they'd been apart, but she still appeared little and vulnerable
Charlotte. Thank God it was over, the separation. How h
they ever stood it?

Vicky, who was very good at being endearing, kept looki
up at Charlotte but said hardly a word until they were out
the terminal complex and in the car.

'Where am I going to go to school?' was her first maj
question.

'In Cambridge, darling. A nice school and not boarding

'Do they have drama?'

'I should imagine so.'

'I've decided what I'm gonna be when I'm grown up. A
actress.'

'Lovely. Vicky, I thought we'd call in and see Grandma
the way home. Would you like that?'

'I don't mind. D'you think she'll have some presents for u

'Vicky! She's not able to go shopping. You know that.'

'Yup, she has everything sent.'

'Avaricious piggy!' Charlotte said, but she was too pleased to have Vicky back to be at all cross with her.

'What's avaricious?'

'Never mind.'

At the North London flat Charlotte's mother went into a wobbly cooing routine in the hallway. The place was more than usually rank with its stewing smells, air kept too still and closed in. Vicky, following her grandmother through to the small living room, turned her head to glance at her mother and grimacing, pinched her nostrils together. Charlotte tried to frown.

'This is lovely,' her mother kept repeating. 'The best Christmas present I could have.'

Charlotte, always conscience-stricken when she saw her mother, heard this reference to Christmas as double edged. There was no possibility of her leaving the confines of the flat and spending Christmas in Cambridge, not that Charlotte wanted her to see Bateman Street or register the absence of Nick, not at this stage; but she and Vicky could have made a Christmas for her, here, in the agoraphobic's cage.

'It's so good to see my baby again,' Mother was saying now, in the most nauseating pram-speak.

'Frances wants a baby but she can't have one. Her philippine tubes are blocked,' Vicky piped up.

Mother looked alarmed and shot a glance at Charlotte as if a four-letter word had been uttered.

'How sad,' Charlotte said, with a genuine wave of pity.

'Leonard told me,' Vicky continued, unabashed but quite aware that she was embarrassing her grandmother. 'He told me all about it, about making babies. He said someone of my age ought to know so they wouldn't be silly about it. Mom, did you know that when the man –'

'Yes,' Charlotte hurriedly cut her short.

'But I haven't told you. When the man –'

'Vicky, I know!'

'Something to eat,' Mother said, taking refuge in food. 'You must have something to eat.'

'No thanks,' Vicky said, pulling a face.

'Very well dear,' Mother said, sounding disappointed, slightly reproving. 'I must say, I think it's a good job you're home. But hasn't she grown, Charlotte, my, what a big girl.'

Vicky twitched the corners of her mouth in a gesture of tedium at this unoriginal, grandmotherly observation.

'Course I've grown,' she said, rudely.

'I'm sorry, Mother,' Charlotte said.

'I expect she's tired after the journey,' Mother said.

'I'm not,' Vicky said.

They couldn't stay too long, Charlotte said. Fortunately Mother seemed determined to remain sugary, making allowances, just so pleased, she kept saying, to have them both home again.

Just before they left she enquired after Dan (never Nick). She'd had a letter from Spain, from his parents, inviting her to spend Christmas with them. So kind – in the circumstances. Yes, thought Charlotte, and they knew she'd never accept. It was mean of her to think this but suppressed spite was still there: Dan's parents had, quite rightly, never taken her to their bosom, although they'd always been kind, done the right thing, which was probably why Charlotte found them insufferable. God, they'd be upset when she and Dan – the thought faded, she mustn't think that far ahead. She was, though, extremely glad they now lived in Spain.

'Daddy will be happy to have you home,' Mother said to Vicky at the front door.

'Yes, he will,' Charlotte said, no longer irritated by her mother's blinkered view, in fact, taking comfort from it. Perhaps, she thought, in a rare flash of unselfish benevolence, they'd build a granny flat on to the house.

Chapter Twenty

Mickey's airmail from New York which had remained unopened the night of the play announced that she was coming home for Christmas.

The letter troubled Dan. Its tone was affectionate, a little wistful, she said she missed being able to talk to him; but this, and the news that she'd be in England again soon, seemed not to be the main reasons for her writing. There was something else lurking between the lines. She said little about what she'd been doing but had filled a whole page with what amounted to a report of the christening, almost as if he hadn't been there. It ended with a long paragraph about Josephine, full of admiration and sympathy – to an unnatural degree. Mickey was without spite, but to be this fulsome . . . he couldn't understand it. After all, Josephine's child was also Mickey's husband's, and conceived before he and Mickey had parted. Attending the christening had been bizarre enough.

Dan's week in London was more than usually hectic, giving him little time to dwell on either Mickey's letter or, more thought-provoking, Charlotte's behaviour. He'd been too badly hurt by her four years earlier to allow himself the joy that might have been his. She'd made it very clear that she wanted him again, though he knew better than she that her sort of wanting was transitory. He was curious as to what had happened with Matthews. What had finished it? It seemed more likely that Matthews had left Charlotte than the other way round. Matthews was that sort of man, a careless disposer of what was no longer sparkling and new, an incorrigible wrecker of other people's lives. Merely to think of him now seemed to slice away the magnanimity that had enabled Dan to hold on to his self-respect when Charlotte had left, and he couldn't help but feel something like satisfaction to know that Charlotte's second marriage hadn't worked, but his dislike of Matthews was far greater than any desire for her to suffer, and vindication would have been sweeter if he could have thought she had done the leaving.

The possibility that she was seeking only comfort, proof of an old point, flawed the enticing scenario. So he would tread carefully and slowly, he decided at the beginning of the week, but this logical caution was at variance with that other, deeper side of his nature, the ardour that ultimately had always dictated the course of his life.

There had been the possibility that he might fly to Spain and spend Christmas with his parents, but he knew he wouldn't now. To see Vicky on Christmas Day was sufficient reason to keep him in England but by the end of the week he could no longer pretend that this alone was why he felt such anticipation.

Additional work on a green paper kept him in London over the weekend and right up until midnight on Christmas Eve. He drove home in the small hours of Christmas morning, unaware of how fast he was going. He'd telephoned Marigold at the weekend and asked her to get a tree and some of those tinselly garlands, and to make sure the bicycle he'd ordered for Vicky was delivered in time.

The police stopped him on the A10 and made him take a breathalyzer test which he rather enjoyed as he'd not had a drink for days. They wished him a merry Christmas and let him go. Another twenty minutes and he was home. It was 2am and the house would be cold but the tree had been placed at the window, its coloured lights twinkling out across the front lawn.

A note from Marigold instructed him to have a happy time. All sorts of food awaited him according to a list she had prepared together with a message to say that Vicky's new bicycle was in the garage.

He went through to the drawing room where the tree Marigold had decorated stood in gawdy splendour. He gazed at it for a while, remembering other Christmases when the

164

house had been full, the years when his parents had come to stay, and Charlotte's mother, the duty Christmases when he and Charlotte had sat in this room at this same hour, when all the others had gone to bed, and promised one another that the next time they'd go to a hotel. He couldn't have had any idea, not then, of what it was like to be alone. Christmas, the loneliest night of the year. He turned away and went upstairs to bed.

The tree, of course, was for Vicky, but in the cold and empty house at the hour of maximum vulnerability Dan suddenly saw it as no more than a pathetic symbol of his own need. What had he hoped for? Some sort of pretence at happy families? To bring Vicky and Charlotte back to the house after the drinks party at James and Audrey's? To keep them there with Marigold's festive tokens? God, what a presumptuous fool he'd been; lining himself up for the whole thing to start again. He should have sold the house long ago, put himself beyond the reach of this nostalgic setting; because all the time he remained there it must seem as if he was holding on to the past.

In the bedroom he'd shared with Charlotte this mood of miserable caution deepened. Supposing he went ahead with the day as planned: it was not so very unlikely that tomorrow night Charlotte could be in this room in the bed, in his arms . . . Vicky in her old room along the corridor . . . but for how long – one night, a week, a month, a year? Maybe he and Charlotte could risk it for themselves but not with Vicky. His thoughts ran on, bypassing the initial euphoria, the potential for happiness in a renewed life together, and saw the misery and mess of a second parting.

He slept badly, falling into a deep sleep in the morning and being woken by the telephone some time after ten. It was his parents ringing from Spain, wanting to know how he would be spending the day, reassuring themselves that he would not be alone. He told them he'd be seeing Vicky.

'We're so pleased,' his mother said in that sad, sympathetic way of hers.

'Give her our love.'

Nobody mentioned Charlotte.

'I hope you're going to have enough to eat,' his mother continued.

165

The long distance between them and infrequent meetings had delayed the transition in their relationship, the point at which responsibility shifts from parent to child, so that Dan, middle-aged, was still promising his mother that he would eat properly.

The call went on. The sun was still shining in Spain. The weather was balmy. They imagined it must be horribly cold and damp in England. It was, wasn't it? Always the same insistent enquiry. Why didn't they concede their mistake and come home? Good weather was no substitute for the habits and friends of a lifetime.

He dressed and went downstairs. The house was so very quiet. Unthinking, he went to the front door to fetch the newspaper, forgetting there weren't any on this day: everything seemed to conspire against people who were alone at Christmas. Then the telephone rang again and it was Mickey.

'Happy Christmas, Dan.'

'Yes,' he said, measuring the word.

'You sound as if you are alone.'

'I am.'

'Can I come over?'

'Of course.'

'Half an hour?'

'Fine.'

It was more like twenty minutes. Mickey arrived, a simultaneous expression of anxiety and relief in her face.

'How are you?' Dan asked, leading her through the hallway to the drawing room.

'OK, but glad to get away from the family for a bit. They treat me like a barometer. They keep looking to see if there's any sign of change.'

Dan laughed.

'I've just had a protracted conversation about weather conditions,' he said.

'I like the tree,' Mickey commented.

'Marigold's effort,' Dan said.

'She's marvellous, that woman,' Mickey said. There was awkwardness between them, but could it have been otherwise?

'Have a drink,' Dan said.

166

They'd spent the previous Christmas together, in this room, as friends, such good friends they'd even been able to talk about being lovers and dismiss the idea with a smile and a joke and a kiss.

'You're not spending the day alone?' Mickey asked.

'Not entirely. I've been invited to pre-lunch drinks with some old friends.'

'You should have said.'

'No, I wasn't sure about going. In fact I've decided against it.'

'Not on my account?'

'No.' He smiled across at her. She looked so anxiously apologetic, but then, to varying degrees, he'd never known her to be without this almost irritating humility, as if she had no right to his time and interest. Since becoming an MP he'd experienced this attitude in all sorts of people, although there were others who demanded too much. Finding the happy medium was always difficult for someone in his position but with Mickey it had nothing to do with who he was; the problem lay in her lack of self-regard, which was why she was so irrevocably a victim. But who was he to judge her so? Hadn't their half-hearted little affair in the autumn failed because each had assumed the same role, and two victims were about as likely to stay together as life after death?

Increasingly he thought in this exasperated fashion while outwardly holding an affable smile, a social drink and the appearance of a listening ear.

'Are you really sure? I mean, I don't want to spoil your plans,' Mickey was still saying.

'No, really.' How agonisingly polite they were to one another now.

'No, I feel awful about this. I feel I've stopped you going,' she persisted.

'Why don't you come with me?' he said then.

Chapter Twenty-One

Stacey Middleton stood in front of the cracked mirror in the public lavatories spraying something not unlike glue into her hair. She'd used practically the whole can but the stalagmite effect she wanted to achieve eluded her in the damp surroundings. Every time she got one bit of hair to stand up a clump she'd already done keeled over like a dog's ear.

'Fuck it!' she said aggressively and had one more go, though her hair was so heavy now with the spray (an unexpected present in her Christmas stocking) her only option was to bend all the spikes that sprouted from the top of her head and make it seem deliberate.

She was in one of her don't know what to do with myself moods, bursting with restless impatience but with nothing in particular upon which to focus her frustration. To make matters worse she'd done a really stupid thing, she'd telephoned Shoot – asked him to come down town to meet her.

She glanced at her watch. Half past eleven. Surely he'd be there, in the park, waiting for her by now. Her mother had thrown a fit. It was Christmas for chrissake! Couldn't she stay in just one day of the year.

'What's it to you?' she'd snarled back at her mother. 'You'll all be stuck in front of the telly box anyway.' Which was just how she'd left them, her mother and father, her two brothers the elder one's new fiancée, the grandparents and that old creep from across the road who'd given her 50p and a big slobber under the mistletoe. They all thought it was such a joke! God, they didn't know about the big lump in his trousers the accidently on purpose hand on her tit. It was after that

168

she'd rung Paul.

'I've got to see you,' she said dramatically, just like one of the grizzlers on Dallas; and now he'd get the wrong idea, think she'd turned keen, which she had.

For ages, at least a week, she'd not seen him. She'd started to worry a bit. Had he gone off her, because if he had he'd no right. It wasn't up to him. Then she'd heard about what he'd done, wrecking the tree in the park. She could hardly believe it. Him! It stuck in her mind, him doing that. He'd have to go to court, like her younger brother when he'd nicked all that stuff from the video shop, only they'd send Paul to borstal because he came from a broken home, hadn't got a dad to give him discipline. Stacey knew how it went, and suddenly Paul was a hero, a victim of society, a stand-alone rebel. She wanted to see him and tell him she'd stand by him, visit him in prison, be waiting when he came out. In her mind's eye she could picture herself standing alone outside a barrack-like building waiting for the big iron doors to be opened and Paul coming out, thin and pale, with a brown paper parcel under his arm – all he possessed in the world, apart from her. The romance of it turned her insides to jelly. She threw the empty can of spray down one of the lavatories and ran out into the park, her heart beating like nobody's business.

And there he was, the only other person in the park, in the world. She ran to him, just like in the films on telly, throwing her arms round his neck then sobbing into his shoulder.

'What's the matter?' he asked, his lovely male arms folding round her back.

'Oh, Paul,' she sobbed, seeing she'd left a deal of make-up on his anorak. 'I'll come away with you now, this minute, if you like. I don't want them to lock you up.' God, she'd got that bit wrong, running away together wasn't as poignantly romantic as a prison parting. 'But if they do, lock you up like, I'll wait for you. I promise.'

'That's very decent of you Stace,' he said. 'Is that why you wanted to see me?'

There was something less than wholehearted in his reaction to her declaration, she felt a little uneasy.

'Could be,' she said, suddenly reverting to her usual manner of belligerent indifference.

Their arms slipped away from one another. She stared at the ground, her right foot twisting back and forth in front of her left. It seemed possible she'd got the whole thing wrong.

'What did you get for Christmas?' she asked, her eyes still down. Had the last few moments really happened or had she sniffed too much of that spray and imagined it all? She glanced up. Course she hadn't. Her make-up was all over him, wasn't it?

'Nothing much,' he answered, dismissively. 'What about you?'

'Oh, the same. They're all watching telly at home. That's all they ever do. I got fed up. There's nowhere to sit anyway, my brother's got his fiancée there. They got engaged today. Romantic, isn't it,' she added, in what she hoped was a cynical tone. She felt a right dip-head now. She could hardly look at him; and it was agony, all this chat about Christmas. Next she'd be telling him about slobberchops and the 50p when she was just bursting to say that she loved him. God, boys were so thick about these things.

'Er, Stace,' he began, hesitantly. 'How did you know — about the police?'

'Everyone knows!'

'But how?'

'I d'know. They just do.'

'Why d'you do it?' she asked then.

'I don't know, it just happened. It was stupid.'

She took a deep breath.

'It don't matter. I still love you.' There, she'd said it, the awful, difficult word.

There was a pause, like something ever so embarrassing had just happened.

'You didn't before,' he said, like he wanted to argue about it.

'I just never said it before,' she retorted.

'Look, I've got to get home' he said next. 'I'm waiting for a phone call.'

She glanced at his face, not believing what he'd said. She felt terrible now, really terrible.

'Oh, fuck you. Fuck you, Shoot Matthews,' she wailed, turning from him and heading back towards the lavatories.

He looked a bit surprised but he didn't move, not right away.

170

In the loos Stacey went straight to the cubicle where the little window was broken. She looked out but not enough so he'd see her. He was still standing there where she'd left him, and he was smiling. Smiling!

She'd cut her throat or take some pills. She'd make him sorry. She'd make them all sorry. She stepped down from the rim of the pan and started to cry. Nothing ever happened! Nothing exciting and big like it was on telly. It was other people. They always let you down.

She went to the cracked mirror and poked at her hair disconsolately. Fuck the lot of them, all she wanted was a bit of romance, something to make her feel special. It was her brother getting engaged that had done it. Why couldn't someone give her a diamond ring!

Paul was not there when she eventually emerged from her refuge. Well, she'd blown that one. She hoped he'd get sent to a really horrid borstal with loads of really rough lads who'd give him a good sorting . . . this thought ran on . . . a hospital bed, Paul lying in it, just about beaten to death . . . her there by his side, keeping a vigil . . . she felt a bit better and made her way home for Christmas dinner.

Paul got home in time to see his grandmother being put in an ambulance.

'I'm sorry,' Marion said to him as she stepped in with Ruby. 'I'll ring you from the hospital, Paul.'

The white doors closed behind her anxious face and the vehicle moved away. Paul went into the empty house and up the stairs to his room, glancing in the landing mirror on his way. Funny how his spots had gone. He lay down on his unmade bed and wondered whether the lie to Stacey about waiting for a phone call had something to do with his grandmother being carted off to hospital, although the fictitiously awaited call was to have come from his father.

Chapter Twenty-two

'How nice to meet you again,' Charlotte said to Mickey.

'Yes,' the girl replied, with a weak smile.

'Happy Christmas, Charlotte,' Dan said.

She looked at him. She wouldn't look at the girl again.

'Yes,' she said. 'Happy Christmas.' Was this revenge? She thought she'd known him better. She felt sick, dizzy. Too much wine. She hadn't been able to eat any of Audrey's renowned mince pies. The anticipation had been too great.

Vicky was standing between them holding Dan's hand. She was very quiet, as if she'd sensed the horrendous delicacy of the moment, its potential for repercussion.

'We can't stay too long,' Charlotte said.

'You said we could,' Vicky piped up in a thin voice.

'Did I?' Charlotte murmured, holding on to a sticky smile. Her jaw ached with the effort.

'You said we'd probably go to Daddy's,' Vicky persisted with infantile wickedness.

'I meant you, darling, that you would probably go to Daddy's.'

'If that's all right,' Dan interjected at this point.

'Yes, of course,' Charlotte answered, her voice sounding brittle and shrill. 'Vicky can go home with you from here and I'll collect her later. I was planning to have the meal this evening. It'll give me a chance to get everything ready.'

'I'll bring her back to you, if that would be easier,' Dan offered.

Such consideration! Make things easy when they were impossibly difficult.

'All right,' Charlotte agreed before remembering that she hadn't wanted him to see where she was living.

It seemed she had dug herself into a deep hole, with Dan and Vicky, the girl, Audrey and James, all standing round the top, peering down at her as if to see what she might do next, how she'd get herself out, unaided, or maybe she'd just dig deeper.

She was stuck. Stuck with this most uncomfortable, no-where to go situation. Even in this room, standing in the polite little semi-circle with the other three, she was held fast, down the hole. Conversation of some sort had to be found, for the sake of appearances, for half an hour, maybe longer, because if she left now everyone would know and talk about it in pitying tones that were also gloating and glad because that was how people were.

'I thought you were in America,' she said in the general direction of the girl. It came out sounding like an accusation.

'No, I came back a couple of days ago,' the girl answered, nervously, like an apology.

'Mickey's spending Christmas here,' Dan said.

'Oh, really,' Charlotte responded. 'Look, will you excuse me, only I think I ought to help Audrey with the food or something.' An inspiration!

'Frances can't have any babies,' she heard Vicky pronounce as she fled, slowly, to the kitchen.

'A bit unexpected,' Audrey said, meeting her in the door-way.

'Sorry?' Charlotte smiled brightly.

Audrey gave her a look.

It was intolerable.

'D'you mind if I don't stay, only I've such a lot to do at home, the turkey and everything.'

'I thought you might like to stay here with us – after all the others have gone,' Audrey said. 'Do stay,' she persisted, gently laying her hand on Charlotte's arm.

Kind complacent cow, Charlotte thought with the memory of James pressed against her across the drawing board, his smelly pipe-smoke breath gusting over her.

'No,' she said. 'I must go.'

In the next moment Audrey had grasped her in something like a bearhug.

173

'I understand,' she whispered, sickeningly. 'Just remember we're here if you need us.'

She returned to the room where Vicky and Dan and the girl were having an animated conversation which abruptly went quiet when the three of them saw her. A conspiracy? Even Vicky?

She told Dan the address of the flat. Vicky her hand still holding on to his, seemed to be watching from the other side of a chasm she knew her mother could not cross.

How suddenly everything to do with hope and happiness could disappear. It was like a death. Back at the flat Charlotte gave in to a sort of wilful hysteria that encompassed the whole lot – Dan and the girl, Vicky, James and Audrey, Nick . . . Ah, Nick. At last she turned angry. She'd not heard a word from him. He could have sent a card, even a telegram or whatever they were called now. Christmas Day and he hadn't the common decency to get in touch, wish her well. He could be dead for all she knew. Panic seized her. Supposing she never heard from him again: she'd be stuck, wouldn't she. Seven years was it, before they assumed the worst?

Time had passed so swiftly over the past few weeks she'd not realised how long it was since he'd left. For a while she'd supposed he'd be back but she'd given him so little thought until now.

Her anger and, plain disappointment, yes, that was what it amounted to, as simple as that, disappointment, with the Dan situation, was no longer a matter of intrigue, only pain; whereas Nick – where was he? What the hell was he playing at!

She tried to think back to their last evening together and the preceeding days and nights. She must have missed something, but there hadn't been very much: he'd said so little. All she could remember was the few last squabbles, though not their content, only the fact of their happening, the distant residue of bitter aftertaste.

It was time to think things out. She sat down in one of the shabby armchairs, lit a cigarette and concentrated her mind, finding that it settled on a single incident which had taken place only a few days after she and Nick had arrived in America and were staying with Frances and Leonard. Frances and Leonard, the works of art in her gallery of friends and acquaintances, the two people with whom she felt most mentally elevated, her own performance lifted by their example.

The four of them had got into one of those late night sessions when the world is so easily dissected and put right. Leonard had argued at length from his Zionist standpoint, she and Frances had taken up a feminist line for the sake of the debate, loftily lamenting the territorial bickering of men, and Nick had thrown in Mrs Thatcher and the Falklands.

Their differences had brought them together on that occasion. Charlotte had sensed her friends' reservation about Nick, but that night they'd all been up there, on the same plain, flexing intellectual muscles with equal aplomb, parading their cleverness and taking delight in the shared perception of abstract concepts.

They'd gone to bed on a high, their minds too enlivened to sleep.

'Was that all right?' Nick said. 'Did I pass the test?'

She was taken aback by his insecurity. Until this point she'd made the mistake of assuming that some sort of invincibility accompanied his money-making success. Perhaps this was because she'd been a little in awe of him. He'd always seemed rather fierce and ruthless to her but it was possible this perception had been made more due to her own state of mind from the time they had met, when she'd been offering him her services as a graphic designer after several years without work. But the image had persisted and the transition from employer to lover had been all the more intoxicating because of it. And if there were any tests she rather thought it was a case of other people having to pass them to his standard, not the other way around.

That was the night they'd talked about having a baby. They'd never discussed it before.

'A joint venture,' Nick had said.

'It might happen anyway, by accident,' she said.

'I'd rather it was intentional,' he said. 'I like the idea of impregnating you.'

'I'm not sure it would be a good idea. I'd get so fat and grumpy.'

'I think it would be rather nice, you being fat there and having milk.' He laid his hand on her flat stomach.

'Ah, so that's it, the milk,' she said lessening the poignancy.

'I've always wanted to,' he said.

'And you couldn't before?'

'No. Not allowed.'

She put her arms round him.

'You're very dear,' she said. 'I didn't know you could be like this.'

And she had forgotten. Subsequent moments of tenderness had been spoilt by a growing defensiveness in her and his increasing preoccupation with business. She'd felt she couldn't keep up with him, that unless she was successful in her own right he'd discount her. Perhaps it was being in America where success was so laudable, failure so dire. Hadn't people shot themselves, jumped out of skyscraper windows when Wall Street had crashed? It would never have been like that in London where only success was despised.

There had been no more talk of a joint venture. She supposed that Vicky's blunt revelation about Frances' problem in that direction must have prompted the memory of that night, but in her own state of despair, she was unable to feel much pity for her friend. Frances had Leonard and Charlotte had always envied the level of that relationship, insular, intense, so that even when she and Nick had been playing out that tender, intimate scene in the other couple's house, a part of her mind was probably comparing the two marriages and feeling that the real thing was in another room.

She'd smoked half a dozen cigarettes with a vicious intensity. The basement room was becoming acrid with suspended strata of exhaled Marlboro. Did she really care if Nick had left her? Wasn't that a quite separate issue from the loss of Dan? With a spark of spite, she hoped fervently that at this very moment Nick was boring the pants off some other woman, ranting on about his wretched work.

She got up, the spark providing her with that restless energy that had always got her through in the past. She wasn't even going to think about Nick any more, she told herself; but Dan was a different matter. The spite expanded. He wanted Vicky, she thought. He might even try and gain custody. The notion was paranoid but her thoughts where Vicky was concerned had always been extreme and possessive. She'd fight him all the way, she decided, no holds barred. *Ménage à trois* with a rapist – wasn't that what Audrey had said?

Chapter Twenty-Three

'When do you go back to New York?' Josephine asked.

'The day after tomorrow,' Mickey answered.

'Alone?'

'Yes.'

They were sitting in Josephine's flat which consisted of a row of rooms at the top of the stately home. They were the rooms vacated only a few decades back by the servants who had run the house; low-ceilinged attic rooms, cold and draughty, probably more so now than in the days when open fires had burnt throughout the labyrinthine edifice.

The two, nineteen eighties women sat in front of a single bar electric fire, their hands wrapped round mugs of instant coffee. Outside it was snowing, big soft lumps sticking to the small, square-paned window.

'It hasn't worked out with Dan?' Josephine enquired tentatively, though always one to come straight to the point.

Mickey stared, unseeing, into her mug.

'No,' she answered 'I would have liked it to, but there are too many ghosts.'

'Such as?' There was a touch of prurience in Josephine's curiosity, though she'd changed a good deal since the days when Mickey had first known her and the questions had been overtly intrusive, deliberately shocking. It had all been part of the attention-seeking desperation of extreme loneliness and in part that had gone since the affair with David and now the existence of Giles, asleep in his cot on the other side of the room.

'Chiefly Dan's wife, I mean ex-wife, though she's rather

more than a ghost.' This was not strictly true, that the main problem was Charlotte, but Mickey didn't want to say anything about her own troubled state of being, the increasing aversion to being touched, man-handled, fingered. She'd become old-fashioned frigid, that was what had happened.

'It's not David then?' The question seemed loaded.

'No, not David.' Mickey's mind travelled back to her husband. Would she be averse to his touch?

Josephine's expression was now one of news to impart.

'That's a relief,' she said, in her crass, honest way. 'Mickey, David has been coming to see me. It started just before Christmas. I think he feels there's a chance we could be together.'

'I see.' The mind journey cut off.

'You don't mind?'

'No, no, of course not.'

'I don't think it's just me. It's Giles as well. He seems fond of him.'

'He knows?'

'That Giles isn't his? Yes, but it doesn't seem to matter.'

David had wanted children. So had Mickey.

'I'm pleased,' she said. 'Pleased for all three of you.' Did this sound too much. She wanted to be sincere.

Noises had started coming from the cot. Both women got up. The baby, his eyes wide open, stared at them in the same disconcerting way Mickey had felt his gaze at the christening. It seemed so wrong that Dan shouldn't know, but how could she say anything now; she'd left it too long. It could be only meddlesome and spoiling after what Josephine had just told her; and yet she felt more strongly than ever that Dan not knowing was a terrible injustice. In fact the main reason she'd come to see Josephine had been to ask her to tell Dan, to involve him, give him a share in the child.

Christmas Day had been such a day. The meeting with Charlotte had touched Mickey in a way she'd not expected, instinctively she disliked Dan's former wife, and not just for the vaguely territorial reasons that perhaps lingered on from the autumn affair. Quite simply, she felt that Charlotte was a bad person; selfish and heedless of the feelings of others. But on Christmas Day, at that dreadful drinks party, Mickey had seen that the woman was in torment. Her edginess, watery eyes, the fact that she had left so abruptly.

Then there was Vicky. This was the first time Mickey had met Dan's daughter. He'd never said much about her, much as she knew the child was in his thoughts, but the impression she had formed was different from the reality. Vicky was a monster.

After the party the three of them had gone back to Dan's house, and Vicky's present, a bicycle, had been brought forth. She'd leapt on it.

'Don't go in the road,' Dan said, and pedalling furiously the child went straight down the drive and into the lane.

Dan ran after her, calling her name. He looked old then, running, out of breath.

'I'm not a baby, Dadda,' Vicky simpered when she came back.

Dadda – why this sudden new name and why so irritatingly coy in its intonation?

Mickey felt uncomfortable with the situation, with herself; uneasy for Dan.

'Can I keep my bicycle here, with you? And can I have a pony and a puppy? Mommy said I'd be able to have pets if I came back to England. And can't I come and live here? Mommy's got a horrid place for us to live. It's small and dark and I don't like it. I want to live here.' She said the last bit with her gaze fixed on Mickey, her eyes glinty and hostile.

Mickey tried to feel sorry for her, to reason that she was only a child and therefore it was unacceptable to dislike her. But Vicky was vibrant with the wheedling ways to wring a parent's blind heart. She knew she was on safe ground with dear Dan no matter what she did, and overt hostility to an outsider was just par for the course.

Dan, besotted, continued running after her, albeit metaphorically. It was partly guilt, for the long separation, but also a deal of emotion inextricably bound up with blood and genes. Vicky was his child. But so was Giles.

On her last day in England Mickey again went to see Dan who was working at home over the Christmas recess.

As soon as he opened the door to her she could see that he was upset. His eyes were dark and deep in their sockets, his

179

smile of greeting no more than perfunctory within the preoccupation of some dreadful anxiety.

'I've come to say goodbye,' she told him. 'I leave tomorrow.'

'So soon? I hadn't realised,' he replied, with minimal interest, but could she expect more?

Again she felt uneasy – and with Dan, her greatest friend and confidant. It was as if the person with her now was a stranger who only looked like the real thing, inhabiting the shell of a departed essence.

'Dan, is everything all right?' she asked in that ridiculous way when things are patently all wrong.

She followed him across the hallway and into the drawing room. The fire was lit and papers of an official-looking nature were strewn over the carpet round the chair where he'd been sitting.

'It's nothing,' he said, attempting to brighten.

'Oh Dan, it is. You look ghastly.'

'It would have been better if you hadn't come,' he said quietly, looking at her now, properly.

'What is it?'

'Charlotte. I think she's become deranged.' He sighed and sat down, everything about him, weary and defeated.

'I made the mistake of telling her, some while back, when she came here – you were here too – that I wanted more formal access to Vicky.'

'That's not so very unreasonable.'

'Maybe not. But Charlotte seems to think so now.' He bent forward and picked up a letter which was on the floor with the other papers. He handed it to her.

When she'd finished reading the single sheet Mickey understood. She felt sick and overcome with remorse, the bitter unfairness of life, the seeming inevitable triumph of evil over and over again. Charlotte was going to fight Dan's access to Vicky by raking up the sordid details of what had happened in this house the night of the rape, linking him with the insanity of Arthur, who Dan had never met, only seen in the dock the day of the trial. She could not have chosen a more hideous weapon.

'I'm sorry,' Dan said. 'I didn't want you to know. The letter arrived a few days ago. Since then I've been trying to decide

180

what to do for the best. I thought about just letting it go. Fighting over children, nobody wins, least of all the child. But Charlotte's behaving like poison and what's that going to do to Vicky? The trouble is I no longer can distinguish between what's right and what I want. Perhaps I want Vicky only for my own sake and I've just been using Charlotte's behaviour as an excuse . . . '

'Excuse?' Mickey echoed. There was to be no end to the misery and repercussions from her affair with Arthur. It had destroyed her marriage, turned her frigid in what might have been a loving relationship with Dan, and now the ripples spread further and with a resurging current.

Dan was watching her. He'd stood up and come across to where she sat. The anxiety in his expression was more immediate now.

'I shouldn't have let you see it,' he said, taking the letter from her hand. 'Mickey, I'm sorry.' He touched her shoulder and she flinched away, leaving his hand in mid air. He seemed startled for a moment but then he didn't know the degree to which she had travelled into isolation.

'It's so unfair,' she murmured, 'so terribly unfair.' She knew as well as Dan that its being untrue would make little difference to a court hearing. It couldn't be proved either way, but any suggestion that he had been involved in such an arrangement would be enough to swing a custody hearing in Charlotte's favour.

'If only . . . ' she began but trailed off.

Dan walked over to the window where the Christmas tree still stood, its lights out and most of its needles shed.

'They never last,' he said. 'Every year I think about planting them but they don't make it to twelfth night.'

'They have to have roots,' Mickey said. 'They can't survive otherwise. Dan, why is Charlotte doing this?'

'I don't suppose she knows herself,' he answered, staring out across the front lawns and beyond to the fields. 'She's unhappy.'

'And that's sufficient reason to make others wretched?'

'Some people can't help it.'

'I wish I could do something.'

'You can't,' he said when he might, so easily, have

181

accused her of already having done too much.

'So you're leaving tomorrow,' he said, turning to face her again.

'Yes.'

'Maybe I'll try and get over to New York later in the year.'

'That would be nice,' she said, knowing he wouldn't come.

Before she left she told him about her visit to Josephine the previous day, but not in the way she'd hoped. Instead she broke the news about David.

'You're not upset?' Dan enquired, kindness and concern second nature even when things were at their worst for him.

'No, I don't think so. Not any more,' she answered, although she was still asking herself the question.

'It'll be better for the child,' he said then. 'And David has a right.'

Somehow Mickey managed to voice agreement. She left the house a few minutes later.

Dan watched her go. He'd wished her well and meant it, and now he had to come to terms with what he'd done. He'd never intended telling her, let alone showing her the contents of Charlotte's letter. At the time of the rape he'd suffered badly over the rumours. His political career had been put in jeopardy, even his professional status as a solicitor, but he'd kept quiet, ridden it out, attended the trial with Mickey because he was damned if he was going to allow tabloid tittle-tattle to dictate his actions, prevent him from standing by a friend. In a way it had been an ennobling experience, although Dan had always been far more noble than he'd ever known and this was one of the reasons Charlotte hadn't liked herself when she was married to him, one of the reasons she'd left him.

All of it was wasted now, he thought. He'd spoilt a lifetime of living by what was right. In a single action he'd crossed the divide. Showing Mickey the letter had been a piece of human frailty he could have tolerated in someone else but not himself. He could imagine Mickey brooding over it, blaming herself for Charlotte's latest treachery, and nothing he might say would stop her. He shouldn't have shown her the letter. Doing so had achieved nothing, only a passing on of guilt.

Despite his anguish, he found it difficult now to keep his thoughts round Mickey for very long. Charlotte intruded all the time, but as he'd known her when they were married and not as she presented herself to him now. He kept drifting off into small reveries that jumbled past with present to create hypothetical exchanges wherein Charlotte played the dark side of his nature, the suppressed self that wanted to shout out Me. Me. What about me?

I don't see why you're so bothered. She doesn't care about you. She's not capable of caring about anyone, he could hear Charlotte say. Why do you always have to make such a big thing of other people's sensibilities?

And Vicky, aren't you using her as a weapon just as much as I am? All this nonsense about wanting the best for her. It's hypocritical. Sure you want the best for her. We both do. You know that, but you want her for yourself as well. Admit it. Go on, admit it. And while you're at it you might just as well come clean over the whole lot. You want me too. The worse I behave the more you think about me. You might feel you hate me but that doesn't alter the fact that you've been only half alive without me. Risk it. Go on. Take a bloody risk and ask me to come back.

Chapter Twenty-Four

My Dear Frances,

It must be years since I wrote you a real letter. I think the last time was when Vicky was a baby and everything was swallowed down into that dark hole called depression. I can't say it is exactly the same now. I suppose the difference is that I feel more in control, but things are middling bleak.

I haven't heard from Nick for nearly two months now (he's back in America – did you know?) and it would seem that things are over between us, though there was so little left towards the end I can't pretend to any great sorrow.

Vicky and I are living in a dismal little flat here in Cambridge but I hope it won't be for long. When I catch up with Nick there should be some sort of share-out which, after all, I am entitled to, but I'm not doing too badly myself at present. I've got a job and there's still Dan's money for Vicky. While I'm working she goes to Audrey, who you may remember. She's big and warm and comforting, rather like a blanket and she makes wonderful home-made biscuits. Vicky will be starting at her new school soon and I think she's looking forward to it.

So, you see, we're all right, your goddaughter and me, except that we both want that which we cannot have. In Vicky's case it's a pony and various other furry things that don't live in flats. In mine it's something at which you may have guessed but right now Dan and I are locked in battle. It's quite hideous really, we're fighting over Vicky four years too late. He's changed, F, he's bitter and angry and I don't know him like that. He's pushed me into a corner and you know what I'm like when that happens. It's not difficult for me to play mean.

What's going to happen I just don't know, but all the time there's something going on, albeit a fight, I keep hoping.

As usual, I've gone on about me. Please forgive. Vicky told me about your problem. Surely there's a chance. The test tube place is near here. I read about someone having twins.

Please give my love to Leonard and my endless thanks to you both for looking after Vicky.

Yours
Charlotte

Chapter Twenty-Five

Dan's letter to Charlotte arrived the next day; the day Mickey flew back to New York, and Charlotte's letter flew to California.

It was a brief note requesting a meeting. Charlotte read it several times, trying to find more than was there in the terse wording. When she dropped Vicky off that morning she asked Audrey if she could keep her a bit later than usual. She rang Dan from the Cambridge studio and told him she would go to the house at six. He sounded icy, out of reach.

All day at the studio the coldness in his voice remained with her. She was working on a fairly straightforward design for a brochure selling vitamin pills but she couldn't get the layout right. Nothing she tried seemed to work. The day dragged. She was nervous. She regretted sending the letter to Dan. Writing it had been a way of venting her bitter disappointment. It shouldn't have been posted. But it had, and now she felt a different sort of resentment: Dan should have understood. His behaviour now seemed like deliberate overreaction. He wanted to punish her by making her feel rotten for what she'd done, not just writing the letter but everything, taking Vicky away in the first place. By five thirty she had got herself into a fighting mood.

The traffic out of Cambridge moved painfully slowly; every set of traffic lights seemed to be against her and at the last major junction she narrowly missed hitting a cyclist. The incident alarmed her, making her heart pound, her hands clammy on the steering wheel. By the time she reached the house she was ready to spit fire.

186

Dan let her in with an expression that observed too perceptively the meanness of her soul.

'Are we alone?' she asked, pointedly.

'Yes, quite alone. I don't think this is something to air in front of other people,' he said in his most pompous, lawyer's voice. That was how it sounded to her.

She found it difficult to look at him. She'd wronged him too much over the years. She wanted to blame him, and surely he was culpable to some extent, just for being the way he was, always doing things the right way and knowing it. The selfless, sacrificing martyrs could make life intolerable for the wretched sinners, but didn't they sin themselves in their greedy grabbing at immortality? Her mind whirled about in crazy hypotheses; she was on thin ground trying to lay blame with Dan.

'Would you like a drink?'

'Yes. No.'

'Which is it to be?'

'You should have thrown out that tree. It's bad luck to keep them in the house after twelfth-night.'

'So I understand.'

'I thought you had a woman who cleaned and did that sort of thing.'

'Marigold is away this week.'

Bend a little. Meet me halfway. Charlotte pleaded inside her head.

'I'll have a scotch,' she said. 'I nearly hit a cyclist on my way out of Cambridge.' It sounded pathetic. Perhaps if she had hit him it would have been better. God, what was she thinking of – the creation of a diverting drama.

Dan looked dreadful, she saw this now. His face was pale, his eyes dark. Had she caused this? She no longer had sufficient egotistical belief in her own power to think it could be so.

'Has something happened?' she asked. 'You don't look too good.'

He moved past her to the table with the decanter, the square crystal one her mother had given them. He had not answered her question.

'Is something wrong?' she persisted foolishly.

He was pouring the scotch. He turned to face her. He held

187

out the tumbler. His hand was shaking. Even more foolishly, she commented on this. Asked why.

The glass dropped between them, shattering over the carpet. 'Oh!'

'What's wrong!' he bellowed. 'What's wrong!'

Her gaze left the broken glass and fixed on his eyes. Her heart began to pound again. She'd never known him to be frightening, never considered it a possibility.

'I didn't intend posting that letter,' she said.

'But you did. Why write it at all if you weren't going to send it?' She had never seen him angry like this and yet all the years she'd known him she'd been doing things to provoke such a reaction. His passive, forgiving acceptance of her behaviour in the past had driven her to distraction. Like leaning on a jelly, that's what Nick had said about Marion.

The passing reference to Nick in her thoughts brought a resurgence of anger:

'You shouldn't have criticised my care of Vicky,' she shouted at him. 'But I don't want to bring her into it.'

'But it's Vicky we're talking about. You're turning her into a spoilt brat.'

'It wasn't me who bought her a bicycle and promised her pets.' She was so angry now she wanted to strike him, hit out at his self-righteous posturing. 'You were happy enough to leave her upbringing to me over the past four years,' she threw at him with gross injustice.

'You took her away. And happy! I'm no more happy than you are.'

'What do you mean?'

'You're an unhappy woman, Charlotte, and you always will be. You'll never be satisfied with anything which is why you go round making others as miserable as yourself. You poison everything, including our daughter. No doubt, you've reduced Matthews to a state of despair.'

'Matthews! Why can't you call him Nick?' was all she could find in the way of retaliation in the wake of such vitriol.

'Surely you don't care now that you've left him as well.'

'I didn't,' she faltered. Even now, in the unguarded passion of hatred, she didn't like to admit that she had been left.

'So he left you. Sensible fellow.'

'Stop it,' she screamed. 'Stop it!' Her body had gone into a violent tremble. Her arm went up, but with too much warning, so that he was able to grab hold of her wrist. She stepped forward to keep her balance and her foot crunched over the broken glass.

Her other arm came up, flailing towards him, but again he met the blow before it could reach its target.

They were grappling then. Charlotte writhed in his restraining grip on her arms. Their bodies moved closer, buffeting one another, as if they weren't quite getting it right for the sort of capitulation that happened in films: a sudden pause, a sigh, a kiss. It wasn't going to happen. Both of them were furious but also shocked and surprised at what they were doing. Neither had ever known this sort of physical violence and after a few moments they stopped, standing back from one another, both panting, wide-eyed.

'We've got to do something about this glass,' Charlotte said, crouching down to pick at the larger pieces, but her hand was unsteady and the first bit she touched pierced her finger. Blood ran down into her palm. Dan was delving in his trouser pocket for a handkerchief. He bent down and pressed it round the cut. They got up, both intent on the small wound; Dan still holding the handkerchief against it.

A little sob escaped from Charlotte, nothing to do with the cut.

'Does it hurt?' he enquired, earnestly.

'No.' Another sob.

'I'll go and fetch something. All that stuff you bought when Vicky was falling over a lot – I think it's still upstairs.'

'Don't go.' She was close to weeping, an activity quite alien to her, as Dan knew. Again the look of surprise. The moment was so raw there had to be some comfort on offer. He stepped towards her again and put his arms round her. She fell against him and sobbed into his neck.

'I think we should go to bed,' he said.

Upstairs was cold but she would have shivered anyway. He removed her clothes, then his own, a ritual he'd never performed when they were married.

In the bed, which they'd shared so many nights, he took her in his arms and moved over her. She gazed up at his face then closed her eyes, taking in the smell of him, as unique as a fingerprint. The impossibility of their not being together: the full realisation of this came to her now with his slow, gentle lovemaking, the familiar feel of his skin. He kissed her face but only came to her mouth in the moment that he penetrated her.

It was the first time for as long as she could remember that it seemed extraordinary, this connection of bodies; his rigid shaft moving back and forth within her, strange and wondrous. She would think about it the next day and for days to come, and she hadn't done that for a long time.

She moved her hands down his back and on to his buttocks, pressing him to enter her still further, to make the invasion as great as possible.

They stayed in the bed for a long time. They were quiet for a while, content and happy, wanting to bask in the bliss of their reunion for a little while before it became necessary to talk.

'You'll come back to me?' he asked.

'I should never have left.'

'There'll be no recriminations.'

'Oh, there might. You'd have to be a saint not to.'

'I'm not going to say that things will be different. Neither of us has really changed.'

'No, thank God.'

'I love you!'

'And I you.'

190

Chapter Twenty-Six

'Well, honey-lamb, time for you to pack your bags.' Germaine stood like an aging Amazon, legs planted apart, hands on hips, gazing down at Nick, who was slumped in a chair.

His bourbon-sodden brain registered that he was being dismissed as house guest. He'd quite lost track of how long he'd been there, how·many days, or was it weeks? Most of the time it seemed he'd been alone. Germaine was always out, and after the second or third party when he'd drunk himself legless she'd stopped taking him to any more. She went by herself and the past couple of days or so he'd been vaguely aware of a newcomer in the house, a gangling youth with a brown body that left a powerful vapour trail of after-shave.

'Here,' Germaine said, thrusting an envelope in his direction. 'This'll get you back to Oakland. I always put things back from the place I got 'em. And Nicky boy, you're gonna have to take a hold of yourself. I'd help you if I could, but I can't bear to see you going down like this. It upsets me. It really does. That's why you gotta leave.'

'You're just piqued 'cos I didn't poke you,' he murmured, then smiled to himself at the neatness of the phrase.

'Wha' did you say?'

'Doesn't matter.' He took the envelope from her.

'The shuttle leaves at four thirty. Be on it.' She'd heard what he'd said.

The chauffeur came into the house to fetch him at some time after midday. Germaine was not about when he left. The big man who'd accompanied them to Rodeo Drive was waiting outside, looking very present and for the first time without his dark glasses.

'Your eyes are too close together,' Nick, still wobbly, said as he stepped past him into the car.

The man did not respond, but Nick felt marginally better. He knew he was drunk and had been like it for days. He'd become maudlin. Nobody loved him. Nobody cared. He was a failure. He seemed to remember saying some of this to Germaine at some point during his stay, and still repeating it, out loud, even after it had dawned on him that she was no longer there. People who felt sorry for themselves were boring. He was boring. 'Boring. Boring. Boring.'

The big man sitting next to him in the back of the car gave him a look. He was thinking out loud again, like the old boy with the long silver hair, the wino he'd passed so often in the street in Cambridge on the way from his office to his car. He wondered whether he was still alive, with his silly, smiling face and sudden expletives. Five, six years ago? How long had it been since those wildly successful money-making days in England? It had seemed too small for him then, the UK. He doubted now whether he'd even get a job back in journalism – on a provincial weekly. He was fit for nothing except pouring alcohol down his throat and embarrassing the world at large with his rambling tongue.

'Nice of you to see me off,' he said to the big hulk of flesh beside him. He tried to look him in the eye as he said it and found he could just about manage both eyes if he focused on the point in the middle where the fellow's brows met. He giggled and put his hand out to pat the poor chap's knee. In the next moment his head was being pushed down on to his own knees and his arm was up his back.

At the airport he was manhandled out of the car and hustled to the departures gate. With stubborn indifference to his fate, he feigned greater drunkenness, thinking he might not be allowed on the plane. What did he care? He'd nowhere to go. People were looking, as they do in America, not like England where everyone tries to pretend they're oblivious.

'Come on fellow, you're on your way,' gorilla-face growled at him, the first time he'd spoken.

Somehow, perhaps bribery, he was got on the plane. No more drink came his way during the flight, but then they didn't always have it on these short hops. When they landed at

Oakland he was somewhat more in control and was able to hire a car. He used a credit card, knowing it had no credit left but they didn't always check. Besides, he was still sufficiently compos mentis to go for a big, fast job that cost a lot. If you were going to cheat then do it in style and you were less likely to be suspected.

So he had wheels but still nowhere to go. He sat in the auto compound and took out his diary. He flipped through the pages of telephone numbers, all of them dead to him. He ripped them out, screwed them into a ball and tossed it out of the car window. There was one number left on a separate page, the non-business section, it was the only non-business contact he had in the whole of America. Frances.

The house on the hill, amidst the trees, was so different from Germaine's overstated white mansion. Frances' restrained villa was as much a monument to good taste as the other place was to bad. Nick, still far from sober, somehow managed to manoeuvre the broad car up the narrow driveway only slightly buffeting the mail box as he turned in off the road.

Frances was in. She always was. What a splendid woman she had to be, forever there. But the reception she gave him was cool. At first he thought it must be because he was still so full of booze, the sluggish coursing of alcohol through his veins slurring his speech and disrupting his equilibrium.

She let him into the house and produced black coffee though he would have preferred another slug of whiskey. It was early evening but there was no sign of Leonard, for which he was thankful: that clever Jew with his thinly disguised sense of superiority had always made him feel uncomfortable.

'Surprised to see me?' he said to Frances, who had placed herself in a chair some distance from the sofa where he sat.

'I suppose I am,' she answered.

'Ah well, full of surprises, that's me,' he said.

She didn't respond.

'How are you then?' he said next, beginning to wonder what he had done, searching the muddled filing in his brain to try and remember whether he'd actually made the pass at her that he'd wanted to the last time they'd been alone together.

'Nick, I received a letter from Charlotte this morning,' she said.

193

'That's nice,' he said. 'How is she?' He didn't know what he was saying, what he was thinking. The mention of Charlotte, the first time out loud in he wasn't sure how long, had a strange, numbing effect upon him.

'I would say she's lonely and uncertain,' Frances responded, choosing these words with slow deliberation. 'She says that you've parted but I gather it's more by default than proper agreement.'

Abruptly Nick stood up.

Frances visibly recoiled in her chair.

'You haven't contacted her for two months, she says.'

'She's not on the phone. She hasn't got a phone,' he said, and it seemed so thin, even to him, that neither of them bothered to expand on so lame an excuse, if excuse it was, and for what? Had he run away from Charlotte, was that how it seemed, how it was? He sank down again. His mind was clearing now.

'I wanted to sort things out,' he said, quietly.

'It might have been better,' Frances commented, coldly.

'I don't mean with Charlotte,' he said. 'I didn't think . . . it wasn't like that. We argued a lot.' Random thoughts voiced. Had he really ever thought that he'd lost her?

'I gather from what she says in her letter that she and Vicky are living in somewhat straitened circumstances.'

At this he laughed. Frances' expression of disapproval deepened.

'You really are a bastard, aren't you,' she said. 'And God knows what you think you're doing coming here.' She was really quite angry now.

'I do apologise,' he said, standing up again, this time to leave. It was no use. For whatever reason he had come to Frances it mattered not any more. Perhaps there had been no clear reason other than the vague, befuddled desire for some sort of sympathy.

He strode towards the door. Frances remained where she was sitting. If she hadn't been so angry with him, not just for the careless way he'd abandoned Charlotte but for being what he was, second-rate, the usurper of Dan, a spoiler, a wrecker, she might have stopped him. He was still too drunk to drive.

She heard the sound of his car, the excessive engine revs. She got up then and went to the window. Daylight had gone but the evening sky was clear and bright and she caught a glimpse of the expensive-looking vehicle as it churned up the end of her drive. Evidently he'd sorted out the business problems he'd hinted at a few months back.

'What the hell!' Nick said out loud as he sped down the hill. He threw back his head, laughing in despair. The yellow cab turning out of a side road would have been easily seen if he'd been looking. He hit it side on, his head thrown forward and through the windshield in the slow motion of a split-second disaster. The steering wheel jammed under his ribcage, holding him, pinioned like a ghoulish parody of a ship's figurehead.

'It's raining,' he thought, in the moment before passing out and the cab's fare screaming at the spectacle of blood pouring down his face.

Chapter Twenty-Seven

Frances met Charlotte at the airport twenty-four hours later. They embraced, the sense of tragedy thick between them.

'How is he?'

'Not good, Lottie.'

They walked in silence to Frances' car.

'Tell me the worst,' Charlotte said as they drove out.

'It's his face,' Frances replied. 'Be prepared for it. He went through the windshield.'

'How does it look?'

'It's very swollen at the moment,' Frances paused. 'Lottie it's not the facial injuries that are the real problem, he's badly hurt internally.'

Charlotte gazed straight ahead at the oncoming headlights. She felt dreadful, a fraud. Frances' evident difficulty in explaining Nick's condition made her feel worse. If the circumstances had been different she could have asked the question: will he live? The thought had been with her ever since Dan's telephone call to the studio: the news of Nick's accident via Frances via Dan, only hours after she'd thought it all settled. Why this, now? The timing was unbelievable. She'd tried very hard not to think the dreadful selfish thoughts but they were there, persistently. If Nick survived, disfigured, disabled – God, she'd be stuck with him for the rest of her life.

On the plane she had tried to imagine what it would be like if it was she who had been in the car crash and Nick who had been summoned: would she want the thing to go on? But it didn't help. The hypothetical notion that she wouldn't want his pity couldn't provide any justification for her own desire to be rid of him.

'Is Vicky all right?' Frances asked.

'Yes, she's with Dan.'

Frances glanced at her.

The strangeness of it all. The sudden changes. Only a few days ago her energy had been bound up in the battle to prevent Dan from having Vicky, and now she had given her over, asked him to take her. Vicky had been full of it, relentless chatter about a pony, a beeline for the bike the moment Charlotte had delivered her to the house. She was spoilt. Dan was right.

'Give me a kiss, darling,' she'd said to her before leaving, but Vicky had pretended not to hear, and the ground was too delicate and new with Dan for any show of insistence.

He'd come out to the car with her, his face full of concern.

'I hope everything will be all right,' he said. 'Don't worry about Vicky. Let me know if there's anything I can do – if Nick needs anything to be done over here.'

She wanted to throw herself into his arms and sob on his shoulder as she had the previous night, but it wouldn't have been seemly. Inappropriate, would be Dan's word, and she had to play by somebody's rules, having none of her own.

'Would you like me to contact Marion and Paul?'

'Yes, I suppose they should be informed.'

Dan, of course, would think of all the right things. It hadn't crossed her mind that there were other people who needed to be told, and even now the inclusion of those others ruffled her possessive instinct.

Outwardly her attitude remained still and calm, maybe too calm, as she sat in the car beside Frances, the awful, guilt-laden muddle teeming in her brain. It was the kindness and sympathy, that's what she found the most unbearable. And supposing when they got to the hospital Nick had died: where to concentrate her mind, on the good or the bad?

Were there any good memories in America or only the bickering and bitterness and that inexplicable resentment that can grow from nowhere, feeding on itself? She supposed it was a combination of many things, jealousy, but not the sort you could make anything of, jealousy of attention elsewhere on business deals, getting in with the right people; exasperation with forever having to be the one waiting rather than waited for; and disappointment, more than anything, disappointment, because it had all started out so differently, with such promise.

Running off with Nick had been the greatest excitement of her life. It had lifted her from her own dullness, which had nothing to do with Dan. It was a deadness inside her which had taken hold round the time Vicky was born. Then the rot had set in. Motherhood had never suited her, much as she adored Vicky, staying at home and doing it all herself had been as bad as being stuck with any job you were no good at, only this job was twenty-four hours a day, seven days a week and with no get out clause. Confidence, of which she'd never had even half as much as others seemed to think, had drained away, the inexorable trickle going on for years until there was hardly a drop left and doing something about it was just about impossible. Then along came Nick, a man who wore jewellery and fancy shoes and whose grammar was suspect. But he had a sexy neck and was surprisingly perceptive. More surprisingly still, he fancied her, and at a time when she didn't fancy herself one bit, so that when he had told her that they had fallen in love she'd agreed, chosen to believe that it was so. The upheaval he offered was too immediately enticing for denial.

A set of oncoming headlights approached with blinding brightness. Frances cursed and said it was no wonder people got killed on the roads, finishing the sentence abruptly, evidently regretting the choice of phrase.

Charlotte's sense of fraudulence stung her anew. Nick dying, dead. She turned her face to the passenger-side window, as if Frances might catch sight of her thoughts. Surely there must have been moments of something in America, some residue from that mad joy so faded in memory . . . sitting in the passenger seat of a car driven by Nick, gazing out at the passing countryside on their way back from skiing in Squaw Valley. It must have been the first year they were there, in America. Two, or was it three days, they'd spent on the ski slopes. Late in the season. It had been hot. Just the two of them. Vicky had been at school.

All the way there Nick had been in a mood of aggression, driving too fast, taking risks with the traffic. The more she asked him to be careful the worse it got, as if he was doing it

198

deliberately to frighten her. She wanted him to get caught by the police. It would have given her satisfaction.

They'd reached the snow, which had come late that year, late and thick on the ground; and he'd refused to stop and put chains on the car, even though she'd got to begging stage. She'd been terrified, slithering about in that great soft car, but he'd seemed intoxicated by her fear. The bastard. God, she'd hated him for it.

It had carried on into the next day, the fight between them, so that she wouldn't speak to him and then he'd used this to get really mean, picking arguments over nothing, just to top up the aggression, knowing she wouldn't be able to hold her tongue for long once it really got going.

She'd done her best, though. The day had dawned bright with warm sunshine, sparkling off the snow like diamonds. She remembered sitting beside him in the chairlift and hating him for spoiling it all, the peace and tranquillity of the place, so out of reach for them. She'd even wondered whether it might be possible to push him off his side of the chair so that he'd fall down one of the ravines spanned by the lift's cable, fall down and break his neck.

They went high that day, up to the slopes at the very top where the snow was always better late season. There weren't many other skiers about. The sun was burning up there, really hot. Nick went tearing off ahead of her and she thought to lose him for the day, get away by herself; but maybe she wanted the aggravation as much as he because she kept watching for him, following on, ready with a set of crushing phrases she'd been putting together all night.

Then she thought she had lost him – and herself. She couldn't work out where she was or see her route down to the bottom of the lift. She'd gone off the main runs and into a lightly wooded area. The air smelt as clean as bath salts. She breathed in deeply and told herself to enjoy what was there, but it wasn't nice, being lost. Others had disappeared in these mountains and not been found until the following spring.

Mild panic had begun to grip her though she'd only been off course for a matter of minutes, but long ones in such circumstances. Then Nick appeared from above her, turning through the trees. He must have been down to the bottom of the slope and up again on the lift.

He reached her at speed, stopping very abruptly right by her, showering her with the soft snow that had settled round the trees.

She snapped at him, angry with relief 'Why couldn't you have waited!'

An evil smile came into his face.

He was breathless from turning through the trees. He flung his arms round her and they fell over into the snow, ski-bindings springing off.

'Come on,' he said, catching his breath. 'I want to do it in the snow.'

'Someone will see,' she hissed, her body flipping on like a light switch, that sudden sweet ache.

'We can't,' she moaned, 'Not in ski suits.' But his hand had plunged down the half open zip of her salopette.

He made her come then slowed the pace, kissing her.

'What about you?' she whispered.

'I'll catch up with you later,' he said 'you sexy bitch.'

They lay there for a few more minutes, the snow a wonderfully cool intervention in the heat from the sun.

'We mustn't be so horrid to one another,' she said. 'We must be more careful.'

He started to kiss her again.

'I like you horrid,' he said. 'I love you for it.' And there was nothing like being told you were loved, especially when it wasn't said often.

His hand went down her again, this time parting the zip to the end, exposing her, but she didn't care, maybe half wanted a stranger to see, though they wouldn't come near, people didn't. And this time she got to him as well, feeling his hardness then letting it free. He pushed snow into her as he rolled on top of her. The sensation was incredible, that split-second plunging cold.

'No more horrid then,' he said when they were done but still weak and panting. 'Not while we're here.'

'Not ever,' she said.

'Don't be so boring,' he said. But she wasn't going to be caught like that.

And Nick could be as nice as it was possible to be, and had been the rest of that day and the next, so that they'd floated about the slopes lovers, with that magical togetherness that cuts off mating creatures from the rest of the world. Each had the capacity for romance, more than most, but they'd expended too little time and energy on it until they lost the way of the trick because neither wanted to be in the weaker position of giving more than the other.

Had that been the last time it had really worked? Charlotte was still gazing out across the darkened landscape, unable to see anything properly and not focused to take it in even if she had. Her eyes were damp. She'd learnt all about it with Nick, the way to stoke up a fire with anger; but it was no good trying to think of him in that way now; it only confused things, selective memories of what had been too spasmodic. She wondered whether she'd done this over Dan, during the last few months, distance lending dangerous enchantment because you'd lost sight of the little things that had turned you off?

She wasn't convincing herself. Logic had never proved much use to her. She wanted Dan. In huge, aching waves, she wanted him and not Nick.

They were nearly at the hospital, the special unit where Nick had been transferred a few hours after the accident. Leonard was paying. It had taken the admissions staff very little time to establish that Nick had no insurance, no credit, no cash. This was a side to America that Frances found abhorrent. Born and bred within a welfare state, she couldn't accept the contradiction of a nation where outwardly everyone was so extravagantly solicitous yet municipally uncaring. She and Leonard had sat down with a calculator and worked out the price of a baby: the cost of the operation that had a less than even chance of being successful; the aftercare; the likelihood of further surgery. Their insurance didn't cover infertility, frustration, despair. Everything that happened these days brought Frances back to the same nagging obsession: even a car crash. Accident-hospital-doctors. Doctors telling her that her tubes were blocked.

She parked the car and switched off the engine. Charlotte turned to her in the sudden quiet.

'You know I've been wishing him dead,' she said.

201

The awfulness of such a statement engulfed them both.

'You don't mean that,' Frances said, because what else could she say.

'I do,' Charlotte cried out. 'I can't bear the dishonesty. Flying to the bedside. All the sympathy and kindness. Twenty-four hours ago I was in bed with Dan. Everything was right again.'

Charlotte's honesty had always been appalling, but she punished herself with it more than others.

Frances reached across and touched her arm. She didn't know what to say, recognising that her friend's agony was far worse than would have been simple grief. Poor Lottie, everything in life always had to be more complicated for her. It was the curse of her nature, this contrary manipulation of tragedy. If she had been unable to conceive, the longing for a child would have been twisted up in some other sort of paranoia. It all had to do with her self-image as a bad person, and that, as the psychiatrists would say, went back to her childhood and the grisly death of her father. For a moment Frances felt almost comfortable with her own straightforward misfortune. She squeezed Charlotte's arm.

'Come on,' she said. 'Stop feeling so guilty. It won't help.' Her voice was very kind. 'You've got to be grown up about this.' She might have been talking to Vicky, though in the child there had never been the same exposure of raw anguish, that aspect of Charlotte which had always been so disarming.

Chapter Twenty-Eight

Paul stood beside his mother in the crematorium chapel. He was deeply embarrassed by the way she was carrying on, weeping copiously into a large white handkerchief that must once have been his father's.

They'd been waiting about in this wretched place for what seemed like half the morning; first of all in a cramped little room full of snivelling strangers, who'd been put in there by mistake, though it was he and Mum who got moved to another, identical cupboard. There was a vase of plastic flowers on the windowsill and a pile of out-of-date parish magazines: the Brownies had made £57.09 at their Christmas bazaar and the money was to be spent on three saplings for waste ground next to the scout hut. The vicar's wife had planted a tree at the old people's home. Paul felt beset by forestry.

Marion, begging him not to fiddle, had called him away from the window, but not before he'd seen that woman, his father's wife getting out of one of the cars.

He stepped back, out of view, and sat down next to his mother. It was only recently he'd begun to think about marriages, why people married the people they did. He couldn't see that his parents had ever had anything in common, but he could see why his father had gone for Charlotte. She reminded him a bit of Stace, not in looks but just in the way he thought she was, sort of stroppy, difficult, unpredictable. Stace had been very peculiar of late, moody. He'd let her come to the house a few times while Marion was at the hospital. A quick one in his bedroom, her all nervous in case his mother came back early, not that he really cared if she did, after all, what would she do about it? Stacey was funny, though, saying that she loved him when he knew she didn't have a clue what that meant, and then getting abusive when he wouldn't say it back to her. He'd begun to enjoy it, this game they played, although he didn't feel the same about himself any more – or her.

He could imagine Charlotte going through the same routine with his father, who, he supposed maybe felt the same as him about it, cold but attracted, by the sex and the strop. And Dan Lovell, Charlotte's first husband, Paul identified his former self with that poor old sod, serious-faced, that lonely look about him. He was a decent enough bloke, but a mug, a sucker for all the rest of it. He'd come round to the house a few times after Dad had left. Paul had resented him a bit then, though he wasn't quite sure why, maybe only because he'd wanted to help.

They hadn't seen him for ages, he and Mum, and then he'd turned up to tell them about the accident in America, and Mum had started sniffing and swallowing, in front of him, as if she still had the right. Then she'd broken down completely and told him about the tree and the police and Ruby being in hospital, as if the whole lot was somehow connected and nothing more than a package of misery solely for her benefit. Christ alive, she made such a meal of it all, like she was now, positively dehydrating herself with so much snivelling.

At last they'd got into the chapel. There'd been some hitch with the electrics, the rollers that took the coffins away, so that there were people hanging about all over the place outside, little clusters of mourners, keeping themselves to themselves, anxious not to trespass into other deaths.

Death. Ruby would have fought it. Paul reckoned she'd gone out scratching and clawing at life. Even now there had to be a delay, as if she'd reached down, or probably up in her case, to tamper with the mechanism that rolled her into the furnace. The notion made him want to laugh. Good old, bad old Gran, always causing trouble, being an embarrassment. Even when this bit was over it was going to carry on. There were about ten people present, he and Mum, Mum's sisters who they never saw, their husbands, the vicar, someone else, and Charlotte and Dad. How were that lot all going to stand round together back at the house eating ham sandwiches?

Though how Dad could stand at all seemed unlikely. He looked bloody awful. It had been a shock, seeing him, his face like that. He didn't think Marion had noticed, not properly, she'd probably throw another trembler when she did, grabbing at anything to hand to be miserable about. He'd never hear the end of it. He'd got to get away. Do something. Escape. It wasn't fair at his age, to have to put up with the tragedies of older generations.

'I don't think we really have to go,' Charlotte had said three days earlier in California.

'I want to,' Nick told her.

It was a month since the accident, the longest and shortest Charlotte had ever known. Backwards and forwards to and from the hospital, every day. It was only the time-demanding routine of it that had kept her going. Nick, withdrawn behind the mask of scars, had been lucky, the doctors and nurses told her, the internal injuries far less severe than they might have been.

That his luck had all run out in every other aspect of his life became clear during the second week when the time she spent at his bedside began to include talking, prohibited in the preceeding days by the stitches round his mouth.

'Why didn't you tell me?' she asked him. 'For God's sake, I had a right to know.'

'I put it off too long,' he murmured, his mouth barely opening.

'Did anyone else know?' Funny the way she referred to the financial tragedy in the past tense, as if it was possible to have only one misfortune at a time.

'Ruby.'

'Ruby? Why Ruby?'

'I think she guessed.' Was this an indictment of herself for not guessing?

She told Frances, at whose house she had a bed during that month. 'I should have realised, shouldn't I?'

'Perhaps.'

'He told Ruby, Marion's mother, wicked old Ruby. Did you know he slept with her when he was married to Marion. Did I tell you that?'

It was late at night, the end of the second week. They were

loading the dishwasher in Frances' kitchen. Leonard had gone to bed.

'No, I think I would have remembered that one,' Frances said. 'But why on earth did he tell you?'

'I guessed,' Charlotte laughed bitterly. 'I'm all right at guessing that sort of thing.'

'You can't be sure, then?'

'Oh yes. I made him admit it. I didn't mind. How could I? It was before my time.'

Frances sighed in affectionate exasperation.

'I know,' Charlotte said. 'I know what you're thinking. What sort of a man sleeps with his mother-in-law. Not the sort you'd marry, but then I've never been like you, more's the pity. I don't think you've ever known how much like you I've always tried to be. What would Frances do? What would Frances chose? Would Frances approve?'

'I'd no idea,' Frances said, evidently taken aback by this sudden sycophantic confession. 'And I don't believe you,' she added, recovering.

'You should. You're the most wonderful role model to work to. A point of reference that's kept me sane on and off over the years, even when we were at school.'

'I still don't believe you. I've always thought you had a greater appetite for life than I've ever had.'

'By that you mean that I'm never satisifed, always casting about for something new.'

'Restless, yes.'

'Inconstant.'

'But constantly so.'

'Constantly so,' Charlotte echoed, suddenly more thoughtful.

'Lottie, have you decided what to do?'

'What would you do?'

'I thought we'd already established that we're different people.'

'I know what you would do, that's the trouble,' Charlotte said, finding a stray teaspoon to put in the machine.

They looked at one another.

'You know you can stay here for as long as you like,' Frances said.

'Just until Nick is out of hospital, but thank you. I don't know how I would have managed without you and Leonard.'

'And after that? When Nick is better?'

'I don't know. I can't think that far. I must get home to Vicky soon, Vicky and,' she hesitated, a fortnight of trying not to think too much about Dan but finding herself remembering, replaying in her mind, even when she was sitting by the bedside, most of all then.

She swallowed hard. Their conversation up until now had been almost bantering, deliberately so.

'I'll have to see,' she continued, on a high, brittle note. 'I'll have to wait and see what's best.'

The telephone began to ring in the other room. Frances went to answer it.

'It's for you,' she called. 'Vicky.'

'Hi, Mom.'

'Hello, darling.'

'Why're you crying?'

'I'm not.'

'You sound as if you are.'

'What are you doing?'

'Talking to you.'

'Oh, Vicky. How are you darling?'

'Okay I guess. Daddy won't give me the same pocket money I usually get. He says it's too much. Mom, I don't think it's fair. Will you tell him?'

'How's school?'

'Boring.'

'How's Daddy?'

'Okay. Mom, you will tell him about the pocket money?'

'Vicky darling, please don't go on about it. Don't you want to know how Nick is?'

'There's something else, Mom, Daddy makes me go to bed too early. Will you tell him that I don't have to go until 9.30.'

'Can I speak to Daddy?'

The receiver was thrown down.

Charlotte's chest had tightened, her heart began to pound.

'Lottie?'

'Dan?'

'How are things?'

'Nick's improving.'

'Good. I'm pleased to hear it.'

'Is Vicky all right? She seems disgruntled about pocket money and bedtime.'

'She's all right, Lottie, she's fine.'

'Detoxicating her, are you?' Charlotte said, remembering the words of their fierce and wonderful row.

'Just a bit,' Dan answered.

There was a pause, the line so clear they could hear each other breathing.

'Nothing's changed here,' he said next. 'Not since we last spoke.'

Charlotte could hear the question in this, the underlying uncertainty now that so much had changed.

'Dan, I've got to wait until Nick is better. As soon as he's out of hospital I'm coming home.'

'Let's hope it's a speedy recovery.'

'Yes.'

'You know my feelings?'

'Yes, they're the same as mine. Vicky's listening is she?'

'How did you guess?' a sigh, a slight chuckle, then, 'but I don't see why that should stop me from saying that I love you.' This was said quite loudly, then Vicky being heard to groan in the background.

'We'd better finish this conversation,' he said. 'Vicky will be late for school.'

'Of course. It's early with you.'

'We'll ring again soon.'

'I miss you both.'

'I'm glad to hear it.'

There were more calls but that was the one Charlotte held on to. At the end of the third week Dan rang with the news that Ruby had died. Nick might have stayed in hospital longer but he was determined to attend the funeral. The degree to which he was affected by Ruby's death came as a surprise to Charlotte. She'd never really understood the relationship. Ruby had infiltrated their life during the early months when it might have been expected she would feel hostility and resentment towards the pair of them. She'd turned up, out of the blue, made herself irresistible, friendly as could be towards Charlotte, who could see she was wicked but couldn't help liking her all the same or perhaps because that was when she'd got the idea, she couldn't remember how, that the mother-in-law/son-in-law relationship had been transgressed. Lasciviously she'd taxed Nick with the notion when they were in bed. It excited her, the unthinkableness of it, and she would have been disappointed if it hadn't been true. What she'd never realised was that Nick had been the love of Ruby's life and in a way Nick had loved her too.

Three days before they were due to fly home for the funeral he discharged himself from the hospital. Charlotte went to fetch him and as soon as they were outside the staring began, those shocked glances. Charlotte thought of the irritation with which she'd noted in the past the vanity that had kept him overlong in bathrooms both sides of the Atlantic. She stared back at the starers, shaming them for their curiosity, their revulsion, and pity.

'Jeez – poor guy,' she heard a woman say.

Nick said nothing. Nothing at all. He'd closed in on himself completely.

They went back to Frances' house but the conversations Charlotte had had there during the previous three weeks seemed to hang in the air: those conversations with Frances that were like communing with her conscience.

'I think it might be an idea to get away for a couple of days, before we go back to England,' she told her friend.

Maybe Frances understood. They'd never had to spell things out to one another.

'Borrow the car and go to Yosemite. It's still out of season up there. Quiet.'

'Not so many people to stare?'

'If you like. Does that bother you very much?'

That Frances asked whether it was she who minded the staring was indicative of the insight that made Charlotte want to get away. Nick appeared to be beyond caring. It seemed he'd set his mind to attending Ruby's funeral as if there was nothing else to concern him either before or after this finite event.

It was a four-hour drive up state to Yosemite, four hours in which Charlotte might have been travelling alone. The freeway was largely empty of other traffic, the landscape open, thinly used, except for the rolling hills a few miles north of San Francisco where acres of anorexic windmills stretched as far as the eye could see. Charlotte had read about this energy-harnessing project but never seen it before. The sight was strange, almost surreal, the sort of thing you wanted to share with someone else, but Nick was asleep on the back seat.

Don Quixote, the setting for a modern-day version, that's what it was. The thought came into her mind as something to be toyed with, a piece of superficiality upon which to dwell for a little: an escapist thought. An impractical idealist. Don Quixote. Lucky, lucky Don Quixote. The man in the back of the car had woken up and was watching her in the rear view mirror.

As Frances had said, Yosemite was quiet, hardly a soul there this time of year. It was a dark, oppressively still place. Huge trees amidst black rocks that dwarfed everything. Small cabins painted camouflage green nestled in woody places. The distant roar of falling water, omnipresent like pink noise. Charlotte had parked the car and walked the couple of hundred yards to the registration office. She breathed in deeply, sniffing the clarity of the air, the clean tang of pine needles; but there was no joy in her. Appreciation of the elements, even at their most magnificent, was not possible. All of it was out of her reach, blocked off by the heaviness within her, as immovable as the massively proportioned landscape into which she had brought them.

She rented a room in one of the larger, two-storey buildings that were a compromise between hotel and cabin, though camouflaged in the same murky olive used on everything man-made up here. The light was beginning to go, for which she was instinctively thankful, then sickened: was this how it was going to be, a twilight existence, waiting for darkness, seeking out shadows in which to hide?

A rack of postcards stood on the registration desk, glorious vistas of nature in the raw, teeming waterfalls, brutal escarpments. It was a place for wonderment with those huge, insurmountable rocks, breathtakingly grotesque. She half turned away then took out a dollar and bought one of the cards, a black and white photo of the bull-nosed El Capitan rock, a mass of scarred granite, awesome, terrible, challenging.

She knew she was indulging her despair in symbolism, but

why shouldn't she? The postcard in her bag, she felt a small surge of defiance as she strode back to the car.

Nick allowed himself to be installed in the room. His internal injuries prevented him from carrying anything. He lay on the bed while Charlotte removed their things from an overnight bag.

'Are you hungry?' she asked.

'No.'

'A drink then?'

'Don't be ridiculous.' His tone was nasty.

Charlotte held back the sort of response that would have come automatically three months ago.

'I'm sorry,' she said instead. 'I forgot.'

'For God's sake, don't start apologising. That was Marion's game.'

'Game?'

'It doesn't matter.' He sighed, wearily.

'Have you taken the pills?'

'Yes,' he snapped.

'Do you want to go to sleep?'

'So that you can go out on your own, you mean.'

'No,' she protested. 'I just thought – your first day out of hospital.'

'Some day!' he said. 'Stuck in the back of a car.'

'We're here now,' she said, hearing appeasement in her voice.

'The bloody back of beyond. Why the hell did you choose this place?'

'It's quiet. Fresh air,' she said, feeling as if she were telling a lie.

'Not so many people to gawp,' he said.

'If you like.' She was beginning to feel prickly.

'I don't like. I've got to live with it, haven't I? I might as well get used to the gawpers sooner rather than later.'

It came into her head to reply with I've got to live with it too, but more as a question than a statement.

'Don't make it worse than it is,' she said, in a pleading sort of way.

She hadn't eaten all day but the recent years of dieting had made it possible for her to go long periods without food. All the same, she was hungry, but didn't feel able to leave him alone in the room. It was as if she had to keep watch over him because if anything happened to him now she wouldn't be able to live with herself ever again.

The room had only one bed, a narrow double. The rest of the furniture was equally mean, two hard, upright chairs, a small table by the window. It was a suitable setting for them now, sparse, without comfort.

'Do you need any help getting undressed?' she asked him.

'No. I can manage.'

She picked up her nightdress and went into the bathroom where the only generous fitting was the mirror. She gazed at her pale face, the strain clear and unblemished. She would have wept then if she'd thought the dividing wall with the bedroom was thick enough to keep in the sound.

When she had undressed and put on the nightie she went back. Nick had turned out the light by the bed and she had to fumble her way across the room. She slid under the sheets beside him and lay very still. His body smelled stale, hospital soap. It was three months since they'd shared a bed: was it possible he might expect her to do something? The thought spread through her body, the relevant zones suddenly stimulated. Her mind ached – she felt like a degenerate.

She fell asleep thinking of Vicky and Dan, picturing them side by side, smiling, standing at the front door of the house in England, like a building society advertisement, and in the half-conscious zone between being awake and being asleep she still managed to deceive herself.

Nick stayed in bed the whole of the following day, sleeping most of the time. Charlotte went out and drove round the valley, not really seeing any of it. She pulled off one of the tracks and stopped the car in a small clearing, there was no one else about. She got out and wandered a little way into the trees. High above her their branches glistened, pearls of rain from the night suspended like jewels catching the light. The ever present roar from unseen torrents pressed in on her. Underfoot the ground was springy with countless layers of pine needles. It was cold. Her breath showed like smoke. The trees were dripping on her. She went back to the car, shivering. Why had she come to this dark, dank, brooding territory, although

212

would anywhere else have seemed any different?

She sat in the car for some while, loath to go back to the room and the man in it. How could it be her fault, any of it, and yet she felt so wretchedly guilty. All she wanted was someone, anyone, to take her by the hand and tell her she could leave, that the place she should be was that building society Utopia with Dan and Vicky.

She was startled out of this shivering reverie by a sudden tapping on the car window, just inches from her shoulder. Her head jerked round and a man's face peered at her, so close his runny nose was all but squashed against the glass.

Panic erupted in her. She fumbled for the ignition. The car lurched forward. Careless of the poor assailant's proximity, she rammed the gear shift into reverse. A horrible graunching sound came from somewhere near her feet. She didn't look to see the man, not even in the mirror, as she veered back on to the track and tore off, the car bouncing and jarring.

She lost her way but eventually found herself approaching the cabins and guest houses from a different direction. They all looked so very much the same, painted their drab green, it was like a military encampment.

She ran up the steps to the room, opening the door with too much force so that it banged against the wall. Nick was staring at her. Had she alarmed him? The distorting disfigurement caused by his wounds precluded discernible expression. God, from one nightmare to another.

She shut the door and leant back against it for a moment. There was no escape.

The night before the flight home she again stood in Frances' kitchen. A few minutes earlier she'd been talking to Vicky over the transatlantic line.

'I'm not going to let anything part us again for a very long time,' she said to her friend. 'I can't bear it F, it's like having a limb torn off. You've no idea how awful it is, to be parted from your child.'

'No, I haven't,' Frances said.

'Oh, I'm sorry. Why do I say these things?'

'It doesn't matter.'

'Oh, it does F, what are you going to do? Adopt? We've hardly talked about it, have we? It's all been about me and my problems.'

'That's the way it's always been. You talk. I listen.'

'Don't you get fed up with being such a saint?'

'Don't be silly. I'm just one of those people who other people tell things.'

The thought that there were others who confided in Frances caused Charlotte an unexpected surge of jealousy, just like when they were girls, at school, in the Guides. Everyone had always wanted Frances as their friend. It was instinctive because she was that rare thing, a good person, without meanness or side, even as a child.

'Leonard doesn't want to adopt,' she said.

'Oh, for goodness sake! Make him. If I were you I'd just go ahead. He'd have to go along with it once you'd started.'

'Oh Lottie, I've never been able to bend people to my will the way you have. I lack your single-minded determination. You've always been able to make things happen. I envy you that.'

This came as a revelation to Charlotte. Thirty years they'd known one another and never once had it occurred to her that Frances could possibly envy the trail of frustration and mess that was how she thought of her life. She'd always assumed the envy to be exclusively hers: Frances' popularity; Frances' academic success; a career that had taken her to America; marriage to a first rate man with the added cachet of being Jewish. Whatever Frances had done, it had always seemed enviable, and all the time she was gazing back and somehow seeing Charlotte's erratic progress through life as making things happen.

Oddly, it left a void, knowing this. Her blueprint for living, idealised as it had been, was suddenly gone. Frances, sad and barren. Her dear friend, but neither saint nor icon, just another troubled woman in pursuit of happiness and finding it wasn't attainable. The difference between them was that Frances had more readily accepted the inevitability of it all.

Oh dear, these were heavy times. There'd been occasions when she was bored, Charlotte had thought she might have a taste for tragedy. Now that she'd got it, the bad happening, she couldn't think of anything more lovely than the peaceful, dull and ordered life of her previous existence.

214

Chapter Twenty-Nine

The funeral done, the ham sandwiches eaten, there was nothing else to delay Charlotte's reunion with Vicky, still with Dan since the two days which had elapsed between the flight back from America and Ruby's cremation.

The collected mourners stood about in Marion's house, cups of tea in their hands, muted sipping and sympathising. The shock of Mick's appearance had provided some diversion from the dutiful grief, the only people truly suffering the loss being Marion, whose nose was red raw, and, surprisingly still, Nick. In his weakened state, exacerbated by the long flight home and the attendant ordeal of staring strangers, he was now pitifully emotional. He was unable to exchange more than a monosyllable with anyone and there had been a moment when Charlotte had suspected tears in his already blood-shot eyes.

Her reaction to this was hard-hearted, recoiling. She felt mean for it, but couldn't help herself. She was no good at pity. She wanted to remove herself and Nick from the wake as soon as was decent; get him back to Bateman Street then go to Vicky and Dan. Ruby's family were not the sort of people she cared for, they had the appearance of poor diets, rotten skins, straggly hair, their Birmingham accents, grating, their conversation inadequate; and they were making a meal of the death, assuaging their guilt with viscid comment on 'the next life – up there' and the suffering being over. Sniff. Hankies out. The only one of them not cast in the same mould was Paul, who she'd not seen for several years. He was very tall now. Thin, but not a bad shape. He didn't look like either of his parents, his face long and narrow, different to Ruby's lot because he had the appearance of intelligence. He looked the serious, studious type, but joyless. Charlotte observed him observing his gathered relatives and thought she detected the same glances of distaste, even contempt. He'd shown no sign of distress at the sight of his father. That was strange. In contrast, Marion had been horribly upset, which had been embarrassing all round, somehow inappropriate.

'Trouble always comes in threes,' she'd wept, without elaborating as to the third, and nobody was going to ask her.

Driving back to Cambridge, Charlotte began to feel nervous, excited. Not long now. Six o'clock she was due to collect Vicky, though the prospect seemed far greater than just that; and because the anticipation made her feel bright, she wanted to talk.

'It didn't go so badly,' she said to the silent Nick, slumped in the passenger seat beside her. 'And nobody was iffy about me being there. They might have been. After all, it was the first time I'd met them.'

'What does it bloody matter?' he murmured.

'I'm sorry?'

'Everything has to be about you, doesn't it?' he said, more strongly.

'Of course not. I was just saying they were all right.'

'All right!' he scoffed, bitterly. 'Right now they'll be picking you to pieces.'

'Why?' Charlotte said, taken aback by this unnecessary vitriol.

'Because they could all see that you're a stuck up bitch who was looking down on them as if they were a bunch of toe-rags.'

Charlotte bit her lip not to respond. Nick was tyrannising her, had been for the past week, and she couldn't fight back. Her hands were tied.

'Of course, they'll be loving this neat little twist of fate,' he went on, indicating his face. 'No more than deserved. They'll enjoy being able to hate us and feel sorry for us at the same time. We should have told them we'd gone bust as well, it would have made their day!'

'Please,' Charlotte pleaded. She didn't want a row. She didn't want to give him the chance of getting round to the

216

future, of saying something that would be undeniable, that would lock her in.

He went quiet. Maybe he didn't want to provoke the undeniable either, he couldn't risk it. She got him home. The flat was cold. She suggested he should go to bed and sleep off the jet lag. He didn't argue, but looked at her in the way a child or a dog will gaze at the person who is leaving them behind.

'Time to fetch Vicky,' she said, smiling.

He didn't respond.

'I'll make up a camp bed for her in here,' she continued, casting about for a suitable space in the living room. 'Perhaps I can borrow something more substantial from Audrey.' She was talking too much. It was difficult to get away, to leave him.

'You'd better go then,' he said, flatly.

'Yes. Will you be all right?'

'I expect so.'

'All right then.' Her heart had started to thud.

Outside she felt as if she'd made an escape. It was the first time for some days that she'd got away from him.

She drove at great speed to the house, her house, slowing only when she turned into the lane, as if to savour by delay the moment of arrival.

She reached the end of the drive. Dan's car wasn't there, but maybe he'd put it in the garage. Her wheels crunched over the gravel – she loved that sound, it was part of the whole, like the dipping shape of the front lawns, the Virginia creeper that clothed the house in summer, the woody smell in the hallway.

She rang the bell at the front door, not quite able, as yet, to go round to the back, the way she'd always entered the house. She could hear someone coming then the clicking of the latch.

The door opened and a woman of indeterminate middle age stood there, looking out at her as if she could be selling encyclopaedias or punting for the Jehovah's Witnesses.

'I've come for Vicky,' Charlotte said, still managing to smile.

The woman still looked enquiring.

'I'm her mother.'

'Ah, I'll fetch her things,' the woman said. 'I'm Mr Lovell's

217

lady what does,' she added. There seemed to be a touch of hostility in her manner.

'May I come in?' Charlotte said, a wave of resentment taking hold of her.

'Right you are,' the woman said, standing wide to let her pass. 'If you'd like to go into the lounge I'll go and see where little Vick's got to.'

'Is my,' Charlotte hesitated. 'Is Dan here?'

'Mr Lovell had to go to London today.'

'Oh. I see.' The balloon deflated.

Obediently, Charlotte went through to the drawing room.

'Mummy!' Vicky flew across the room.

'Darling!'

They hugged and kissed one another.

'What have you brought me?'

'Nothing, darling. It wasn't a holiday.'

'Oh,' Vicky said, as if her balloon had just lost its air as well.

'Anyway, you shouldn't be so avaricious.'

'Still don't know what that means.'

'Wanting things all the time. Aren't you pleased to see me?'

'I guess so.'

Charlotte sighed. 'We'd better put your things in the car. You don't know what time Daddy's coming home?'

'Late, I think. He's always late when he goes to London.'

'No point in waiting then, but I expect we'll see him in the next day or so.'

'There's no one to play with round here,' Vicky said. 'My friends at school all live in Cambridge.'

'You can have them to tea,' Charlotte said, without thinking.

'When?'

'Soon,' Charlotte answered, realising that she'd meant tea here, not at the flat in Bateman Street.

'Come on, let's get back,' she said.

With everything loaded into the car they set off back to Cambridge.

'See you soon,' the woman called Marigold had said to Vicky as they left.

'Do you like her?' Charlotte asked, unwisely, as they turned out of the lane.

'She's all right,' Vicky answered, noncommittally. 'I like it better when Daddy's there,'

'Of course,' Charlotte said.

Before they got into Cambridge she managed to broach the subject of Nick's appearance.

'You must try not to stare,' she said.

'How did it happen? Was he drunk?' Vicky enquired, loudly.

'Why should he have been?' Charlotte said after a pause.

'It's on the telly. Don't drink and drive. I think he was drunk.'

'Don't say so to him. Vicky, darling, Nick's a bit short-tempered right now. His face hurts. Don't say anything to make him cross.'

'He's always in a temper.'

'Not always.'

'Mostly.'

'Just keep out of his way, if you can. I'm afraid we're going to be a bit cramped with three of us.'

They were. Vicky, on her makeshift bed had a nightmare the first night and went running into the bedroom, to the wrong bed. Her scream was another sound Charlotte wouldn't forget.

Two days passed. Vicky went to school. Charlotte went to the studio to see if her job was still there, which it was. Nick stayed tight shut in the flat, his self-pity turning it into a tinder box of indefinable recrimination, making it more confining than it was already. When they were all there together it was only Charlotte who spoke, with that false brightness cultivated from guilt and desperation. Nick was increasingly morose, and Vicky, quiet, watchful, and terrified. Each of them was waiting for the explosion but none of them knew how it might come.

On the third day, with still no word from Dan, Charlotte felt bound to act. She telephoned from the studio, two numbers before she got through to his secretary at the House of Commons.

'Mr Lovell is in court today. In Cambridge.'

'I don't understand.'

'He's representing a client.'

219

'But I thought he . . . '

'It's a special case.' There was inscrutability in the woman's voice, smooth as smooth could be.

'May I say who called?'

'No, it's all right.' It hurt now, hearing voices that were familiar to him and not to her. Voices and attitudes that seemed to want to shut her out.

It was nearly one o'clock. She left the studio and walked the two streets to the magistrates' court where Dan had once spent a good deal of his time, in the early years, when they were newly married. She didn't know it would be the right place but the compulsion to see him took her there as if it had to be. She reached the entrance but the doors were locked. She took a step back and saw the notice on the wall. This building was no longer in use. The writing that told her so was faded, weather-beaten. She crossed the street and went into a bank, but it was lunchtime and there was a queue. Outside again, she saw a newspaper vendor.

'Can you tell me where the magistrates' courts have gone?'

The man looked at her with suspicion, or maybe she imagined it.

'On the top of the car park, the multi-storey,' he said.

'Are you sure?'

'Lady, if you don't believe me . . . '

She hurried away. Why were people so hostile? She made her way round to the multi-storey car park, not really believing what the man with the newspapers had said, but finding it to be true. The new court complex sat squat on top of the car park, and emerging from the main entrance she saw Marion and Paul and then Dan.

Finding him, seeing him, gave the surroundings a sudden fullness that took her by surprise. She could feel her heart beating and her face felt flushed. She hadn't expected this sort of reaction: it was almost adolescent.

He saw her and left the other two who walked on in the opposite direction. As he came up to her he smiled, though in his face there was more sympathy than pleasure. How closely she observed these things, now, if not in the past.

'Lottie,' he said, conclusively.

They might have embraced but neither was publicly demonstrative, and he looked inexplicably untouchable in his dark suit.

'How did you hear about this?' he asked.

'About what? You being here? A newspaper seller told me.'

He moved closer and took her arm.

'That sounds too unlikely to go into. Let's go somewhere less public.'

Bed, she thought. A bed somewhere. God, I love you.

She said. 'Yes. Somewhere less public.'

They found a pub which was about as public as anywhere could be, but full of other people with their own concerns and preoccupations. She managed to get a table in a corner while he fetched drinks.

'What about the others, Marion and Paul, and what were they doing there?' she asked him as he sat down.

'Marion wanted to get home.' He paused. 'So you don't know?'

She waited for him to continue.

'When I saw you I thought you must have been told. Marion decided it was better that Nick shouldn't know, not until he's properly recovered from his injuries. Paul's been in a bit of trouble. That's all. Nothing too serious, but upsetting for Marion.'

'I'd no idea,' Charlotte said. 'What's he done?'

'Vandalised a tree.'

'You're not serious?'

'Well, it was a bit more serious than it sounds,' he said and went on to explain the particular tree's significance. 'It's all been made worse because there's been so much vandalism. We were concerned that the courts might decide to make an example of Paul, especially as he's of high intelligence.'

'And have they?'

Dan hesitated. He looked down at the glass in his hand. 'No, Lottie, they haven't,' he said, as if this was only part of the answer. 'He's got to do a few hours' community service, that's all.'

'You were representing him, weren't you?' she said.

'Yes.'

'What did you tell them?' she asked, quietly, watching him. 'Did you tell them that he came from a broken family, all that sort of stuff?'

221

'The case is finished,' he said. 'No point in going over it.'

Charlotte felt as if her blood had frozen. Did her culpability extend to a vandalised Christmas tree?

'How is Nick?' Dan asked now, changing the subject, though wasn't it all part of the same?

'I can't tell,' Charlotte said, her voice suddenly high and breaking. 'He's gone like my mother, you know, agoraphobic, only he's got more cause.' She laughed because it was all too awful not to.

'Lottie, I'm sorry, really sorry,' Dan said with sympathy.

'Oh, I expect he'll get over it,' she said, carelessly, but Dan wasn't deflected or fooled by her manner.

'If there's anything I can do,' he said. 'Help with Vicky . . . '

'That would suit you, wouldn't it?' she uttered, accusingly, trying to hold on to her bursting emotions.

He didn't respond.

The noise of the pub intruded then receded. People were looking.

Chapter Thirty

Behind the bicycle sheds Paul was smoking a slim panatella.

'Give us a drag,' one of the other lads said.

Holding the cigar between thumb and forefinger, Paul passed it to him. The boy sucked in the smoke and began to choke. The rest of the little gathering fell about laughing. Stacey slapped his back.

'Not man enough for it,' she said.

'For what!' someone else chipped in. More laughter.

Stacey moved away from the coughing boy and back to her allotted position next to Paul. She was getting very possessive. She shuffled up close to him then glanced at Karen, a tall girl with a pale face and straight blonde hair, and blue eyes that were too often gazing in the direction of Paul.

The bell went and the gang dispersed. Paul nipped the end of the cigar between his fingers and put it in his pocket.

'Watch you don't catch fire,' someone shouted.

'Shit for brains,' Stacey yelled back at them.

Paul experienced that uncomfortable creeping disgust which had increasingly affected him in recent weeks every time Stacey opened her big mouth.

'See you later, then,' she was saying now in her soft voice, which was beginning to have the same effect. He'd preferred her when she was mean. Over by the school door he saw Karen glancing back at him.

'Maybe,' he said to Stacey.

The afternoon was a free period for study, not that he had any intention of doing any work. He'd come out of his straight

223

phase, what was the point, it didn't get you anywhere; if he hadn't been such a boff in the past chances were the tree thing would never have gone to court. He'd have got a ticking off maybe, but not this penitential garbage, twelve hours over six weeks digging flower beds outside the hospital. What a way to go!

He sloped off across the netball courts. Stacey had gone in to her home economics, sponge cakes, who ate sponge cakes these days? Certainly not him.

Things at home had been different since Ruby'd gone, nearly a month ago now. Mum had taken up jogging – jogging! Her! She got up early and went out in a white tracksuit that had taken on a few browny-pink streaks since going into the washing machine with his socks. She'd actually got upset about it, the streaks (perhaps she knew now how he felt), and tried to bleach them out, without success. Something was going on. She'd had her hair cut and even put on a bit of make-up – at seven o'clock in the morning – to go jogging. He reckoned she'd met someone and it was secret assignations on the Heath at the crack of dawn, a quick roll in the dew. He didn't like to think about it.

Another thing that had changed at home was the food. It was all roughage and vitamins these days, better than before, but he wouldn't have minded the occasional lump of cake or a nice greasy chip. Still, his spots had stayed away.

He'd moved into Ruby's room, which was bigger than his old bedroom. He'd stuck fifties style posters on the walls and found an old chrome car bumper which had polished up well and now lay on the floor as an *objet d'art*. Otherwise he was conscientiously untidy, the only way to keep out his mother who refused to dust and clean unless the mess was cleared up.

Paul had begun to think about his future, even if he pretended to himself that he didn't care. He worried now about having sex with Stacey, not, as in the past, about his performance, but about the possibility of making her pregnant and being stuck with her and it if she wouldn't have an abortion. As soon as he'd done his 'A' levels, pass or fail, he wanted to travel, to go round the world, to get as far away from this place as he could. After that, well, he'd see what turned up. One thing he wasn't going to do, and that was to stay on with his mother if she was going to shack up with some bloke in running shorts.

Feeling grudging and petulant was getting to be a habit with him. He didn't like it, feeling this way, but it kept him going, that and his new-found nonchalance that covered up the self-pity and had changed things through one hundred and eighty degrees at school.

Today was a digging day. Half past four he was due at the hospital. At least it wasn't raining this week. He caught the bus straight after school. His hands had blistered a bit the first couple of digging sessions. He looked at them now and was pleased by their hardened appearance. Perhaps he'd do a spot of labouring here and there to get him round the world. He'd never admit it to anyone, but he quite enjoyed the rhythmic action of forking over clods of earth.

He was halfway through the session when he saw his father; you couldn't miss him these days. The first time he'd seen him, at the funeral, it had been a shock, the damage to his face, but there'd been a feeling of, sort of satisfaction, justice, because hadn't he been hoping for something vile to happen, and it had.

It troubled him though, that feeling, as did just about every other emotion he had. He wasn't really up to callous indifference, hard as he might concentrate on achieving it. Even the Stacey thing, the developing revulsion, was more to do with not really wanting to hurt her.

Seeing his father this second time, he wanted to hide. He stood very still, bent over his fork, watching Nick step out of the ambulance that collected up outpatients.

What if he saw him? What would he do? What would he say?

Two women were coming by. Paul saw them looking at his father, then a comment between them and looking again. Suddenly the confusion in him seemed to harden into a bursting feeling in his chest. He wanted to rush over to the women and smash them with his fork.

Chapter Thirty-One

The third week back in Cambridge Charlotte saw Audrey and Jean in Eaden Lilley's coffee shop. It was lunchtime and there was a queue, strangers having to share tables.

'Come and join us,' Audrey called to her.

'How are things?' she asked, her head tilted in sympathy.

'Oh, not too bad,' Charlotte said, taking the seat next to Jean. She was thankful that she'd only a cup of coffee, no food, no reason to have to remain with the two of them more than a few minutes. She'd avoided Audrey since getting back from America this last time, avoided most contact with the familiar and friendly because all that was for the permanent future and not her present existence. It was like a superstition, the keeping to herself, though she'd not thought of it as such, not thought much at all in recent days.

'How is your husband?' Jean asked in that hushed, almost reverential tone that is reserved for tragedy and bereavement.

'He's getting better, thank you,' she replied stiffly. She didn't want to talk about Nick in case she had to admit the truth to herself. His face was improving but in himself he was no better, so withdrawn now that he rarely said a word, though his eyes followed her everywhere in the tiny flat, accusing her, as if he knew, like the condemned man waiting for sentence to be carried out.

Charlotte thought she saw the other two women exchange glances, as if they too knew what was in her heart. They seemed vaguely standoffish, even disapproving, Audrey with her red mouth set in that false smile, Jean who probably didn't like her after the unsatisfactory evening they'd spent together a lifetime ago.

'We're planning a new production,' Audrey announced, overtly changing the subject.

'Yes,' Jean concurred, all enthusiasm. 'My turn this time. Joe will have to stay at home and look after the kids.' This said gleefully, as if it was all a point-scoring exercise. Charlotte wasn't fooled. They didn't know how to be. They kept watching her then looking away, but why should they care? What was any of it to them?

God, she looks terrible, they'd say, when she'd gone. Brought it on herself. Doesn't eat enough. Silly to go without lunch. Should never have done what she did . . .

'*Pride and Prejudice*,' Audrey said. 'What do you think?'

'Lovely parts for women,' Jean observed.

'Would you like to be in it?' Audrey asked. 'You don't have to decide this minute, just give it some thought.'

'Must go,' Charlotte said, jolting the table as she got up. 'Got to get back to work.'

'Of course. Lovely to see you. James and I were talking about you last night, wondering how things were going.' What did she mean by that? Nothing but kindness, probably. Charlotte experienced a small piece of hope for herself to have been able to think of this last possibility.

She worked hard all afternoon. Mercifully there was a great deal to occupy her at the studio and had been ever since she'd got back. She was earning good money as well and needed every penny, not only to keep the three of them going at the flat but to begin the long haul of paying off Nick's credit card debts and everything they owed Frances and Leonard, who would never ask.

Dan had been away in Brussels since the day of Paul's case, though he was due back this evening. His departure had felt like the loss of faith at the time, the removal of that invisible leaning post to which Charlotte had been attempting to cling for weeks that had become months. His attitude to her situation had left her in mid air after their meeting in the pub. He could be patronisingly calm; she remembered that now, old familiarity beginning to colour the ideal with the darker shades as well as the light, not that this helped: she longed to see him again, to feel the completeness within herself that came from being with him, even when there was irritation. But that last meeting troubled her. She'd wanted to see him because she couldn't bear not to for another second and yet she felt as if he'd failed her in some way. She wanted him to tell her what to do, take on the responsibility for her actions. She was like a child in an unfair situation: somebody else had to say she didn't have to go on with it, only nobody would because this was a grown-up unfairness and everything twisted round so that right was wrong and vice versa, or so it seemed because she couldn't bring herself to face what maybe Dan had already.

'I'll always be here,' he'd said, when they'd parted outside the pub, but why, oh why had he had to say it with that inflection of his, that sigh of resignation?

Vicky was already home when she got back to the flat at the end of the afternoon. Charlotte tried to be there before her but it was becoming increasingly difficult to work a short day. Nick was in the bedroom. She called to him that she was home but he didn't respond. Vicky was in the tiny kitchen, making herself a Marmite sandwich.

'Nice day at school?' Charlotte asked.

'Suppose so,' Vicky mumbled, concentrating on her spreading.

Charlotte plugged in the electric kettle she'd bought. She drank too much coffee these days, smoked too many cigarettes.

'When are you going to bring a friend home for tea? D'you remember, we talked about doing that?' she said, watching her daughter lick the knife then plunge it back into the small black pot.

'I don't want to,' Vicky said.

'Why not?' Charlotte persisted, foolishly, as if she needed to hear the reason.

'I just don't.'

'It's up to you,' Charlotte sighed. 'Do you want to watch television while I get supper ready?' She'd bought a small colour set from Woolworth's, though the reception was not good with only an indoor aerial and the flat being below ground level.

Vicky took her sandwich and went through to the cramped living room that was also her bedroom. She'd been very good

228

about that, hadn't complained. Charlotte had told her that it was a temporary thing, that soon she'd have her own room again, though she'd not said where this might be in case Vicky said anything to Nick.

She'd just finished scraping the carrots when it happened, the explosion. She turned from the sink and ran into the living room. The scene that confronted her was frozen like a tableau. The television, its screen smashed in, was on the floor. In the nearest corner Vicky was crouched up in the manner of a terrified lunatic in a padded cell. Standing in the centre of the room, Nick, his fist bleeding, was staring at her, his bloodshot eyes glazed over as if he'd passed into a different consciousness beyond her reach.

So it had happened. Breaking point all round. And even in the immediate reaction of terror, Charlotte welcomed it like a violent thunderstorm breaking into a heavy and airless atmosphere. She didn't hesitate more than the few seconds it took to take in what had been done. She gathered up Vicky and left the flat. Something was said as she slammed the door, but she didn't want to hear it.

She ran down the street, holding on to Vicky, pulling her along. She couldn't use the car because the keys were still in the flat and she wouldn't go back. Her body tingled with fright and a wonderful sense of release: she couldn't risk going back and hearing what he had said.

In the telephone box she rang for a taxi, no hesitation as to the destination. Her mind was working with the clarity that can come with shock: from which direction would the taxi come? she asked. She and her daughter would be walking to meet it. She didn't really believe that Nick would pursue them, but she wanted to get as far away from Bateman Street as she could, the need immediate, overwhelming, reinforcing the sense of escape.

Twenty minutes later they were at the house. Vicky hadn't spoken but in the taxi she had begun to tremble. Charlotte had her arms round her, holding her tightly.

'We're going back to Daddy,' she whispered to her. 'We're going home.'

Chapter Thirty-Two

'Don't go. Please. Don't,' was what Nick had said, and hard as she'd tried not to hear, the words had lodged in Charlotte's head.

'I can't stay, can I?' she said to Dan, some three or four hours later, when Vicky was asleep in her own bedroom upstairs.

They were sitting on the gold sofa, that small stage which had held rather too many moments of extreme emotion over the course of Charlotte's adult life. It had been the scene of inept and frustrating lovemaking, but that was when it was still in Dan's parents' home; it had been the place where Charlotte had sat watching television through a blur of misery during that period of inexplicable despair after Vicky was born; and it had been the place from which she'd sat and listened to Nick telling Dan that he wanted her and was taking her. How deceptively comfortable its soft cushions were.

If she thought of all this now, it was with an overall longing for everything to have been different, because she was still prey to her own idealised belief that other people lived in a more proper fashion, somehow less troubled by the ebbs and flows.

Sitting beside Dan she suddenly shivered.

'Are you cold?'

'A little. I preferred it when the fire was real,' she added, gazing at the imitation log fire with its gas flame.

'It wasn't practical, not after you left.' It was only now that they could talk in this way, openly referring to that period of their past. It came into Charlotte's mind then to wonder if this would have been the case if she had been going to stay: perhaps they might have continued to avoid reference to that shared

230

failure, but now it didn't matter, not because they were careless of one another, but because the past had been superceded so completely by their brief reunion.

'Do you think this is worse than if we hadn't made it up?' she asked him.

'Made it up,' he repeated, sadly. 'You make us sound like school chums.'

'That's only because I can't bring myself to say the other sort of words, the heavy ones.'

'I don't think there's any comparison,' he said, answering her question. 'This is like knowing you've won by not getting the prize. Before, I wasn't even sure I was in the contest.'

'You see, you can't use the real words either.'

He smiled and sighed and leant back into the cushions, sliding his arm round her shoulders.

'Perhaps one day,' he said, not finishing the sentence, though she understood his meaning.

'Lottie, there won't be anyone else, not for me.'

'It seems so unfair,' she said, unable to tell him that he should try and find another woman, or, at least not to discount the possibility. She would have liked to think there might be a chance for them some day but having at last come to terms with her responsibility towards Nick, how could she put a time limit on it?

She felt quite different now from anything she'd experienced before, sort of removed from the raw immediacy. She was almost calm. Horribly sad, but for the first time in months, maybe even years, she felt clean of guilt, certain that she was doing what was right. The hardest part of course, was Vicky, that darling, darling little beast, who had not been nearly beastly enough lately. Not having Vicky with her was going to be the major sacrifice. The merest thought in this direction made her feel so hollow inside that she might easily renege, even now.

She'd told Dan everything but he'd waited for her to say that Vicky should live with him, softening this by suggesting boarding school, to which she was already accustomed.

'We can share her in the holidays,' he said. 'I think she needs us both.'

'A brother or a sister, that's what she's always needed,'

231

Charlotte murmured, wistfully, dangerously.

'My goodness, one monster's enough,' Dan said, because the tenor of the conversation had been too vital and intense not to ease it in this way.

'You would have liked another child,' Charlotte persisted, her tone too reflective for him to doubt that she was speaking only of what might have been. 'A son. You wanted a son.'

'I don't think I ever said so.'

'Perhaps not. I just felt it.'

She left him just before midnight. He was uneasy about her going back to the flat alone but she wasn't frightened any more because her fear had been to do with making a decision and that was taken.

'I feel a bit of a saint,' she said to him just before the taxi came. 'That's not good, is it?'

'I'm sure you'll get over it,' he answered.

They heard the car turn into the drive.

'Do you think it will be all right?' she asked him, at the last moment. 'Do you think I'll be able to do it?'

'Of course. Think how bored you used to be with me.'

'Was I?'

'Dreadfully so.'

'Oh Dan, I wish . . . '

He stopped her.

'Don't start wishing now.'

She put her arms round his neck and pressed her cheek against his, very hard.

'Tell me that it wouldn't work for us, not with Nick the way he is.'

Gently, he eased her away from him.

'Not a chance,' he said. 'Neither of us would be able to live with it.'

'Maybe a year from now?' she asked, very nearly going back on her resolve.

'You'll probably be in love with Matthews again by then,' he answered her, a little roughly.

'And you'll probably have married your American mouse.'

They gazed at one another in the wake of these uncertainties, neither believing what each had said, but who could tell how things might be in another year.

Chapter Thirty-Three

'You don't really want chips?' Charlotte said.

'Of course! I haven't had a good greasy chip for months. Not since Heathman.'

Charlotte opened the cupboard in search of some sort of pan. Most of the stuff was still wrapped in newspaper, the Cambridge Evening News, of which they had a liberal supply.

'I'll chop up the potatoes, if you like,' Paul said.

'That's big of you.'

'Ah, well . . . '

They smiled at one another. Extraordinary how well they got on. Extraordinary that here they were, wicked stepmother, miscreant stepson, about to make chips in Marion's old kitchen.

'You ought to call him George,' Charlotte said.

'I do to his face.'

Marion had married her jogger from the Heath and they'd run off back to Birmingham from whence both had originated. Paul, in his final year at school, had come up with the bizarre suggestion that Charlotte and Nick move in with him. The house was still half Dad's wasn't it, and Heathman had pots of money to buy something huge and vulgar in Brum.

The idea took hold, not least because Charlotte was aware that the past twelve months had been survivable largely due to Paul. It wasn't just the time he spent with Nick, the hours he'd been at the Bateman Street flat in the evenings while she stayed on at the studio. God knows what went on during those evenings, what they talked about, what they did, but it made all the difference. Charlotte had never fully realised how hard it had been for Nick, the American years not seeing his son. She'd made a lot of assumptions about Nick's feelings, mostly that they were nonexistent, outside business.

Paul had just come round to the flat one Saturday morning and stayed, not saying much or doing anything in particular; it had been awkward at first, for all of them. The visits had gone on from there, once, twice, sometimes three times a week. Sometimes he'd come with his homework, saying it was impossible to work at home with Marion singing all over the house. Maybe he'd used them as an escape from Heathman but Paul was deeper than that, there was a need in him to give as well as take.

In the other kitchen, the tiny one in Bateman Street, he sometimes stayed on when Charlotte got in late and Nick was already asleep. He talked to her about his plans to travel. He told her about a girl called Stacey Middleton who sounded dreadful but funny and who Charlotte suspected provided him with some sort of sex life. There was another girl he mentioned but with a different tone. Then he stopped talking about either of them and the kitchen conversations were about everything else under the sun, interspersed with companionable silences. Without noticing or trying, they'd become like family, except they were more careful and considerate of one another than blood relations, and always, even when he was asleep, there was the ever present sense of Nick, their shared responsibility.

Maybe it was wrong, allowing this to happen, but didn't everyone need some kind of support, and the only other possibilities for Charlotte were Audrey and Dan. The former, good friend that she was, could not conceal an element of pity in her kind concern; and Dan, how difficult it was seeing him within the tacitly agreed but unacceptable limitations of platonic reconciliation. The occasional meeting was unavoidable because of Vicky, now sufficiently settled at the boarding school to be behaving badly.

Charlotte and Dan had met at the house only a few days ago for yet another discussion over a piece of po-faced feedback from Vicky's house mistress.

It didn't get any better, the anticipation, the heart-twisting longing that led to each visit; then the moment of seeing him, the quick search for some kind of evidence in his expression that it was all still there for him too.

Naughty Vicky to worry them so and necessitate more frequent meetings than they would otherwise have been able to justify. In fact, her regression to badness was something of a relief to Charlotte who had been far more concerned about her daughter during the weeks of silent watchfulness leading up to Nick's explosion. After all, she herself had been wicked at school.

Sometimes she wondered what would happen when Vicky grew up, how she and Dan might continue their bittersweet contrivance, because she couldn't conceive of a time when it might end, or, with a slow realisation that was almost perverted, change. The thing was that over the past year she had not actually been unhappy. There had been huge potential for misery and despair but she couldn't really claim either. The plain fact was she'd been too busy for the restless regret that had plagued her before. Every moment of her time had a demand upon it. She'd made a success of her job and by the end of the summer she was planning to start her own studio. The prospect excited her in a way nothing in the past had engrossed her energy and enthusiasm.

And so to Nick, the canker in her existence, the balance in an otherwise largely self-seeking pattern of activities and emotions.

She'd felt pretty saintly when she'd left Vicky with Dan and gone back to the flat, but if she'd expected anything like gratitude, a night of sobbing into her hard, hitherto pitiless shoulder, abject murmurings about life being impossible without her, it had not been like that at all; and anything so nauseatingly irresistible within the context of this new sense of self-sacrifice would have been hideously bad for both of them.

Nick had been as sullen and as silent as before and it was only gradually, over the course of weeks and months, that he emerged from the well of self-pity down which he'd thrown himself with such abandon. It had been hugely difficult living with him during that time, like tiptoeing round a volcano, because at any moment Charlotte expected some sort of eruption, even began to hope for it with a strange and enticing terror.

They'd not slept together for months, then one night the

235

feeling of isolation got to Charlotte so acutely that she left her own narrow bed and crossed the great divide. That she had gone to him made all the difference and after that they bought a proper bed and from it Nick's recovery began.

Of course there were sleepless times when Charlotte lay in the dark thinking of Dan and in much the same way she'd had thoughts of Nick four years earlier during the last days and nights at her old house, that previous time of travelling in hope.

The chips were frying, filling the house with the smell of the past when Nick got home, so that for a moment it seemed as if Marion might be in the kitchen and Ruby upstairs, propped up on her pillows but her hair red and abundant, her lips cherry red, moist and sensuous. He smiled to himself at this piece of selective imagery and thought how Ruby would have appreciated it.

He took off his coat and hung it in the hall cupboard, catching sight in the mirror of the strange expressionless face from which his own eyes saw the reflection. The white scar tissue could not accommodate the manifestation of happiness or sorrow or any of the range of emotions that had returned to him over the past year. If it had, then maybe in this moment the muscular messages would be indicating a combination of something approaching contentment plus a degree of regret for the episodes of the past, time ill used and lost forever.

It was a Saturday, a dread day in the recent past because it was the time when he'd waited to see if Charlotte would choose to spend this non-working day with him or find an excuse for escape. This Saturday it was different, the first of his one in four that had to be worked. He removed the newspaper from his coat pocket and surveyed the front page which he had laid out and given a headline a few hours earlier. It was all there, all the misery and mess of life, people doing things they'd regret; but what else was there to write about? These things happened.

He went through to the kitchen and seeing his wife, wondered for the umpteenth time how much longer it might be before she felt able to let him go.